From the Pages of Alice's Adventures in Wonderland and Through the Looking-Glass

The rabbit-hole went straight on like a tunnel for some way, and then dipped suddenly down, so suddenly that Alice had not a moment to think about stopping herself before she found herself falling down what seemed to be a very deep well.

(Alice's Adventures in Wonderland, page 13)

Tied round the neck of the bottle was a paper label, with the words "DRINK ME" beautifully printed on it in large letters.

(Alice, page 17)

"Shall I *never* get any older than I am now? That'll be a comfort, one way—never to be an old woman—but then—always to have lessons to learn! Oh, I shouldn't like *that!*"

(Alice, page 45)

The Caterpillar and Alice looked at each other for some time in silence: at last the Caterpillar took the hookah out of its mouth, and addressed her in a languid, sleepy voice.

(Alice, page 55)

"All right," said the Cat; and this time it vanished quite slowly, beginning with the end of the tail, and ending with the grin, which remained some time after the rest of it had gone.

(Alice, page 76)

The Queen turned crimson with fury, and, after glaring at her for a moment like a wild beast, began screaming "Off with her head!"

(Alice, page 93)

"Every thing's got a moral, if only you can find it."

(Alice, page 103)

The King and Queen of Hearts were seated on their throne when they arrived, with a great crowd assembled about them—all sorts of little birds and beasts, as well as the whole pack of cards.

(Alice, page 125)

'Twas brillig, and the slithy toves
Did gyre and gimble in the wabe;
All mimsy were the borogoves,
And the mome raths outgrabe.

"Beware the Jabberwock, my son!
The jaws that bite, the claws that catch!
Beware the Jubjub bird, and shun
The frumious Bandersnatch!"

(Through the Looking-Glass, page 164)

"It's a poor sort of memory that only works backwards."

(Looking-Glass, page 204)

"They gave it me—for an un-birthday present."

(Looking-Glass, page 218)

"You don't know how to manage Looking-glass cakes," the Unicorn remarked. "Hand it round first, and cut it afterwards."

(Looking-Glass, page 235)

"Then fill up the glasses with treacle and ink,
Or anything else that is pleasant to drink;
Mix sand with the cider, and wool with the wine—
And welcome Queen Alice with ninety-times-nine!"

(Looking-Glass, page 261)

Alice's Adventures in Wonderland

and

Through the Looking-Glass and What Alice Found There

Lewis Carroll

With an Introduction and Notes by Tan Lin
Illustrated by John Tenniel

George Stade
Consulting Editorial Director

ЛВ
BARNES & NOBLE CLASSICS
NEW YORK

JB

BARNES & NOBLE CLASSICS

NEW YORK

Published by Barnes & Noble Books
122 Fifth Avenue
New York, NY 10011

www.barnesandnoble.com/classics

Alice's Adventures in Wonderland was first published in 1865. *Through the
Looking-Glass and What Alice Found There* was first published in 1871.

Originally Published in trade paperack format in 2003 by
Barnes & Noble Classics with new Introduction, Notes, Biography, Chronology,
Inspired By, Comments & Questions, and For Further Reading.
This hardcover edition published in 2005.

Alice's Adventures in Wonderland and Through the Looking-Glass
ISBN-13: 978-1-59308-345-8
ISBN-10: 1-59308-345-9
LC Control Number 2004110466

Produced and published in conjunction with:
Fine Creative Media, Inc.
322 Eighth Avenue
New York, NY 10001

Michael J. Fine, President and Publisher

Printed in the United States of America

WCM

11   13   15   17   19   20   18   16   14   12   10

Lewis Carroll

Lewis Carroll was born as Charles Lutwidge Dodgson on January 27, 1832, in Daresbury, Cheshire, England, the eldest son of eleven children raised in a devout English household. He had an inquisitive mind, and his early poems, plays, and paintings display the genius that characterizes his mature works; he seems to have had a happy childhood. Charles was often in charge of the activities of his younger siblings, and he showed a great gift for entertaining and instructing children—one that would persist and deepen throughout his life. Young Charles had a sharp intellect and, tutored by his father, was well ahead of the other students when he enrolled in grade school. He became fluent in Latin and had a propensity for complex mathematics that would likewise distinguish him when in 1850 he entered university at Christ Church college of Oxford University. After graduation, he taught mathematics and logic at Christ Church. In 1856, he created the pseudonym "Lewis Carroll" (versions of his first and middle names in reverse order). He conducted his academic career and published mathematical works as Charles Dodgson but signed his literary works as Lewis Carroll.

Carroll was known for his piety (he was ordained as a deacon in 1861), and he suffered from a stutter and deafness in one ear. A sensitive man with many interests, he was an amateur painter and inventor, and an avid theatergoer who moved in London's artistic circles. A talented art photographer, he made portraits of various luminaries of the day, including Tennyson and the Rossettis. Most frequently, however, he turned his lens upon his favorite subjects and companions: young girls. Carroll's love of purity and guilelessness and his early experience with his many siblings made him prefer the company of children to that of adults. Whatever other impulses may have led Dodgson to seek out the companionship of young girls, these relationships were by all accounts innocent and kindly. Indeed, Dodgson's young friends were inspirational—the games and stories he invented to please them led to the creation of *Alice's Adventures in Wonderland* and *Through the Looking-Glass*, among other works of fantasy and high nonsense.

Carroll never married, maintained close relationships with his siblings, and led a charitable, productive life unshaken by the political and social upheavals of the day. His more than 300 published works comprise poetry, mathematics, logic, and his beloved children's stories. Lewis Carroll died in Guildford, England, on January 14, 1898.

Table of Contents

The World of Lewis Carroll,
Alice's Adventures in Wonderland
and Through the Looking-Glass

1832 The third of eleven children, Lewis Carroll is born Charles Lutwidge Dodgson on January 27 in Daresbury, Cheshire, England, the eldest son of the Reverend Charles Dodgson and Frances Jane Lutwidge Dodgson.

1843 The family moves to Croft, Yorkshire, where Charles senior takes the position of rector. While looking after his siblings, young Charles shows signs of his creative gifts. He paints, puts on puppet shows, and writes plays and sophisticated poems.

1844 Charles enrolls in the Richmond School, Yorkshire, where he also boards. Previous instruction by his father makes him an excellent student of Latin and mathematics.

1846 He enters the Rugby public (in American terms, "private") school; he has a difficult time acclimating socially but performs admirably in his courses.

1847 Charlotte Bronte's *Jane Eyre* and Emily Bronte's *Wuthering Heights* are published.

1850 Charles enrolls at Christ Church college of Oxford University.

1852 He is made a life fellow of Christ Church.

1854 He graduates with honors. Alfred, Lord Tennyson's "The Charge of the Light Brigade" is published.

1855 Charles becomes a lecturer in mathematics at Christ Church, Oxford. He writes the first stanza of "Jabberwocky."

1856 He invents the nom de plume "Lewis Carroll," versions of his first and middle names in reverse order. Throughout his life, he will publish mathematical works as Charles Dodgson and literature as Lewis Carroll. (For the sake of simplicity, from here on we refer to him as Lewis Carroll.)

1856 Carroll first meets the Liddell family when Alice Liddell's father takes a position at Oxford. He buys a camera and eventually becomes an excellent photographer.

1857 He earns his MA degree.

1859 Charles Darwin's *On the Origin of Species* is published. Charles Dickens's *A Tale of Two Cities* is published.

1861 Carroll is ordained as a deacon but never becomes a priest. Around this time, he begins to keep a log of his correspondence; by the end of his life, his meticulous accounting records nearly 100,000 letters.

1862 Carroll and a friend take the Liddell sisters, including Alice, on a summertime river-boat ride. Carroll tells the girls the tale *Alice's Adventures Under Ground.* Alice asks him to write down the story for her.

1863 By February he has written a first draft. In June he discusses publishing the book with the Clarendon Press.

1864 Carroll has expanded the manuscript and engages *Punch* magazine cartoonist John Tenniel as illustrator.

1865 Tenniel finishes the illustrations and the Clarendon Press prints 2,000 copies of the book as *Alice's Adventures in Wonderland.* Despite the book's great success, Carroll prefers to stay out of the public eye.

1869 Long fascinated by occultism, Carroll introduces ghosts into his work with the publication of *Phantasmagoria and Other Poems.*

1871 As a sequel to *Alice's Adventures in Wonderland,* Carroll publishes *Through the Looking-Glass and What Alice Found There.* George Eliot's *Middlemarch* is published.

1876 Carroll's long poem *The Hunting of the Snark, An Agony in Eight Fits,* a classic of nonsense literature, is published.

1879 *Euclid and His Modern Rivals* is published; demonstrating the usefulness of Euclid's *Elements* in the teaching of geometry, it is written as a play with the ghost of Euclid as one of the characters.

1881 Carroll resigns his mathematical lectureship to focus on his writing.

1882 He takes the demanding position of curator of the Senior Common Room at Christ Church, Oxford.

1883 The poetry collection *Rhyme? And Reason?* is published.

1885 Carroll publishes *A Tangled Tale,* ten stories for children featuring linguistic play and mathematical "knots" to undo.

1886 The original manuscript of *Alice's Adventures Under Ground* is published.

1888 *Curiosa Mathematica, Part I: A New Theory of Parallels* is published.

1889 *Sylvie and Bruno,* a story for children, is published.

1890 *The Nursery Alice,* Carroll's adaptation for younger children, with twenty enlargements from Tenniel's illustrations, is published. Oscar Wilde's *The Picture of Dorian Gray* is published.

1892 Carroll resigns as curator of the Senior Common Room.

1893 *Sylvie and Bruno Concluded* and *Curiosa Mathematica, Part II: Pillow Problems Thought Out during Sleepless Nights* are published.

1896 *Symbolic Logic,* which shows how to visually represent propositions in mathematical logic, is published.

1898 Lewis Carroll dies of pneumonia at Guildford, England, on January 14.

Introduction

BOREDOM AND NONSENSE IN WONDERLAND

"What do you suppose is the use of a child without any meaning?"
(p. 253)

Alice's Adventures in Wonderland and *Through the Looking-Glass and What Alice Found There* pursue what lies beyond and down rabbit holes and on reverse sides of mirrors. But mainly their subject is what comes after, and in this sense the books are allegories about what a child can know and come to know. This quest, as in many great works of literature, unwinds against a larger backdrop: what can and what cannot be known at a particular historical moment, a moment that in Lewis Carroll's case preceded both Freud's speculations on the unconscious and Heisenberg's formulation of the uncertainty principle. Yet because the books were written by a teacher of mathematics who was also a reverend, they are also concerned with what can and cannot be taught to a child who has an infinite faith in the goodness and good sense of the world. But Alice's quest for knowledge, her desire to become something (a grown-up) she is not, is inverted. The books are not conventional quest romances in which Alice matures, overcomes obstacles, and eventually gains wisdom. For when Alice arrives in Wonderland, she is *already* the most reasonable creature there. She is wiser than any lesson books are able to teach her to be. More important, she is eminently more reasonable than her own feelings will allow her to express. What comes after for Alice? Near the end of *Through the Looking-Glass,* the White Queen tells Alice, "Something's going to happen!" (p. 265).

Quests for mastery are continually frustrated in the Alice books. In comparison with the ever-sane Alice, it is the various Wonderland creatures who appear to be ridiculous, coiners of abstract word games. Yet Carroll also frustrates, with equal precision, Alice's more reasonable human desires. Why, after all, cannot Alice know why the Mad Hatter is mad? Or why will Alice never get to 20 in her multiplication tables? In Carroll, the logic of mathematical proofs runs counter to the logic of reasonable human desire—and neither logic is easily mastered. To his radical epistemological doubt, Carroll added a healthy dose of skepticism for the conventional children's story—a story that in his day came packaged with a moral aim and treated the child as an innocent or tabula rasa upon which the morals and knowledge of the adult could be tidily imprinted.

Alice embodies an idea Freud would later develop at length: What Alice the child already knows, the adult has yet to learn. Or to be more precise, what Alice has not yet forgotten, the adult has yet to remember as something that is by nature unforgettable. In other words, in *Alice* childhood fantasy meets the reality of adulthood, which to the child looks as unreal and unreasonable as a Cheshire Cat's grin or a Queen who yells "Off with her head!" But even as she calls adult reality unreal, Alice, as the most reasonable creature in her unreasonable dreams, doesn't quite yet realize that the adult's sense of reality has already taken up residence in her. The principal dream of most children—the dream within the dream, as it were—is the dream of not dreaming any longer, the dream of growing up. For the adult, the outlook is reversed. The adult's quest is an inverted one: to find those desires again, in more reasonable forms—and this involves forgetting the original childhood desires (to become an adult) in order to remember them as an adult. The psychoanalyst Adam Phillips notes: "Freud is not really saying that we are really children, but that the sensual intensities of childhood cannot be abolished, that our ideals are transformed versions of childhood pleasures. Looking forward . . . is a paradoxical form of looking back. The future is where one retrieves the pleasures, the bodily pleasures of the past."[1] The Alice books manage to show both these quests—that of the child to look forward, and of the adult to look back—simultaneously, as mirror logics of each other.

Like both Freud and the surrealists, Carroll implicitly understood that a child's emotions and desires appear omnipotent and boundless to the child—and thus make the adult's forgetting of them difficult if not illogical. Growing up poses psychological and logical absurdities. The quandary of a logically grounded knowledge constituted out of an illogical universe pervades both books. The questions that Alice asks are not answered by the animals in Wonderland nor by anyone after she wakens. It is likely that her questions don't have answers or that there are no right questions to ask. *Alice's Adventures in Wonderland* and *Through the Looking-Glass* remain the most prophetic of the nineteenth century's anti-narratives, inverted quest romances, circular mathematical treatises on the illogical logic of forgetting one's desires. They display a logic that the child must master in order to grow up. As the White Queen remarks of the Red Queen: "She's in that state of mind . . . that she wants to deny *something*—only she doesn't know what to deny!" (p. 254).

For the child, the future lies undeniably beyond her (in a world of ever more sophisticated language skills), whereas for the adult, the future is something she must remember to return to. Carroll seems to be saying that children, in their rush to grow up, can pretend to be adults too soon; and adults can also, in a very different kind of game, forget how to be children—that is, forget the sensual, even nonsensical desires of childhood, which endure in language as in life. It is not surprising that children love puns and riddles, just as kings and oracles do. Carroll's books of words and pictures, puns and riddles, indefinitely prolong the time of childhood nonsense. Carroll's Alice books have a moral nonetheless: Like childhood, they end. And yet both books, which end with measured recollection and memory, seem to continue into the future.

Alice's Adventures in Wonderland was published in 1865; *Through the Looking-Glass* appeared six years later in 1871. The first of the books began as an oral tale, told on a rowboat expedition up the Thames on a "golden afternoon," most likely July 4, 1862. The party in the boat included Charles Lutwidge Dodgson (the mathematician, logician, and photographer who had already created the storytelling pen name Lewis Carroll), his friend the Reverend Robinson Duckworth, and the three Liddell sisters: Alice, who was ten; Lorina Charlotte, who was thirteen; and Edith, who was eight. Carroll was thirty at the time and had been ordained as a deacon the year before. Hardly a recluse, he enjoyed traveling, frequented the theater, took pleasure in giving un-birthday presents on any day of the year, wrote a large number of letters, invented mathematical puzzles, and was an avid amateur photographer who liked "making up pictures,"[2] often composing his subjects in tableau-like settings that suggested make-believe stories. His sitters included Tennyson, Ruskin, the Rossettis, Millais, Queen Victoria's son, Prince Leopold—as well as his favorite subject: Victorian children, particularly young girls. He gained First Class Honours in mathematics and produced a number of treatises on mathematics and symbolic logic, beginning with *A Syllabus of Plane Geometry*, which appeared in 1860. He was a polymath, albeit a conservative one. He considered Tuesday his lucky day.

The boat trip on that July day covered about three miles. The story that would become *Alice,* according to Carroll, was extemporized as they went along that day and over several subsequent trips. Carroll remembers how, "in a desperate attempt to strike out some new line of fairy-lore," he sent Alice "straight down a rabbit-hole, to begin with, without the least idea what was to happen afterwards."[3] On one boat trip, Carroll tried to amuse the girls with a game but was forced to "go on with my interminable fairy-tale of *Alice's Adventures.*"[4] With some prompting by Alice Liddell, Carroll began penning the story he initially called *Alice's Adventures Under Ground.* For reasons that are not clear, Carroll was banned from the Liddell household before completing the book, making the Alice books very much about a child as absent muse rather than as recipient of either of the books. The book—the title now changed to *Alice's Adventures in Wonderland*—was published on July 4, 1865, to commemorate the date of that first boating expedition.

Despite their differences, both books chronicle the adventures of a girl named Alice, modeled on Alice Liddell, whose father was the dean of Christ Church, Oxford, where Carroll taught. Carroll first came to Christ Church in 1850. He stayed for nearly fifty years. During that time, Dean Liddell was busy attempting to modernize the college, turning it from a kind of genteel seminary into something more like a German university, a process Carroll resisted in characteristic fashion: He produced a series of comic pamphlets in protest. However, he was made a don after only five years, a feat remarkable even then. Carroll met Alice in 1856, when she was four. From that time onward, Carroll took a number of photographs of Alice and her siblings. Both *Alice's Adventures in Wonderland* and *Through the Looking-Glass* begin with Alice on the verge of dreaming, but the books transpire in different seasons and evoke different moods.

Alice commences on a warm spring day, while *Through the Looking-Glass* is set in midwinter. The looking glass—as an analogue for the confusion of things that are knowable—was probably a relatively late addition by Carroll, added at a time when, according to Alice Liddell, the three sisters were themselves learning to play chess and Carroll was entertaining all three with stories about chess playing, among other things. The initial appearance of the looking glass was prompted by Carroll's meeting with another young Alice, his cousin Alice Raikes, most likely in August 1868. In his biography of Carroll, Derek Hudson recounts the following incident:

The room they entered had a tall mirror standing in one corner. [Carroll] gave his cousin an orange and asked her which hand she held it in. When she replied 'The right,' he asked her to stand before the glass and tell him in which hand the little girl in the mirror was holding it. 'The left hand', came the puzzled reply. 'Exactly,' said [Carroll], 'and how do you explain that?' . . . 'If I was on the *other* side of the glass,' [Alice] said, 'wouldn't the orange still be in my right hand?' . . . 'Well done, little Alice,' [Carroll] said. 'The best answer I've had yet.'[5]

Carroll completed work on the sequel quickly; a manuscript entitled *Behind the Looking-Glass, and What Alice Saw There* was posted to Macmillan in January 1869. It appeared, with its present title, in time for Christmas 1871, though its publication date reads 1872. The book was a wild success, selling out its initial print run of 9,000 copies almost immediately. By 1893 it had sold 60,000 copies.

TAMING CHANCE VS. ENDING BOREDOM

"I can't remember things before they happen." (p. 204)

"Can you row?" the Sheep asked, handing her a pair of knitting-needles as she spoke.

"Yes, a little—but not on land—and not with needles—" Alice was beginning to say. (p. 209)

Alice's Adventures in Wonderland began as an oral tale told by Lewis Carroll to the three Liddell sisters, although it is often forgotten that Carroll's fantasia of reading and upside-down geography lessons begins with a book, and specifically the aversion to reading one. In the first chapter, Alice, bored to tears and sitting on a river bank, peeks at and then turns away from her sister's book because it lacks "pictures or conversations" (p. 13). She thinks to make a daisy chain, thus taking charge of her own boredom by ending it. Of course, Alice never does make herself a daisy chain, and in this she implicitly acknowledges that it may not be enough to *want* to end boredom to bring it to an end. It might be more accurate to say that boredom is ended *for her* by something she cannot entirely provide by herself. Not surprisingly, Alice's dream, like the landscape of Wonderland itself, feels both expansive and boxed in, wonderfully curious and frustratingly opaque, an imaginary landscape that is located under as opposed to above ground.

For a child, boredom may be the biggest non-event or riddle to solve because its solution must come from without—while seeming to come from within. As Walter Benjamin wrote, "We are bored when we don't know what we are waiting for."[6] Like the various creatures in Wonderland, boredom is a curious riddle of wanting something to want. Like a good many "acceptable" neuroses, boredom is indeterminate. It resists analysis. Not surprisingly, when Alice first sees the Rabbit she answers as any bored child might: "There was nothing so *very* remarkable in that" (p. 13). As the psychoanalyst Adam Phillips suggests, it may be a pedagogical and therapeutic mistake (*Alice in Wonderland* is filled with both) to try to cure boredom.[7]

If boredom is difficult to dispel, the boredom all children feel is not easily tolerated by adults, who insist that children have things to do, that they have interests. The field of symbolic logic and the adult's attempts to eradicate boredom turn out to be equally coercive. Alice's English and her manners are corrected relentlessly. Alice is bossed about: The rabbit orders her to fetch his handkerchief, a note on a bottle enjoins her to "drink me," the caterpillar demands that she explain herself, the Queen summons her to play croquet. The result of such coercion is generally terror followed by tears, and there is much crying in *Alice in Wonderland*. Nearly all the players in Wonderland, with the exception of the Duchess and the Queen, are male, older than Alice, and contentious, imperious, or condescending in their adherence to strict rules. Even in play, logic reigns rigidly in Wonderland in a kind of spoof of the analytical philosophical logic popular at Oxford in Carroll's day. One of the dangers in ending a child's boredom is that the adult's gesture will be, like a bad psychoanalytic session, too coercive, a kind of monstrous bestiary of loud-mouthed creatures and half-human authority figures—like Humpty Dumpty and a tyrannical Queen whose favorite line is "Off with her head!" What is Alice to do with *other* people's wishes, other people's logical desires? As Humpty Dumpty puts it, "The question is . . . which is to be master—that's all" (p. 219).

Lewis Carroll was a teacher of symbolic logic at Oxford, and he loved to make mathematical knots for his pupils to wriggle out of. Carroll's fondness for mathematical puzzles and classical logic admits of both the curious and trivial. He found logical problems and amusements in port prices, postal calculations, even lawn tennis. In 1883 he published a pamphlet, *Lawn Tennis Tournaments,* in which he proved, logically of course, that a player who lost in the first round might find that the finalist was an inferior player to herself. The lessons in *Alice's Adventures in Wonderland* are clever impositions upon the logic, which is to say the reasonableness, of a child. Over the course of the two books, what might at first appear to the child as boring lessons in geography, anatomy, botany, astronomy, linguistics, geology ("What volcano?" [p. 161]), physics, and mathematics are transformed into the form most favored by oracles, kings, and children—riddles: Are flowers alive? Can a kitten play chess? Is saying what one means the same as meaning what one says? Is looking-glass milk good to drink? Both books commence with things that cannot be known, and both are thus about the curiosity and the desires provoked by unnamed somethings. In Alice, such somethings take the form of riddle-like creatures like Cheshire cats without bodies and rabbits with pocket watches. They may be something posing as nothing, or vice versa. In the book's opening chapters, Alice falls literally into a riddle or void of insolubility: She cannot know how long her fall will be nor what is in the bottle on a small glass table, nor what will happen when she drinks from it.

Yet annoying and worrisome enticements are also—and Carroll seems to have understood this perfectly—incitations to desire, curiosity, and empathy—that is, open invitations *not* to be bored, *not* to remain the same as one was but to transform oneself, to relate to things and people outside oneself—and thus bring an end to one's boredom. The book, like a camera obscura, mechanically and miraculously manufactures its exact mirror opposite. Out of Alice's boredom arises a series of events defined by their whimsical changeableness, a series of frenetic and ridiculous lessons in bringing about the disappearance of the thing known as boredom itself. Nonsense, like boredom, turns out to be vast and chaotic, spanning inside and outside and defying notions of time and place, scale and sense, rightness and rudeness, rightness and leftness. Boredom seems a temporary non-event defined by a span of near-indeterminate waiting. Is Alice bored because she is desiring nonsensically or unreasonably?

In place of the dullness of an unread book and a large tract of time she doesn't know how to fill, Alice confronts an officious White Rabbit who is worried about being late, a long or slow fall (it is impossible to tell which) down a hole lined with cupboards and empty jars of marmalade, a bottle that might or might not contain poison, and the frightful—that is, illogical—possibility of drowning in a pool of her own tears. Alice's adventures are mathematically elaborate literary comfits or problem-sets, frustratingly opaque, more or less timeless events that are not quite events, with people who are not quite people, which is to say they are ridiculous obstacles to Alice's desires.

What is the mirror opposite of boredom? It turns out to be a book, after all, one that mirrors and somehow inverts the most insoluble, and hence unforgettable, problems of the day: the extinction of species, the shifting, relative sizes of things, the loss of one's identity and gravitas, and the speed of falling bodies. By chapter IV of *Alice*, "The Rabbit Sends in a Little Bill," Carroll appears to have worked wonders upon his heroine and pupil Alice. In one of her most remarkable early bouts of reasoning, Alice concludes that if she drinks from the bottle, "*something interesting is sure to happen*" (p. 44). Before the end of *Alice's Adventures in Wonderland*, the good-natured Alice will have been distracted from her boredom and will have experienced a host of emotions, from bewilderment over bottles and the right vs. left sides of mushrooms, exasperation with the Mad Hatter's table manners, anger over the rudeness of countless inhabitants of Wonderland, enchantment with miniature gardens, fear of an enormous puppy, and loneliness at having driven a mouse away. Like riddles, the creatures generate an odd mix of pity, curiosity, and exasperation in Alice. The opposite of boredom turns out to be unsettling and frustrating. Ending boredom may be more dangerous a pastime than it at first appears. In this way, Carroll suggests that Alice must be careful that her desires don't turn into worries. The boredom of the world is indeterminate, whereas worrying, because we tend to worry *about* something, is not—and this suggests that the subject of our boredom is somehow intrinsically insoluble, at least by worry.

One of the many paradoxes of both Alice books is that what at first appears trivial, nonsensical, or even boring might have some quite untrivial and curious lesson to deliver after all, and that the idea of the Victorian children's book—whose aim is to educate young readers in the world of morality—might be turned entirely upside down and yet somehow fulfilled at the same time. Lessons in change are paradoxical, as Alice attests:

I wonder if I've been changed in the night? Let me think: *was* I the same when I got up this morning? I almost think I can remember feeling a little different. But if I'm not the same, the next question is, "Who in the world am I?" Ah, *that's* the great puzzle!" (pp. 24–25).

In theory, lessons are imposed so that eventually they may be learned and mastered. Humpty Dumpty claims to be the master of the universe he discourses about. Such a position is precarious. The Liddell sisters would understand the failures of mastery from their scientific geography and mathematical books, some of which Carroll most likely copied into the Alice books. Alice's various encounters and conversations, the mock trials and sporting events—such as croquet games with flamingos as mallets—tend not to go anywhere conclusive. Races are conducted that nobody wins. People sit down to dine but end up not eating anything. Alice or one of her interlocutors will simply walk away from a conversation. These episodes suggest an alternate and much less rational model of our lives, a cornucopia of blunders, non-conversations, and frustrating encounters. Beneath our rational, day-to-day arrangements and reasonable expectations lies something else entirely: a kind of slapstick psychopathology of our own everyday lives. Mastering boredom turns out to be no easier than mastering desire.

WELL-MEANING SPEAKERS AND THE MASTERY OF LANGUAGE

"You won't make yourself a bit realler by crying." (p. 197)

Unlike most of the creatures in Wonderland, Alice tries to use words, perhaps illogically, to express concern for those around her. When Alice asks Humpty Dumpty a question about the *relative* safety of the wall vs. the ground because she is worried about the *likelihood* of his falling off the wall, Humpty Dumpty answers that "there's no chance of" (p. 215) his falling off, and then proceeds to explain what will happen if he does. In this exchange, which Alice feels is not like a conversation because Humpty Dumpty never "said anything to *her;* in fact, his last remark was evidently addressed to a tree" (p. 214). Alice's questions, unlike Humpty Dumpty's, are asked not "with any idea of making another riddle," or a kind of linguistic dueling, "but simply in her good-natured anxiety for

the queer creature" (p. 215). Morality, like laws and manners, are ways
of living with one's own and others' desires. Yet Humpty Dumpty in his
rudeness may be right. Perhaps all desires are riddles, especially to others. For if our desires are inexpressible, then the language with which
we try to communicate our desires will appear, at least to others, as a
kind of linguistic nonsense. The words for our anxieties may be an
incomprehensible poetry of which only the speaker is master.

Although Alice's feelings for others are almost never reciprocated,
they are bizarrely *like* the creatures she speaks to, who could also be
said to be too literal and perhaps too trivial for ordinary words. After
her various encounters, Alice probably wonders what would it mean
for her feelings to feel real? Wonderland abounds with rules, but are
there any logical rules to having feelings? How should Alice talk to a
Cheshire Cat or a Mad Hatter or a pet kitten named Dinah? Children
tend to see animals as fellow creatures and are quite as comfortable
talking to them as they are to people. It must be remembered that the
kitten does not answer Alice's questions and most of Alice's conversations are unsatisfying:

> She quietly walked away: but she couldn't help saying to herself as she
> went, "Of all the unsatisfactory—" (she repeated this aloud, as it was a
> great comfort to have such a long word to say) "of all the unsatisfactory
> people I *ever* met—" She never finished the sentence, for at this moment
> a heavy crash shook the forest from end to end (p. 225).

Like chess and a logical argument, a conversation is a game having a
beginning, middle, and end, and is conducted according to certain
rules or rituals (manners). Most of Alice's non-human interlocutors
(chess pieces, mice, eggs, toads, walrus, lion, unicorn, flowers), however, seem to be playing a different game than Alice. They claim to not
know what Alice "means" or else proclaim, as Humpty Dumpty does,
that a word "means just what I choose it to mean—neither more nor
less" (p. 219). Alice's conversations, when they don't end unsatisfactorily
in silence, tend to go in a circle.

For the child, the ability to have and share feelings might even
be inversely related to language acquisition, so that paradoxically the
more skilled the child is in language, the *less* able she is to express the
intensity of her first feelings, which are by definition primal and non-
verbal. The creatures of Wonderland, from kittens to mad hatters, con-

stitute a kind of mute allegory for the things like hunger, love, and sex that Alice feels, and they seem difficult to communicate to her interlocutors. An unsure speaker is simply one whose words don't feel real. But in *Alice* what is real and what is fantasy? Language enables the child to name the world and exert mastery over it; but in relation to feelings, language can seem impoverished, like a starving of one's desires. The language of one's own dream may not be all nourishing, after all. After waking, Alice's sister tells her to run in and have some tea. And in *Looking-Glass,* Alice promises the kitten a breakfast accompanied by a tale of the Walrus and his oysters—as if poetry were nourishment.

In *Alice* tears are shed, creatures are taken for a stroll and then devoured, and Queens scream their heads off. Yet if strong feelings and unreasonable desires abound in the Alice books, understanding the feelings of others is scarce. In chapter I of *Looking-Glass,* the Queen, after looking at the King's memorandum book that Alice has written in, proclaims to the King: "That's not a memorandum of *your* feelings!" (p. 163). After the mouse tells his sad tale of persecution, Alice asks, "But why do you call it sad?" (p. 36). Having feelings is one thing; understanding someone else's is another. After hearing Tweedledee and Tweedledum's story of the Walrus and the Carpenter, even the compassionate Alice says: "I like the Walrus best . . . because you see he was a *little* sorry for the poor oysters" (p. 195). Alice is uncertain *what amount* she should feel, which is to say her feelings feel like guesses. Alice first spied the Mock Turtle

> sitting sad and lonely on a little ledge of rock. . . . She pitied him deeply. "What is his sorrow?" she asked the Gryphon. And the Gryphon answered, very nearly in the same words as before, "It's all his fancy, that: he hasn't got no sorrow, you know." . . .
>
> "This here young lady," said the Gryphon, "she wants for to know your history, she do."
>
> "I'll tell it her," said the Mock Turtle in a deep, hollow tone. "Sit down, both of you, and don't speak a word till I've finished."
>
> So they sat down, and nobody spoke for some minutes. Alice thought to herself, "I don't see how he can *ever* finish, if he doesn't begin" (p. 108).

When is a feeling not a feeling? Perhaps when you want to share a feeling that you can't. Alice's feelings and her conversations go nowhere because they have no one to go to. Alice generally experiences her emotions by herself—that is, her emotions, like pity, are usually rapidly substituted by a chain of dissatisfaction and worry. For this reason, they appear shallow and unreal.

INEDIBLE PUNS AND WORDPLAY IN WONDERLAND

"That's a great deal to make one word mean," Alice said in a thoughtful tone.

"When I make a word do a lot of work like that," said Humpty Dumpty, "I always pay it extra." (p. 219)

It is not surprising that *Alice's Adventures in Wonderland,* like any drama about growing up, is also a drama of the arbitrary, nonsensical, and unending transformations and erasures that characterize games, conversations, and literature. Thus *Alice* is a novel of growing up that is populated with twins and twinned occurrences, speakers who repeat exactly what another says, people appearing and disappearing out of nowhere, birthday presents that don't feel like presents, and Carroll's parodies of conventionally didactic school verses. Many of the characters in *Alice* don't just speak in rude puns and insoluble riddles—they are puns and riddles that have been transformed into characters. Both characters and narrative events are at times indistinguishable from nonsensical linguistic transformations. In the Humpty Dumpty chapter in *Looking-Glass*:

The egg only got larger and larger, and more and more human: when [Alice] had come within a few yards of it, she saw that it had eyes and a nose and mouth; and when she had come close to it, she saw clearly that it was HUMPTY DUMPTY himself. "It can't be anybody else!" she said to herself. "I'm as certain of it, as if his name were written all over his face!"

To which Carroll disingenuously adds: "It might have been written a hundred times, easily, on that enormous face" (p. 214).

Growing up, like writing a pun or falling in love, is the occasion for perhaps some of the most absurd of human feelings. These feelings are suggested by the non-conversations, questions answered with riddles, and wordplay of the Alice books: paronomasia, linguistic substitution, antanaclasis, anagrams, punning, palindromic progression and erasure, repetition with minor variation, spurious etymological derivations, and reverse mirroring. These linguistic "events" take place in a time that is not clearly the present ("in about half no time!" [p. 106] as the Queen puts it) but which seems to reference an endless becoming. Such activities are related to Alice's erroneous multiplication tables, the "sweet little nothings" whispered by lovers, Alice's unwitting jibes, and the unforeseen appearance of the Cheshire Cat's grin. A short excerpt from one of the Duchess's speeches in "The Mock Turtle's Story" is exemplary. The passage begins with an injunction not to imagine something, passes through the vicissitudes of understanding, and finally ends with an entreaty to not speak; this series of transformations is similar to growing out of childhood itself, which is suggested here by a birthday present one doesn't want to have:

> "I quite agree with you," said the Duchess; "and the moral of that is—'Be what you would seem to be'—or, if you'd like it put more simply—'Never imagine yourself not to be otherwise than what it might appear to others that what you were or might have been was not otherwise than what you had been would have appeared to them to be otherwise.' "
>
> "I think I should understand that better," Alice said very politely, "if I had it written down: but I ca'n't quite follow it as you say it. . . . Pray don't trouble yourself to say it any longer than that," said Alice.
>
> "Oh, don't talk about trouble!" said the Duchess. "I make you a present of everything I've said as yet."
>
> "A cheap sort of present!" thought Alice. "I'm glad people don't give birthday-presents like that!" But she did not venture to say it out loud (p. 105).

Growing up, which is what Alice is in the midst of, is a strange, nonsensical, and paradoxical event in which boredom and interest, possibility and probability, childish fantasy and adult reality intermingle. If possibility is about desire, then probability is about its limitations, the things Alice can't say or do. And that is where nonsense, which is where the probable becomes indistinguishable from the possible, comes into play, along with anxiety, misunderstanding, puns, and death. Our desires, like puns, are absurd to think about, imagine, speak, or exchange. Moreover, our desires are almost impossible to realize. The things that happen in the Alice books are not quite events or exchanges; they are more like meta-events, things that are logically conceivable within a specified range of actions (possible) or things that are logically likely within a range of actions (probable). All events in the Alice books thus feel like non sequiturs. What kind of sense does growing up make to the child trapped in a present that has not yet become future? "I don't know when I began it, but somehow I felt as if I'd been singing it a long long time!" (p. 190). Freud noted in *The Interpretation of Dreams* that "in the unconscious, nothing can be brought to an end, nothing is past or forgotten."[8] As Adam Phillips notes, for children, "answers merely interrupt questions."[9] The opposite of endless waiting may be endless and infinite becoming, with Alice growing larger one moment and shrinking the next. If Alice's wishes were merely boring repetitions of things she already knew, rather than nonsensical re-expressions or puns of her never-ending desires, she would have nothing more to be curious about or quibble with—in others or in herself—and not being able to do these things, she would be left with something anomalous and inhuman.

In the second "fit" of Carroll's *The Hunting of the Snark: An Agony in Eight Fits*, the poet calls attention to the division, seen as a kind of "interruption," inherent in the (verbal) definition of a thing. The narrator of the poem proposes "one" of the characteristics of a snark but like a magician ends up by specifying two: "It will sigh like a thing that is deeply distressed: / And it always looks grave as a pun." With its doubled meanings contained (accidentally) in a single word, the pun suggests the inexpressible, a kind of irreducible argument that takes shape as a single word which, rather than repeating its meaning, splits violently into two senses. Like desire, the pun is inexpressible. Its meanings sprawl endlessly, non-purposively, and violently. Our wishes, which take grammatical form as questions,[10] are a kind of metaphysical nonsense about the unspecified things they may become. Childhood desires exist to be transformed into something else: a book, a pet kitten, a lover, a grown-up sister, even a Cheshire Cat or a White Knight.

The story of Alice is a story of what her desires, her curiosity, will find and how, in the process, they become something else." Elizabeth Sewell notes of nonsense words, "If a word does not look like a word . . . , the mind will not play with it."[11] Yet nonsense, like fertility, "has a fear of nothing."[12] Or, as Jacques Lacan noted, "the signifier is stupid" and in the pun engenders "a stupid smile."[13] In a world where desires are like puns, the dispute between true versus false becomes absurd, like a puzzle without a solution, a game without rules, effects without causes, desires without satisfactions—or a grin without the cat. Such a condition is grave; the Queen, upon witnessing the chaos of a croquet game, demands to trump the untrumpable by having "everybody executed, all round" (p. 99). Carroll conceived of the Queen "as a sort of embodiment of ungovernable passion—a blind and aimless Fury."[14] Thus much of the nonsense, curiosity, and desire of the Alice books can be answered only with silence or death—or other radical misinterpretations. But, of course, one wants to know if death is a misinterpretation of nonsense—or is it the other way around? To put it in terms relevant to Alice, is death nonsensical, or is nonsense a cloak for death? The Mouse's tale is at bottom something to read. It is an emblematic poem about injustice, shaped like a mouse's tail. It begins on a Monday morning with Fury having "nothing to do" (p. 37) and culminates with the unspeakable: Fury's illogical persecution of and condemnation of a mouse to death—a deadly joke about the literal and figurative end of a tale/tail, which is to say a joke about nothing.

Unlike the endless substitutions of the pun, death "confronts us with the fact that, despite the capacity for substitution that development, in psychoanalytic terms, depends upon, there are no substitutes."[15] The joke and pun put up a shabby, even stupid resistance to things that must die, and so they are a paean to continuing misinterpretation. The pun is grave; but so is all language, which ceases at the borders of rudeness in order to conceal the fact that after a certain point, there are no more things to be said, that talking is a nonsensical covering for the rude silence that cannot be concealed. As Freud noted, unlike the child, the "civilized adult . . . can hardly even entertain the thought of another person's death without seeming to himself hard-hearted and wicked."[16] Alice mentions her cat Dinah and unwittingly brings silence to her interlocutors. Alice is not yet fearful of death or bodily changes. She is learning that to be subjected to the desires of others is to be subjected to unbearable puns and nonsensical commands. To the Queen's frantic calls for a beheading, and to her query about why people are lying face down on the ground, Alice responds:

"How should *I* know?" said Alice, surprised at her own courage. "It's no business of *mine.*"

The Queen turned crimson with fury, and, after glaring at her for a

moment like a wild beast, began screaming "Off with her head! Off
with—"

"Nonsense!" said Alice, very loudly and decidedly, and the Queen
was silent (p. 93).

Alice is not surprised by what she doesn't know because she has no
desire to know it ("It's no business of *mine*"), and this serves as an anti-
dote to the Queen's fury. But fury may be no less and no more express-
ible than the other emotions Alice has. One can no more choose to be
or not be angry than worried or curious. Among many other things,
good manners may be Alice's pragmatic way of living within her own
wishes. Saying no is merely a polite way of saying no to more nonsense
than the mind can bear.

INDETERMINISM AND THINGS NOT EATEN

"I like the Walrus best," said Alice: "because you see he was a *little*
sorry for the poor oysters." (p. 195)

A world consumed by non-stop punning is an indeterministic world
where chance rules and creates what the nineteenth-century French
statistician Poisson termed the very rare event—what became known as
the Poisson distribution. Following such a mathematical curve, *all*
events in the Alice books are equally unexpected concatenations, and
many characters are improbable hybrids of animals and people and
insects, most of whom speak reasonably well. Being a pragmatist, Alice
wonders, and then worries, about what she will eat. She also, less nor-
mally, wonders and worries if she will be eaten, though she fails to realize that for something to eat, something else must be eaten. Thus she
mentions her cat Dinah to a mouse and birds. Many of the creatures
behave like strange recipes for inedible foods, food that would prefer to
talk back than be consumed. The tove is a badger with the "short horns
of a stag," and a borogrove is an extinct "kind of Parrot" that "lived on
veal."[17] Wonderland and the world beyond the looking glass is home to
a Rocking-horse-fly that is made of wood and swings from branch to
branch, a Dragon-fly whose body is formed of plum pudding, and a
Bread-and-butter fly whose wings are thin slices of bread and whose
head is a lump of sugar. Edible lobsters dance the quadrille. The chief

ingredient of Mock Turtle soup sings a rather sad and piquant song, and Alice travels in a carriage compartment that holds a goat, a gentleman dressed in white paper, a horse, a beetle, and a gnat that is large as a chicken but whose voice sounds like that of a horse. All this follows upon Alice's seeing a "regular bee" that was quite irregular: "in fact, it was an elephant" (p. 177).

These cross-pollinated creatures are sui generis beings who resemble another strange creature in Carroll's works: the portmanteau word—the highly individuated, one-of-a-kind linguistic phenomenon that is predictably unreliable at communicating meaning. Like most things whose actions are improbable, such creatures can hardly be believed. They appear to be governed neither by rule nor by law. In this sense, very little can be inferred about their nature or their genus. The contemplation of life forms turns out to be frustratingly abstract; the creatures are as unpredictable as unsolved problems. And like most anomalous specimens and unappeasable desires, they seem to have gone extinct before their proper time, as witness the Dodo and borogrove. Yet such is the accidental nature of organic life itself, the life of desire, which the French philosopher Bichat noted defies "every kind of calculation, for it would be necessary to have as many different rules as there are different cases."[18] In this sense, Wonderland is a belated nineteenth-century ecosystem, a pastoral mathematical formula on the verge of logical extinction. In this system, determinism, as an immutable law, is being subjected to the twentieth century's "laws" of chance. There is a simpler way to state this: Many creatures in the Alice books are edible things that remain inedible to Alice: lobsters, mock turtle soup, a rabbit, a duck, a pig, a fish, oysters, a whiting, an egg—Alice has no desire to eat them. Our appetites are arbitrary. If our desires are not surprising to ourselves, they probably don't work very well as desires. One of the first things Alice eats is something that is, from a botanical standpoint, neither living nor dead and so, from a logical standpoint, incapable of having desire: a mushroom.

For all her worrying, Alice does little eating, and this suggests three things: that her desire to eat remains unresolved (a kind of self-punning on her wants); that her consumption patterns are anarchic rather than habitual; and that she is too reasonable with her appetites, conversing with foods (that she should be eating). Being a pragmatist with one's emotions is dangerous play. Instead of feeling, Alice tends to worry, just like the White Rabbit who is a parody of an adult male who worries too much. Worries are a form of policing one's desires, often before they become desires. Yet worries are not easy to see for what they are. Like a pun, the White Rabbit keeps disappearing. Worries are almost feelings. Like minor disturbances, they disappear and begin again and disappear and begin again. They are the feelings we don't want to be having—but are.

From a Darwinian perspective, many creatures of Wonderland are both inedible *and* extremely rare. Yet they exist. They constitute a bestiary of related things, though their family lineages are murky. They inhabit the same world and dine at the same table, yet they are antithetical to community. They do not share their feelings, and this makes them likely to be forgotten. For Carroll, like most nineteenth-century probability experts, eccentricity is another word for deviance, opposed to the normal, and bad for reproduction. The identical twins Tweedledee and Tweedledum threaten to become the victims of a fratricide. Not surprisingly, when Alice sees them she wonders if they are alive. The same could be said of Wonderland and the world beyond the looking glass, which, like childhood and the life of a gnat, verge on expiration. Unlike a bored child, the White Rabbit is in a very big hurry, in a race with the watch he carries on his person. In a gesture of compassionate conservation, Carroll terminates *Through the Looking-Glass* with a manual of extinction, his unending desire couched as a memorial poem for Alice herself: "Long has paled that sunny sky: / Echos fade and memories die: / Autumn frosts have slain July" (p. 272).

Near the end of the books, Alice angrily calls quits to the pack of cards and pulls the tablecloth out from under the diners' meal. Indeterminism creates a world where there is no end to worrying about what Alice was unable to consume, and the most non-consumable thing about ourselves is our own passions. What is to be done with them? Desire resembles a game not with subjects who reciprocate our feelings but with losers and winners. Both books end violently, with the upsetting of a table and of a pack of cards, acts that suggest the end of an unsuccessful game and the figurative death of Alice's desires. So the final book ends—with a poem that signals Carroll's farewell.

PROBABLE ENDINGS AND IMPROBABLE BEGINNINGS

"And if he left off dreaming about you, where do you suppose you'd be?"

"Where I am now, of course," said Alice.

"Not you!" Tweedledee retorted contemptuously. "You'd be nowhere. Why, you're only a sort of thing in his dream!"

"If that there King was to wake," added Tweedledum, "you'd go out—bang!—just like a candle!" (p. 197)

Both Alice books begin with dullness, pass through fantasy and end with waking (back to dullness). Boredom is a part of the indeterminate stuff of this world, a kind of question that cannot be answered by our desires. The various animal and human-like creatures in *Alice's Adventures in Wonderland* and *Through the Looking-Glass* are in the end difficult to locate in any real place. Yet Carroll fastidiously brackets each book to suggest that the vagaries of dreaming and nonsense occur within the boundaries of a book and the head of a sleeping child. Alice wakes to a world of dull reasonableness, which is to say that chance has yet to become the chief quality of the world out there, what the philosopher Ian Hacking terms "objective chance." Yet for the child, curiosity, like love, is defined by boundlessness. Dullness without, chaos and wonder within—or is it the other way around?

Alice and *Looking-Glass* are nineteenth-century works; they regard disorder and chaos as problems to be tucked away in regressive moments of dreaming and remembering. And yet, as Ian Hacking points out, the problems of one century become the solutions of the next. The dangers of possibility and chaos in the nineteenth century become the immutable laws of chance and uncertainty in the twentieth. Determinism erodes throughout both books: The world becomes a place not where things happened but where fantastic things might have happened. But then, of course, looking at it from the nineteenth-century perspective of Alice's looking glass, they might not have happened at all. Alice is unsure if it even was her dream.

The final chapter of *Alice*, "Alice's Evidence," ends with the Queen's coercive command for "Sentence first—verdict afterwards" followed with Alice's reply: "Stuff and nonsense!" (p. 140). The line between "stuff" and "nonsense" is not so clear, although Alice tries to make the distinction. Precisely at this moment the nonsense, after reaching an insufferable level, ends, and Alice awakens with her head in her sister's lap. She tells her sister her dream, whereupon her sister dreams Alice's dream. But this second dream is different from Alice's, for it is a dream in which the dreamer is half awake and acknowledges that the dream cannot last forever and will "change to dull reality" (p. 143). Alice, her sister surmises, will wake and grow up into everyday reality, within which the dull and boring world no longer seems opposed to desires but must be reconciled to them. Earlier the extinct Dodo had solemnly called for "more energetic remedies" (p. 35), but clearly the time for such remedies has passed. Alice's sister entertains one last image of Alice, another invention but more tempered than earlier ones: "Lastly, she pictured to herself how this same little sister of hers would, in the after-time, be herself a grown woman; and how she would keep, through all her riper years, the simple and loving heart of her childhood" (p. 144).

It is a mistake to read these books, as many critics have, as lessons in growing up or in mastering or coercing experience (particularly boredom), through play or other means. If anything, the books suggest what the reasonable Alice, at the end of the book, still doesn't know. It is, after all, not Alice but her sister who sees in Alice's waking a probable future that Alice has herself yet to experience. Mastery turns out to be a communal rather than solitary affair. Alice's sister has a reminiscence of Alice the child before Alice has taken leave of childhood. Thus do inexorable probabilities creep in and replace the highly improbable creatures of Alice's dream. The reader knows that Alice's sister is *probably* right: Boredom and dull reality will return when Alice wakens and then grows into an adult. And yet a memory that is not yet a memory is a highly improbable event. What control over the things we remember will we ultimately have? What for Alice has been lost but not yet lost? Of course, we often seem to know something is lost before we lose it—and this feeling suffuses childhood and the adult's recollection of what that childhood was, which is probably the only childhood he or she can have. Such is the nature of desire: One desires things that have yet to be and that are in some sense already lost to the moment of desire. When the Queen pricks her finger, Alice asks why she doesn't scream. The Queen replies, "Why, I've done all the screaming already" (p. 206).

In a paradoxical way, the book suggests that one has desires *in order to* forget them and thus grow into the future rather than merely repeat one's past. In the moments before Alice wakes, both books delineate unsatisfying and indeterminate chaos: In *Through the Looking-Glass,* the guests are being devoured by their foods; in *Alice's Adventures in Wonderland,* the Queen orders Alice's execution and a pack of cards flies upon poor Alice, who finally exclaims, reasoning backward as it were into a realm of diminishing possibilities: "You're nothing but a pack of cards!" (p. 140). Here Alice reverses the logical argument of the earlier chapters, in which she (or something inside her) turned nothing into something. After this point, the story of Alice's "real" life is set to unfold. This suggests that Alice is no longer trapped in someone else's dream (of her). Like a good many children who are on the verge of not being children, Alice is learning forgetfulness, as a prelude to something (the future of one's desires) that cannot be known with certitude. Childhood desires thus comprise a nonsense of a different order.

For Carroll, boredom still manages a moral impetus: It teaches the adult (Alice is an adult before her time) that nonsense is *both* possible and necessary; it also teaches the adult that nonsense is a regressive fiction that one wakes from and waking from, then mourns. For an adult, the nonsense of childhood is the nonsense of its loss. Competing necessities govern the end of each book, and they govern the strategies involved in regulating one's desires, which also need to be forgotten so they can be retold. Only by forgetting childhood desires can a certain amount of sense be gained. But, of course, the absence of those desires has to be regulated too; perhaps boredom is a preemptive strike at desires we may never have. None of the games that Alice plays suggests mastery, a narrative thread, the end of conflict, the resolution of a misunderstanding, or a satisfying answer to the questions her desires pose. It is Alice's sister who forgets for her, rather than Alice herself.

Of the two books, *Through the Looking-Glass* is the bleaker; it ends with a question, whereas *Alice's Adventures in Wonderland* ends with a sister's loving reminiscence, delivered in Wordsworthian fashion as a premature eulogy for a childhood not yet lost, a lost childhood whose losses were *already* being deferred, as it were, by a familial caretaker. One of the ways to learn to give up an unbearable personal fantasy (and Alice can barely bear hers) is to make it the subject of a story. But once that is done, a mystery ends and with it a part of desire. What story can be told to get desire back? Perhaps storytelling offers a clue to deferring desires for something that has not yet arrived. To speak is to speak, as Carroll does, of imaginary things. *Alice's Adventures in Wonderland* is, after all, a story told by Carroll to children, and Alice in turn tells her sister her dream, another kind of story. At the close of both Alice books, the adult reader/listener again confronts Alice the child, someone on the verge of becoming someone else, someone the grown-up reader knows well, someone who is "loving and gentle . . . courteous to *all*, high or low . . . trustful, ready to accept the wildest impossibilities with all that utter trust that only dreamers know; and lastly, curious—wildly curious, and with the eager enjoyment of Life that comes only in the happy hours of childhood."[19] Understanding desires turns out to be a communal rather than a solitary experience. For Alice's dream language to make sense, Alice must escape it first. The easiest way to escape is to make it the subject of a sharing; the language of the dream must be given to someone else.

Like Alice's sister's act of remembering, the reader's recognition is a repetition with a difference, because the repetition involves retelling. Repetition is about eternity and stopping time; repetition with a difference presupposes change and time passing. Carroll tellingly pairs impossibility with curiosity—even if such impossibilities are something not entirely forgotten. The adult is a child whose childhood desires are something she hasn't learned to forget. Such acts of forgetting, like acts of mastery, turn out to be equally contingent as the futures the child hasn't yet had. The problems Alice confronts, for all their seeming reality, are the stuff of fantasy, but the fantasy may be merely a screen for banal fears and anxieties the adult world generates: how to put on shoes when your feet are too far off; how to get into a door that is too small; how to reach a golden key; how to get out of a pool of one's own tears? In this sense the nonsensical obstacles of childhood, the things known as fantasies, become the more reasonable problems of adulthood, but they remain problems to be solved nonetheless. If the problems we have never go away and are in some sense insoluble—that is, unforgettable—what moral stories might we tell as consolation? One of the things the adult imagines is, of course, an adulthood that never quite arrived to take the place of Wonderland.

Tan Lin is a writer, artist, and critic. He is the author of two books of poetry, *Lotion Bullwhip Giraffe,* and *BlipSoak01*. He received his Ph.D. from Columbia University and teaches creative writing at New Jersey City University.

NOTES TO THE INTRODUCTION

1. Adam Phillips, *The Beast in the Nursery* (New York: Basic Books, 1998), pp. 134–135.
2. Mark Haworth-Booth, "The Photographic Moment of Lewis Carroll," in Morton N. Cohen, ed., *Reflections in a Looking-Glass: A Centennial Celebration of Lewis Carroll, Photographer* (New York: Aperture, 1998), p. 127.
3. Derek Hudson, *Lewis Carroll: An Illustrated Biography* (London: Constable, 1976), p. 114.
4. Hudson, p. 114.
5. Hudson, p. 152.
6. Walter Benjamin, *The Arcades Project*, translated by Howard Eiland and Kevin McLaughlin (Cambridge, MA: Harvard University Press, 1999), p. 105.
7. Adam Phillips, *On Kissing, Tickling, and Being Bored* (Cambridge, MA: Harvard University Press, 1993), p. 78.
8. Adam Phillips, *Terrors and Experts* (Cambridge, MA: Harvard University Press, 1996), p. 1.
9. Phillips, *Terrors and Experts*, p. 1.
10. Adam Phillips, *Promises Promises* (London: Faber, 2000), p. 175.
11. Elizabeth Sewell, "The Balance of Brillig," in *Alice in Wonderland*, edited by Donald J. Gray, second edition (New York: Norton, 1992), p. 384.
12. Sewell, p. 384.
13. Gregory Ulmer, "The Puncept in Grammatology," in *On Puns*, edited by Jonathan Culler (Oxford: Blackwell, 1988), p. 176.
14. Martin Gardner, *The Annotated Alice* (New York: Clarkson N. Potter, 1960), p. 109.
15. Adam Phillips, *On Flirtation* (Cambridge, MA: Harvard University Press, 1994), p. xx.
16. Phillips, *On Flirtation*, p. xx.
17. Gardner, p. 191.
18. Ian Hacking, *The Taming of Chance* (New York: Cambridge University Press, 1990), p. 14.
19. Hudson, p. 156.

Alice's Adventures in Wonderland

PREFACE

To The

EIGHTY-SIXTH THOUSAND

Enquiries have been so often addressed to me, as to whether any answer to the Hatter's Riddle (see p. 79) can be imagined, that I may as well put on record here what seems to me to be a fairly appropriate answer, viz. "Because it can produce a few notes, though they are *very* flat; and it is nevar put with the wrong end in front!" This, however, is merely an after-thought: the Riddle, as originally invented, had no answer at all.

All in the golden afternoon
Full leisurely we glide;
For both our oars, with little skill,
By little arms are plied,
While little hands make vain pretence
Our wanderings to guide.

Ah, cruel Three! In such an hour,
Beneath such dreamy weather,
To beg a tale of breath too weak
To stir the tiniest feather!
Yet what can one poor voice avail
Against three tongues together?

Imperious Prima flashes forth
Her edict "to begin it":
In gentler tones Secunda hopes
"There will be nonsense in it!"
While Tertia interrupts the tale
Not MORE than once a minute.

Anon, to sudden silence won,
In fancy they pursue
The dream-child moving through a land
Of wonders wild and new,
In friendly chat with bird or beast—
And half believe it true.

And ever, as the story drained
The wells of fancy dry,
And faintly strove that weary one
To put the subject by,
"The rest next time—" "It IS next time!"
The happy voices cry.

Thus grew the tale of Wonderland:
Thus slowly, one by one,
Its quaint events were hammered out—

And now the tale is done,
And home we steer, a merry crew,
Beneath the setting sun.

Alice! A childish story take,
And, with a gentle hand,
Lay it where Childhood's dreams are twined
In Memory's mystic band,
Like pilgrim's wither'd wreath of flowers
Pluck'd in a far-off land.

CHRISTMAS-GREETINGS.

[FROM A FAIRY TO A CHILD.]

Lady dear, if Fairies may
For a moment lay aside
Cunning tricks and elfish play,
'T is at happy Christmas-tide.

We have heard the children say—
Gentle children, whom we love—
Long ago, on Christmas Day,
Came a message from above.

Still, as Christmas-tide comes round,
They remember it again—
Echo still the joyful sound
"Peace on earth, good-will to men!"

Yet the hearts must childlike be
Where such heavenly guests abide;
Unto children, in their glee,
All the year is Christmas-tide!

Thus, forgetting tricks and play
For a moment, Lady dear,
We would wish you, if we may,
Merry Christmas, glad New Year!

Christmas, 1867.

Contents

I

Down the Rabbit Hole

A lice was beginning to get very tired of sitting by her sister on the bank, and of having nothing to do; once or twice she had peeped into the book her sister was reading, but it had no pictures or conversations in it, "and what is the use of a book," thought Alice, "without pictures or conversations?"

So she was considering, in her own mind (as well as she could, for the hot day made her feel very sleepy and stupid), whether the pleasure of making a daisy-chain would be worth the trouble of getting up and picking the daisies, when suddenly a White Rabbit with pink eyes ran close by her.

There was nothing so *very* remarkable in that; nor did Alice think it so *very* much out of the way to hear the Rabbit say to itself "Oh dear! Oh dear! I shall be too late!" (when she thought it over afterwards, it occurred to her that she ought to have wondered at this, but at the time it all seemed quite natural); but, when the Rabbit actually *took a watch out of its waistcoat-pocket,* and looked at it, and then hurried on, Alice started to her feet, for it flashed across her mind that she had never before seen a rabbit with either a waistcoat-pocket, or a watch to take out of it, and, burning with curiosity, she ran across the field after it, and was just in time to see it pop down a large rabbit-hole under the hedge.

In another moment down went Alice after it, never once considering how in the world she was to get out again.

The rabbit-hole went straight on like a tunnel for some way, and then dipped suddenly down, so suddenly that Alice had not a moment to think about stopping herself before she found herself falling down what seemed to be a very deep well.

Either the well was very deep, or she fell very slowly, for she had plenty of time as she went down to look about her, and to wonder what was going to happen next. First, she tried to look down and make out what she was coming to, but it was too dark to see anything: then she looked at the sides of the well, and noticed that they were filled with cupboards and book-shelves: here and there she saw maps and pictures hung upon pegs. She took down a jar from one of the shelves as she passed: it was labeled "ORANGE MARMALADE," but to her great disappointment it was empty: she did not like to drop the jar, for fear of killing somebody underneath, so managed to put it into one of the cupboards as she fell past it.

"Well!" thought Alice to herself. "After such a fall as this, I shall think nothing of tumbling down-stairs! How brave they'll all think me at home! Why, I wouldn't say anything about it, even if I fell off the top of the house!" (Which was very likely true.)

Down, down, down. Would the fall *never* come to an end? "I wonder how many miles I've fallen by this time?" she said aloud. "I must be getting somewhere near the centre of the earth. Let me see: that would be four thousand miles down, I think—" (for, you see, Alice had learnt several things of this sort in her lessons in the schoolroom, and though this was not a *very* good opportunity for showing off her knowledge, as there was no one to listen to her, still it was good practice to say it over) "—yes, that's about the right distance—but then I wonder what Latitude or Longitude I've got to?" (Alice had not the slightest idea what Latitude was, or Longitude either, but she thought they were nice grand words to say.)

Presently she began again. "I wonder if I shall fall right *through* the earth! How funny it'll seem to come out among the people that walk with their heads downwards! The antipathies, I think—" (she was rather glad there *was* no one listening, this time, as it didn't sound at all the right word) "—but I shall have to ask them what the name of the country is, you know. Please, Ma'am, is this New Zealand? Or Australia?" (and she tried to curtsey as she spoke—fancy, *curtseying* as you're falling through the air! Do you think you could manage it?) "And what an ignorant little girl she'll think me for asking! No, it'll never do to ask: perhaps I shall see it written up somewhere."

Down, down, down. There was nothing else to do, so Alice soon began talking again. "Dinah'll miss me very much to-night, I should think!" (Dinah* was the cat.) "I hope they'll remember her saucer of milk at tea-time. Dinah, my dear! I wish you were down here with me! There are no mice in the air, I'm afraid, but you might catch a bat, and that's very like a mouse, you know. But do cats eat bats, I wonder?" And here Alice began to get rather sleepy, and went on saying to herself, in a dreamy sort of way, "Do cats eat bats? Do cats eat bats?" and sometimes "Do bats eat cats?", for, you see, as she couldn't answer either question, it didn't much matter which way she put it. She felt that

---

*The Liddells had a cat named Dinah.

she was dozing off, and had just begun to dream that she was walking hand in hand with Dinah, and was saying to her, very earnestly, "Now, Dinah, tell me the truth: did you ever eat a bat?", when suddenly, thump! thump! down she came upon a heap of sticks and dry leaves, and the fall was over.

Alice was not a bit hurt, and she jumped up on to her feet in a moment: she looked up, but it was all dark overhead: before her was another long passage, and the White Rabbit was still in sight, hurrying down it. There was not a moment to be lost: away went Alice like the wind, and was just in time to hear it say, as it turned a corner, "Oh my ears and whiskers, how late it's getting!" She was close behind it when she turned the corner, but the Rabbit was no longer to be seen: she found herself in a long, low hall, which was lit up by a row of lamps hanging from the roof.

There were doors all round the hall, but they were all locked; and when Alice had been all the way down one side and up the other, trying every door, she walked sadly down the middle, wondering how she was ever to get out again.

Suddenly she came upon a little three-legged table, all made of solid glass: there was nothing on it but a tiny golden key, and Alice's first idea was that this might belong to one of the doors of the hall; but, alas! either the locks were too large, or the key was too small, but at any rate it would not open any of them. However, on the second time round, she came upon a low curtain she had not noticed before, and behind it was a little door about fifteen inches high: she tried the little golden key in the lock, and to her great delight it fitted!

Alice opened the door and found that it led into a small passage, not much larger than a rat-hole: she knelt down and looked along the passage into the loveliest garden you ever saw. How she longed to get out of that dark hall, and wander about among those beds of bright flowers and those cool fountains, but she could not even get her head through the doorway; "and even if my head *would* go through," thought poor Alice, "it would be of very little use without my shoulders. Oh, how I wish I could shut up like a telescope! I think I could, if I only knew how to begin." For, you see, so many out-of-the-way things had happened lately, that Alice had begun to think that very few things indeed were really impossible.

There seemed to be no use in waiting by the little door, so she went back to the table, half hoping she might find another key on it, or at any rate a book of rules for shutting people up like telescopes: this time she found a little bottle on it ("which certainly was not here before," said Alice), and tied round the neck of the bottle was a paper label, with the words "DRINK ME" beautifully printed on it in large letters.

It was all very well to say "Drink me," but the wise little Alice was not going to do *that* in a hurry. "No, I'll look first," she said, "and see whether it's marked 'poison' or not"; for she had read several nice little stories about children who had got burnt, and eaten up by wild beasts, and other unpleasant things, all because they *would* not remember the simple rules their friends had taught them: such as, that a red-hot poker will burn you if you hold it too long; and that, if you cut your finger *very* deeply with a knife, it usually bleeds; and she had never forgotten that, if you drink much from a bottle marked "poison," it is almost certain to disagree with you, sooner or later.

However, this bottle was *not* marked "poison," so Alice ventured to taste it, and, finding it very nice (it had, in fact, a sort of mixed flavour of cherry-tart, custard, pine-apple, roast turkey, toffy, and hot buttered toast), she very soon finished it off.[1]

* * * * * * * * * * * * * *

"What a curious feeling!" said Alice. "I must be shutting up like a telescope!"

And so it was indeed: she was now only ten inches high, and her face brightened up at the thought that she was now the right size for going through the little door into that lovely garden. First, however, she waited for a few minutes to see if she was going to shrink any further: she felt a little nervous about this; "for it might end, you know," said Alice to herself, "in my going out altogether, like a candle. I wonder what I should be like then?" And she tried to fancy what the flame of a candle looks like after the candle is blown out, for she could not remember ever having seen such a thing.

After a while, finding that nothing more happened, she decided on going into the garden at once; but, alas for poor Alice! when she got to the door, she found she had forgotten the little golden key, and when she went back to the table for it, she found she could not possibly reach it: she could see it quite plainly through the glass, and she tried her best to climb up one of the legs of the table, but it was too slippery; and when she had tired herself out with trying, the poor little thing sat down and cried.

"Come, there's no use in crying like that!" said Alice to herself rather sharply. "I advise you to leave off this minute!" She generally gave herself very good advice (though she very seldom followed it), and sometimes she scolded herself so severely as to bring tears into her eyes; and once she remembered trying to box her own ears for having cheated herself in a game of croquet she was playing against herself, for this curious child was very fond of pretending to be two people. "But it's no use now," thought poor Alice, "to pretend to be two people! Why, there's hardly enough of me left to make *one* respectable person!"

Soon her eye fell on a little glass box that was lying under the table: she opened it, and found in it a very small cake, on which the words "EAT ME" were beautifully marked in currants. "Well, I'll eat it," said Alice, "and if it makes me grow larger, I can reach the key; and if it makes me grow smaller, I can creep under the door: so either way I'll get into the garden, and I don't care which happens!"

She ate a little bit, and said anxiously to herself "Which way? Which way?", holding her hand on the top of her head to feel which way it was growing; and she was quite surprised to find that she remained the same size. To be sure, this is what generally happens when one eats cake; but Alice had got so much into the way of expecting nothing but out-of-the-way things to happen, that it seemed quite dull and stupid for life to go on in the common way.

So she set to work, and very soon finished off the cake.

*   *   *   *   *   *   *   *   *   *   *   *   *   *   *

II

The Pool of Tears

C uriouser and curiouser!" cried Alice (she was so much surprised, that for the moment she quite forgot how to speak good English). "Now I'm opening out like the largest telescope that ever was! Good-bye, feet!" (for when she looked down at her feet, they seemed to be almost out of sight, they were getting so far off). "Oh, my poor little feet, I wonder who will put on your shoes and stockings for you now, dears? I'm sure *I* sha'n't be able! I shall be a great deal too far off to trouble myself about you: you must manage the best way you can—but I must be kind to them," thought Alice, "or perhaps they wo'n't walk the way I want to go! Let me see. I'll give them a new pair of boots every Christmas."

And she went on planning to herself how she would manage it. "They must go by the carrier," she thought; "and how funny it'll seem, sending presents to one's own feet! And how odd the directions will look!

Alice's Right Foot, Esq.
*Hearthrug, near the Fender,**
(with Alice's love).

Oh dear, what nonsense I'm talking!"

Just at this moment her head struck against the roof of the hall: in fact she was now rather more than nine feet high, and she at once took up the little golden key and hurried off to the garden door. Poor Alice! It was as much as she could do, lying down on one side, to look through into the garden with one eye; but to get through was more hopeless than ever: she sat down and began to cry again.

"You ought to be ashamed of yourself," said Alice, "a great

---

*Screen that prevents ashes from spilling out of a fireplace.

girl like you," (she might well say this), "to go on crying in this way! Stop this moment, I tell you!" But she went on all the same, shedding gallons of tears, until there was a large pool all round her, about four inches deep, and reaching half down the hall.

After a time she heard a little pattering of feet in the distance, and she hastily dried her eyes to see what was coming. It was the White Rabbit returning, splendidly dressed, with a pair of white kid-gloves in one hand and a large fan in the other: he came trotting along in a great hurry, muttering to himself, as he came, "Oh! The Duchess, the Duchess! Oh! *Wo'n't* she be savage if I've kept her waiting!"—Alice felt so desperate that she was ready to ask help of any one: so, when the Rabbit came near her, she began, in a low, timid voice, "If you please, Sir——" The Rabbit started violently, dropped the white kid-gloves and the fan, and skurried away into the darkness as hard as he could go.

Alice took up the fan and gloves, and, as the hall was very hot, she kept fanning herself all the time she went on talking. "Dear, dear! How queer everything is to-day! And yesterday things went on just as usual. I wonder if I've been changed in the night? Let me think: *was* I the same when I got up this morning? I almost think I can remember feeling a little different.

But if I'm not the same, the next question is 'Who in the world am I?' Ah, *that's* the great puzzle!" And she began thinking over all the children she knew that were of the same age as herself, to see if she could have been changed for any of them.

"I'm sure I'm not Ada," she said, "for her hair goes in such long ringlets, and mine doesn't go in ringlets at all; and I'm sure I ca'n't be Mabel, for I know all sorts of things, and she, oh, she knows such a very little! Besides, *she's* she, and *I'm* I, and—oh dear, how puzzling it all is! I'll try if I know all the things I used to know. Let me see: four times five is twelve, and four times six is thirteen, and four times seven is—oh dear! I shall never get to twenty at that rate! However, the Multiplication-Table doesn't signify: let's try Geography. London is the capital of Paris, and Paris is the capital of Rome, and Rome—no, *that's* all wrong, I'm certain! I must have been changed for Mabel! I'll try and say *'How doth the little—',"* and she crossed her hands on her lap, as if she were saying lessons, and began to repeat it, but her voice sounded hoarse and strange, and the words did not come the same as they used to do:—

> *"How doth the little crocodile*
> *Improve his shining tail,*
> *And pour the waters of the Nile*
> *On every golden scale!*
>
> *"How cheerfully he seems to grin,*
> *How neatly spreads his claws,*
> *And welcomes little fishes in,*
> *With gently smiling jaws!"*[2]

"I'm sure those are not the right words," said poor Alice, and her eyes filled with tears again as she went on, "I must be Mabel after all, and I shall have to go and live in that poky little house, and have next to no toys to play with, and oh, ever so many lessons to learn! No, I've made up my mind about it: if I'm Mabel, I'll stay down here! It'll be no use their putting their heads down and saying 'Come up again, dear!' I shall only look up and say 'Who am I, then? Tell me that first, and then, if I like being that person, I'll come up: if not, I'll stay down here till I'm somebody else'—but, oh dear!" cried Alice, with a sudden burst of tears, "I do wish they *would* put their heads down! I am so *very* tired of being all alone here!"

As she said this she looked down at her hands, and was surprised to see that she had put on one of the Rabbit's little white kid-gloves while she was talking. "How *can* I have done that?" she thought. "I must be growing small again." She got up and went to the table to measure herself by it, and found that, as nearly as she could guess, she was now about two feet

high, and was going on shrinking rapidly: she soon found out
that the cause of this was the fan she was holding, and she
dropped it hastily, just in time to save herself from shrinking
away altogether.

"That *was* a narrow escape!" said Alice, a good deal frightened at the sudden change, but very glad to find herself still
in existence. "And now for the garden!" And she ran with all
speed back to the little door; but, alas! the little door was shut
again, and the little golden key was lying on the glass table as
before, "and things are worse than ever," thought the poor
child, "for I never was so small as this before, never! And I
declare it's too bad, that it is!"

As she said these words her foot slipped, and in another
moment, splash! she was up to her chin in salt-water. Her first
idea was that she had somehow fallen into the sea, "and in that
case I can go back by railway," she said to herself. (Alice had
been to the seaside once in her life, and had come to the general conclusion that, wherever you go to on the English coast,
you find a number of bathing-machines in the sea, some children digging in the sand with wooden spades, then a row of
lodging-houses, and behind them a railway-station.) However,
she soon made out that she was in the pool of tears which she
had wept when she was nine feet high.

"I wish I hadn't cried so much!" said Alice, as she swam about, trying to find her way out. "I shall be punished for it now, I suppose, by being drowned in my own tears! That *will* be a queer thing, to be sure! However, everything is queer to-day."

Just then she heard something splashing about in the pool a little way off, and she swam nearer to make out what it was: at first she thought it must be a walrus or hippopotamus, but then she remembered how small she was now, and she soon made out that it was only a mouse, that had slipped in like herself.

"Would it be of any use, now," thought Alice, "to speak to this mouse? Everything is so out-of-the-way down here, that I should think very likely it can talk: at any rate, there's no harm in trying." So she began: "O Mouse, do you know the way out of this pool? I am very tired of swimming about here, O Mouse!" (Alice thought this must be the right way of speaking to a mouse: she had never done such a thing before, but she remembered having seen, in her brother's Latin Grammar, "A mouse—of a mouse—to a mouse—a mouse—O mouse!") The mouse looked at her rather inquisitively, and seemed to her to wink with one of its little eyes, but it said nothing.

"Perhaps it doesn't understand English," thought Alice. "I daresay it's a French mouse, come over with William the

Conqueror." (For, with all her knowledge of history, Alice had no very clear notion how long ago anything had happened.) So she began again: "Où est ma chatte?",* which was the first sentence in her French lesson-book. The Mouse gave a sudden leap out of the water, and seemed to quiver all over with fright. "Oh, I beg your pardon!" cried Alice hastily, afraid that she had hurt the poor animal's feelings. "I quite forgot you didn't like cats."

"Not like cats!" cried the Mouse in a shrill, passionate voice. "Would *you* like cats, if you were me?"

"Well, perhaps not," said Alice in a soothing tone: "don't be angry about it. And yet I wish I could show you our cat Dinah. I think you'd take a fancy to cats, if you could only see her. She is such a dear quiet thing," Alice went on, half to herself, as she swam lazily about in the pool, "and she sits purring so nicely by the fire, licking her paws and washing her face—and she is such a nice soft thing to nurse—and she's such a capital one for catching mice——oh, I beg your pardon!" cried Alice again, for this time the Mouse was bristling all over, and she felt certain it must be really offended. "We wo'n't talk about her any more, if you'd rather not."

"We, indeed!" cried the Mouse, who was trembling down to the end of its tail. "As if *I* would talk on such a subject! Our family always *hated* cats: nasty, low, vulgar things! Don't let me hear the name again!"

"I wo'n't indeed!" said Alice, in a great hurry to change the subject of conversation. "Are you—are you fond—of—of dogs?" The Mouse did not answer, so Alice went on eagerly: "There is such a nice little dog, near our house. I should like to show you! A little bright-eyed terrier, you know, with oh, such long curly brown hair! And it'll fetch things when you throw them, and it'll sit up and beg for its dinner, and all sorts of things—I ca'n't remember half of them—and it belongs to a farmer, you know, and he says it's so useful, it's worth a hundred pounds! He says it kills all the rats and—oh dear!" cried Alice in a sorrowful tone. "I'm afraid I've offended it again!" For the Mouse was swimming

---

*Where is my cat? (French).

away from her as hard as it could go, and making quite a com-
motion in the pool as it went.

So she called softly after it, "Mouse dear! Do come back
again, and we wo'n't talk about cats, or dogs either, if you don't
like them!" When the Mouse heard this, it turned round and
swam slowly back to her: its face was quite pale (with passion,
Alice thought), and it said, in a low trembling voice, "Let us get
to the shore, and then I'll tell you my history, and you'll understand why it is I hate cats and dogs."

It was high time to go, for the pool was getting quite
crowded with the birds and animals that had fallen into it:
there was a Duck and a Dodo, a Lory and an Eaglet, and several
other curious creatures. Alice led the way, and the whole party
swam to the shore.

III

A Caucus Race & a Long Tale*

---

*Private political meeting among party members.

They were indeed a queer-looking party that assembled on the bank—the birds with draggled feathers, the animals with their fur clinging close to them, and all dripping wet, cross, and uncomfortable.

The first question of course was, how to get dry again: they had a consultation about this, and after a few minutes it seemed quite natural to Alice to find herself talking familiarly with them, as if she had known them all her life. Indeed, she had quite a long argument with the Lory, who at last turned sulky, and would only say "I'm older than you, and must know better." And this Alice would not allow, without knowing how old it was, and, as the Lory positively refused to tell its age, there was no more to be said.

At last the Mouse, who seemed to be a person of some authority among them, called out "Sit down, all of you, and listen to me! *I'll* soon make you dry enough!" They all sat down at once, in a large ring, with the Mouse in the middle. Alice kept her eyes anxiously fixed on it, for she felt sure she would catch a bad cold if she did not get dry very soon.

"Ahem!" said the Mouse with an important air. "Are you all ready? This is the driest thing I know. Silence all round, if you please! 'William the Conqueror, whose cause was favoured by the pope, was soon submitted to by the English, who wanted leaders, and had been of late much accustomed to usurpation and conquest. Edwin and Morcar, the earls of Mercia and Northumbria——' "

"Ugh!" said the Lory, with a shiver.

"I beg your pardon!" said the Mouse, frowning, but very politely. "Did you speak?"

"Not I!" said the Lory, hastily.

"I thought you did," said the Mouse. "I proceed. 'Edwin and Morcar, the earls of Mercia and Northumbria, declared for him; and even Stigand, the patriotic archbishop of Canterbury, found it advisable——' "

"Found *what?*" said the Duck.

"Found *it*," the Mouse replied rather crossly: "of course you know what 'it' means."

"I know what 'it' means well enough, when *I* find a thing," said the Duck: "it's generally a frog, or a worm. The question is, what did the archbishop find?"

The Mouse did not notice this question, but hurriedly went on, " '——found it advisable to go with Edgar Atheling to meet William and offer him the crown. William's conduct at first was moderate. But the insolence of his Normans——' How are you getting on now, my dear?" it continued, turning to Alice as it spoke.

"As wet as ever," said Alice in a melancholy tone: "it doesn't seem to dry me at all."

"In that case," said the Dodo solemnly, rising to its feet, "I move that the meeting adjourn, for the immediate adoption of more energetic remedies——"

"Speak English!" said the Eaglet. "I don't know the meaning of half those long words, and, what's more, I don't believe you do either!" And the Eaglet bent down its head to hide a smile: some of the other birds tittered audibly.

"What I was going to say," said the Dodo in an offended tone, "was, that the best thing to get us dry would be a Caucus-race."

"What *is* a Caucus-race?" said Alice; not that she much wanted to know, but the Dodo had paused as if it thought that *somebody* ought to speak, and no one else seemed inclined to say anything.

"Why," said the Dodo, "the best way to explain it is to do it." (And, as you might like to try the thing yourself, some winter-day, I will tell you how the Dodo managed it.)

First it marked out a race-course, in a sort of circle, ("the exact shape doesn't matter," it said,) and then all the party were placed along the course, here and there. There was no "One, two, three, and away!", but they began running when they liked, and left off when they liked, so that it was not easy to know when the race was over. However, when they had been running half an hour or so, and were quite dry again, the Dodo suddenly called out "The race is over!", and they all crowded round it, panting, and asking "But who has won?"

This question the Dodo could not answer without a great deal of thought, and it stood for a long time with one finger pressed upon its forehead (the position in which you usually see Shakespeare, in the pictures of him), while the rest waited in silence. At last the Dodo said "*Everybody* has won, and *all* must have prizes."

"But who is to give the prizes?" quite a chorus of voices asked.

"Why, *she*, of course," said the Dodo, pointing to Alice with one finger; and the whole party at once crowded round her, calling out, in a confused way, "Prizes! Prizes!"

Alice had no idea what to do, and in despair she put her hand in her pocket, and pulled out a box of comfits (luckily the salt water had not got into it), and handed them round as prizes. There was exactly one a-piece, all round.

"But she must have a prize herself, you know," said the Mouse.

"Of course," the Dodo replied very gravely. "What else have you got in your pocket?" it went on, turning to Alice.

"Only a thimble," said Alice sadly.

"Hand it over here," said the Dodo.

Then they all crowded round her once more, while the Dodo solemnly presented the thimble, saying "We beg your acceptance of this elegant thimble"; and, when it had finished this short speech, they all cheered.

Alice thought the whole thing very absurd, but they all looked so grave that she did not dare to laugh; and, as she could not think of anything to say, she simply bowed, and took the thimble, looking as solemn as she could.

The next thing was to eat the comfits: this caused some noise and confusion, as the large birds complained that they could not taste theirs, and the small ones choked and had to be patted on the back. However, it was over at last, and they sat down again in a ring, and begged the Mouse to tell them something more.

"You promised to tell me your history, you know," said Alice, "and why it is you hate—C and D," she added in a whisper, half afraid that it would be offended again.

"Mine is a long and a sad tale!" said the Mouse, turning to Alice, and sighing.

"It *is* a long tail, certainly," said Alice, looking down with wonder at the Mouse's tail; "but why do you call it sad?" And she kept on puzzling about it while the Mouse was speaking, so that her idea of the tale was something like this:——

"Fury said to
      a mouse, That
            he met in the
                  house, 'Let
                     us both go
                     to law : *I*
                        will prose-
                        cute *you*.—
                        Come, I'll
                        take no de-
                        nial: We
                     must have
                  the trial;
            For really
         this morn-
         ing I've
      nothing
      to do.'
      Said the
         mouse to
            the cur,
               'Such a
                  trial, dear
                     sir. With
                        no jury
                        or judge,
                           would
                           be wast-
                           ing our
                        breath.'
                  'I'll be
               judge,
         I'll be
      jury,'
      said
      cun-
      ning
      old
      Fury:
      'I'll
         try
            the
               whole
               cause'
               and
               con-
               demn
            you to
      death.'"

"You are not attending!" said the Mouse to Alice, severely. "What are you thinking of?"

"I beg your pardon," said Alice very humbly: "you had got to the fifth bend, I think?"

"I had *not!*" cried the Mouse, sharply and very angrily.

"A knot!" said Alice, always ready to make herself useful, and looking anxiously about her. "Oh, do let me help to undo it!"

"I shall do nothing of the sort," said the Mouse, getting up and walking away. "You insult me by talking such nonsense!"

"I didn't mean it!" pleaded poor Alice. "But you're so easily offended, you know!"

The Mouse only growled in reply.

"Please come back, and finish your story!" Alice called after it. And the others all joined in chorus "Yes, please do!" But the

Mouse only shook its head impatiently, and walked a little quicker.

"What a pity it wouldn't stay!" sighed the Lory, as soon as it was quite out of sight. And an old Crab took the opportunity of saying to her daughter "Ah, my dear! Let this be a lesson to you never to lose *your* temper!" "Hold your tongue, Ma!" said the young Crab, a little snappishly. "You're enough to try the patience of an oyster!"

"I wish I had our Dinah here, I know I do!" said Alice aloud, addressing nobody in particular. "*She'd* soon fetch it back!"

"And who is Dinah, if I might venture to ask the question?" said the Lory.

Alice replied eagerly, for she was always ready to talk about her pet: "Dinah's our cat. And she's such a capital one for catching mice, you ca'n't think! And oh, I wish you could see her after the birds! Why, she'll eat a little bird as soon as look at it!"

This speech caused a remarkable sensation among the party. Some of the birds hurried off at once: one old Magpie began wrapping itself up very carefully, remarking "I really must be getting home: the night-air doesn't suit my throat!" And a Canary called out in a trembling voice, to its children, "Come away, my dears! It's high time you were all in bed!" On various pretexts they all moved off, and Alice was soon left alone.

"I wish I hadn't mentioned Dinah!" she said to herself in a melancholy tone. "Nobody seems to like her, down here, and I'm sure she's the best cat in the world! Oh, my dear Dinah! I wonder if I shall ever see you any more!" And here poor Alice began to cry again, for she felt very lonely and low-spirited. In a little while, however, she again heard a little pattering of footsteps in the distance, and she looked up eagerly, half hoping that the Mouse had changed his mind, and was coming back to finish his story.

IV

The Rabbit Sends in a Little Bill

It was the White Rabbit, trotting slowly back again, and looking anxiously about as it went, as if it had lost something; and she heard it muttering to itself, "The Duchess! The Duchess! Oh my dear paws! Oh my fur and whiskers! She'll get me executed, as sure as ferrets are ferrets! Where *can* I have dropped them, I wonder?" Alice guessed in a moment that it was looking for the fan and the pair of white kid-gloves, and she very good-naturedly began hunting about for them, but they were nowhere to be seen—everything seemed to have changed since her swim in the pool; and the great hall, with the glass table and the little door, had vanished completely.

Very soon the Rabbit noticed Alice, as she went hunting about, and called out to her, in an angry tone, "Why, Mary Ann, what *are* you doing out here? Run home this moment, and fetch me a pair of gloves and a fan! Quick, now!" And Alice was so much frightened that she ran off at once in the direction it pointed to, without trying to explain the mistake that it had made.

"He took me for his housemaid," she said to herself as she ran. "How surprised he'll be when he finds out who I am! But I'd better take him his fan and gloves—that is, if I can find them." As she said this, she came upon a neat little house, on the door of which was a bright brass plate with the name "W. RABBIT" engraved upon it. She went in without knocking, and hurried upstairs, in great fear lest she should meet the real Mary Ann, and be turned out of the house before she had found the fan and gloves.

"How queer it seems," Alice said to herself, "to be going messages for a rabbit! I suppose Dinah'll be sending me on messages next!" And she began fancying the sort of thing that would happen: "'Miss Alice! Come here directly, and get ready for your walk!' 'Coming in a minute, nurse! But I've got to watch this mouse-hole till Dinah comes back, and see that the mouse doesn't get out.' Only I don't think," Alice went on, "that they'd let Dinah stop in the house if it began ordering people about like that!"

By this time she had found her way into a tidy little room with a table in the window, and on it (as she had hoped) a fan and two or three pairs of tiny white kid-gloves: she took up the fan and a pair of the gloves, and was just going to leave the room, when her eye fell upon a little bottle that stood near the looking-glass. There was no label this time with the words "DRINK ME," but nevertheless she uncorked it and put it to her lips. "I know *something* interesting is sure to happen," she said to herself, "whenever I eat or drink anything: so I'll just see what this bottle does. I do hope it'll make me grow large again, for really I'm quite tired of being such a tiny little thing!"

It did so indeed, and much sooner than she had expected: before she had drunk half the bottle, she found her head pressing against the ceiling, and had to stoop to save her neck from being broken. She hastily put down the bottle, saying to herself "That's quite enough—I hope I sha'n't grow any more— As it is, I ca'n't get out at the door—I do wish I hadn't drunk quite so much!"

Alas! It was too late to wish that! She went on growing, and growing, and very soon had to kneel down on the floor: in another minute there was not even room for this, and she tried the effect of lying down with one elbow against the door, and the other arm curled round her head. Still she went on growing, and, as a last resource, she put one arm out of the window, and one foot up the chimney, and said to herself "Now I can do no more, whatever happens. What *will* become of me?"

Luckily for Alice, the little magic bottle had now had its full effect, and she grew no larger: still it was very uncomfortable, and, as there seemed to be no sort of chance of her ever getting out of the room again, no wonder she felt unhappy.

"It was much pleasanter at home," thought poor Alice, "when one wasn't always growing larger and smaller, and being

ordered about by mice and rabbits. I almost wish I hadn't gone
down that rabbit-hole—and yet—and yet—it's rather curious,
you know, this sort of life! I do wonder what *can* have happened
to me! When I used to read fairy tales, I fancied that kind of
thing never happened, and now here I am in the middle of one!
There ought to be a book written about me, that there ought!
And when I grow up, I'll write one—but I'm grown up now," she
added in a sorrowful tone: "at least there's no room to grow up
any more *here*."

"But then," thought Alice, "shall I *never* get any older than I
am now? That'll be a comfort, one way—never to be an old
woman—but then—always to have lessons to learn! Oh, I
shouldn't like *that*!"

"Oh, you foolish Alice!" she answered herself. "How can you
learn lessons in here? Why, there's hardly room for *you*, and no
room at all for any lesson-books!"

And so she went on, taking first one side and then the other,
and making quite a conversation of it altogether; but after a few
minutes she heard a voice outside, and stopped to listen.

"Mary Ann! Mary Ann!" said the voice. "Fetch me my gloves
this moment!" Then came a little pattering of feet on the

stairs. Alice knew it was the Rabbit coming to look for her, and she trembled till she shook the house, quite forgetting that she was now about a thousand times as large as the Rabbit, and had no reason to be afraid of it.

Presently the Rabbit came up to the door, and tried to open it; but, as the door opened inwards, and Alice's elbow was pressed hard against it, that attempt proved a failure. Alice heard it say to itself "Then I'll go round and get in at the window."

"*That* you wo'n't!" thought Alice, and, after waiting till she fancied she heard the Rabbit just under the window, she suddenly spread out her hand, and made a snatch in the air. She did not get hold of anything, but she heard a little shriek and a fall, and a crash of broken glass, from which she concluded that it was just possible it had fallen into a cucumber-frame,* or something of the sort.

Next came an angry voice—the Rabbit's—"Pat! Pat! Where are you?" And then a voice she had never heard before, "Sure then I'm here! Digging for apples, yer honour!"

"Digging for apples, indeed!" said the Rabbit angrily. "Here! Come and help me out of *this!*" (Sounds of more broken glass.)

"Now tell me, Pat, what's that in the window?"

"Sure, it's an arm, yer honour!" (He pronounced it "arrum.")

"An arm, you goose! Who ever saw one that size? Why, it fills the whole window!"

"Sure, it does, yer honour: but it's an arm for all that."

"Well, it's got no business there, at any rate: go and take it away!"

There was a long silence after this, and Alice could only hear whispers now and then; such as "Sure, I don't like it, yer honour, at all, at all!" "Do as I tell you, you coward!", and at last she spread out her hand again, and made another snatch in the air. This time there were *two* little shrieks, and more sounds of broken glass. "What a number of cucumber-frames there must be!" thought Alice. "I wonder what they'll do next! As for pulling me out of the window, I only wish they *could!* I'm sure *I* don't want to stay in here any longer!"

She waited for some time without hearing anything more: at last came a rumbling of little cart-wheels, and the sound of a good many voices all talking together she made out the words: "Where's the other ladder?—Why, I hadn't to bring but one. Bill's got the other—Bill! Fetch it here, lad!—Here, put 'em up at this corner—No, tie 'em together first—they don't reach half high enough yet—Oh, they'll do well enough. Don't be particular—Here, Bill! Catch hold of this rope—Will the roof bear?—Mind that loose slate—Oh, it's coming down! Heads below!" (a loud crash)—"Now, who did that?—It was Bill, I fancy—Who's to go down the chimney?—Nay, *I* sha'n't! *You* do it!—*That* I wo'n't, then!—Bill's got to go down—Here, Bill!

*Small building that resembles a greenhouse.

The master says you've got to go down the chimney!"

"Oh! So Bill's got to come down the chimney, has he?" said Alice to herself. "Why, they seem to put everything upon Bill! I wouldn't be in Bill's place for a good deal: this fireplace is narrow, to be sure; but I *think* I can kick a little!"

She drew her foot as far down the chimney as she could, and waited till she heard a little animal (she couldn't guess of what sort it was) scratching and scrambling about in the chimney close above her: then, saying to herself "This is Bill," she gave one sharp kick, and waited to see what would happen next.

The first thing she heard was a general chorus of "There goes Bill!" then the Rabbit's voice alone—"Catch him, you by the hedge!" then silence, and then another confusion of voices—"Hold up his head—Brandy now—Don't choke him—How was it, old fellow? What happened to you? Tell us all about it!" Last came a little feeble, squeaking voice ("That's Bill," thought Alice), "Well, I hardly know—No more, thank ye; I'm better now—but I'm a deal too flustered to tell you—all I know is, something comes at me like a Jack-in-the-box, and up I goes like a sky-rocket!"

"So you did, old fellow!" said the others.

"We must burn the house down!" said the Rabbit's voice. And Alice called out, as loud as she could, "If you do, I'll set Dinah at you!"

There was a dead silence instantly, and Alice thought to herself "I wonder what they *will* do next! If they had any sense, they'd take the roof off." After a minute or two, they began moving about again, and Alice heard the Rabbit say "A barrowful will do, to begin with."

"A barrowful of *what?*" thought Alice. But she had not long to doubt, for the next moment a shower of little pebbles came rattling in at the window, and some of them hit her in the face. "I'll put a stop to this," she said to herself, and shouted out "You'd better not do that again!", which produced another dead silence.

Alice noticed, with some surprise, that the pebbles were all turning into little cakes as they lay on the floor, and a bright idea came into her head. "If I eat one of these cakes," she thought, "it's sure to make *some* change in my size; and, as it ca'n't possibly make me larger, it must make me smaller, I suppose."

So she swallowed one of the cakes, and was delighted to find that she began shrinking directly. As soon as she was small enough to get through the door, she ran out of the house, and found quite a crowd of little animals and birds waiting outside. The poor little Lizard, Bill, was in the middle, being held up by two guinea-pigs, who were giving it something out of a bottle. They all made a rush at Alice the moment she appeared; but she ran off as hard as she could, and soon found herself safe in a thick wood.

"The first thing I've got to do," said Alice to herself, as she wandered about in the wood, "is to grow to my right size again; and the second thing is to find my way into that lovely garden. I think that will be the best plan."

It sounded an excellent plan, no doubt, and very neatly and simply arranged: the only difficulty was, that she had not the smallest idea how to set about it; and, while she was peering about anxiously among the trees, a little sharp bark just over her head made her look up in a great hurry.

An enormous puppy was looking down at her with large round eyes, and feebly stretching out one paw, trying to touch her. "Poor little thing!" said Alice, in a coaxing tone, and she tried hard to whistle to it; but she was terribly frightened all the time at the thought that it might be hungry, in which case it would be very likely to eat her up in spite of all her coaxing.

Hardly knowing what she did, she picked up a little bit of stick, and held it out to the puppy: whereupon the puppy jumped into the air off all its feet at once, with a yelp of delight, and rushed at the stick, and made believe to worry it: then Alice dodged behind a great thistle, to keep herself from being run over; and, the moment she appeared on the other side, the puppy made another rush at the stick, and tumbled head over heels in its hurry to get hold of it: then Alice, thinking it was very like having a game of play with a carthorse, and expecting every moment to be trampled under its feet, ran round the thistle again: then the puppy began a series of short charges at the stick, running a very little way forwards each time and a long way back, and barking hoarsely all the while, till at last it sat down a good way off, panting, with its tongue hanging out of its mouth, and its great eyes half shut.

This seemed to Alice a good opportunity for making her escape: so she set off at once, and ran till she was quite tired and out of breath, and till the puppy's bark sounded quite faint in the distance.

"And yet what a dear little puppy it was!" said Alice, as she leant against a buttercup to rest herself, and fanned herself with one of the leaves. "I should have liked teaching it tricks very much, if—if I'd only been the right size to do it! Oh dear! I'd nearly forgotten that I've got to grow up again! Let me see—how *is* it to be managed? I suppose I ought to eat or drink something or other; but the great question is 'What?' "

The great question certainly was "What?" Alice looked all round her at the flowers and the blades of grass, but she could not see anything that looked liked the right thing to eat or drink under the circumstances. There was a large mushroom growing near her, about the same height as herself; and, when she had looked under it, and on both sides of it, and behind it, it occurred to her that she might as well look and see what was on the top of it.

She stretched herself up on tiptoe, and peeped over the edge of the mushroom, and her eyes immediately met those of a large blue caterpillar, that was sitting on the top, with its arms folded, quietly smoking a long hookah, and taking not the smallest notice of her or of anything else.

V

Advice from a Caterpillar

The Caterpillar and Alice looked at each other for some time in silence: at last the Caterpillar took the hookah out of its mouth, and addressed her in a languid, sleepy voice.

"Who are *you*?" said the Caterpillar.

This was not an encouraging opening for a conversation. Alice replied, rather shyly, "I—I hardly know, Sir, just at present—at least I know who I *was* when I got up this morning, but I think I must have been changed several times since then."

"What do you mean by that?" said the Caterpillar, sternly. "Explain yourself!"

"I ca'n't explain *myself,* I'm afraid, Sir," said Alice, "because I'm not myself, you see."

"I don't see," said the Caterpillar.

"I'm afraid I ca'n't put it more clearly," Alice replied, very politely, "for I ca'n't understand it myself, to begin with; and being so many different sizes in a day is very confusing."

"It isn't," said the Caterpillar.

"Well, perhaps you haven't found it so yet," said Alice; "but when you have to turn into a chrysalis—you will some day, you know—and then after that into a butterfly, I should think you'll feel it a little queer, wo'n't you?"

"Not a bit," said the Caterpillar.

"Well, perhaps *your* feelings may be different," said Alice: "all I know is, it would feel very queer to *me*."

"You!" said the Caterpillar contemptuously. "Who are *you*?"

Which brought them back again to the beginning of the conversation. Alice felt a little irritated at the Caterpillar's making such *very* short remarks, and she drew herself up and said, very gravely, "I think you ought to tell me who *you* are, first."

"Why?" said the Caterpillar.

Here was another puzzling question; and, as Alice could not think of any good reason, and the Caterpillar seemed to be in a *very* unpleasant state of mind, she turned away.

"Come back!" the Caterpillar called after her. "I've something important to say!"

This sounded promising, certainly. Alice turned and came back again.

"Keep your temper," said the Caterpillar.

"Is that all?" said Alice, swallowing down her anger as well as she could.

"No," said the Caterpillar.

Alice thought she might as well wait, as she had nothing else to do, and perhaps after all it might tell her something worth hearing. For some minutes it puffed away without speaking; but at last it unfolded its arms, took the hookah out of its mouth again, and said "So you think you're changed, do you?"

"I'm afraid I am, Sir," said Alice. "I ca'n't remember things as I used—and I don't keep the same size for ten minutes together!"

"Ca'n't remember *what* things?" said the Caterpillar.

"Well, I've tried to say *'How doth the little busy bee,'* but it all came different!" Alice replied in a very melancholy voice.

"Repeat *'You are old, Father William,'*"[3] said the Caterpillar.

Alice folded her hands, and began:—

> *"You are old, Father William," the young man*
>   *said,*
> *"And your hair has become very white;*
> *And yet you incessantly stand on your head—*
> *Do you think, at your age, it is right?"*

"In my youth," Father William replied to his
       son,
"I feared it might injure the brain;
But, now that I'm perfectly sure I have none,
Why, I do it again and again."

"You are old," said the youth, "as I mentioned
       before,
And have grown most uncommonly fat;
Yet you turned a back-somersault in at the door—
Pray, what is the reason of that?"

"In my youth," said the sage, as he shook his
       grey locks,
"I kept all my limbs very supple
By the use of this ointment—one shilling the box—
Allow me to sell you a couple?"

"You are old," said the youth, "and your jaws
       are too weak
For anything tougher than suet;

Yet you finished the goose, with the bones and
   the beak—
Pray, how did you manage to do it?"

"In my youth," said his father, "I took to the law,
And argued each case with my wife;
And the muscular strength which it gave to my jaw
Has lasted the rest of my life."

"You are old," said the youth, "one would
   hardly suppose
That your eye was as steady as ever;
Yet you balanced an eel on the end of your
   nose—
What made you so awfully clever?"

"I have answered three questions, and that is
   enough,"
Said his father. "Don't give yourself airs!
Do you think I can listen all day to such stuff?
Be off, or I'll kick you down-stairs!"

"That is not said right," said the Caterpillar.

"Not *quite* right, I'm afraid," said Alice, timidly: "some of the words have got altered."

"It is wrong from beginning to end," said the Caterpillar, decidedly; and there was silence for some minutes.

The Caterpillar was the first to speak.

"What size do you want to be?" it asked.

"Oh, I'm not particular as to size," Alice hastily replied; "only one doesn't like changing so often, you know."

"I *don't* know," said the Caterpillar.

Alice said nothing: she had never been so much contradicted in all her life before, and she felt that she was losing her temper.

"Are you content now?" said the Caterpillar.

"Well, I should like to be a *little* larger, Sir, if you wouldn't mind," said Alice: "three inches is such a wretched height to be."

"It is a very good height indeed!" said the Caterpillar angrily, rearing itself upright as it spoke (it was exactly three inches high).

"But I'm not used to it!" pleaded poor Alice in a piteous

tone. And she thought to herself "I wish the creatures wouldn't be so easily offended!"

"You'll get used to it in time," said the Caterpillar; and it put the hookah into its mouth, and began smoking again.

This time Alice waited patiently until it chose to speak again. In a minute or two the Caterpillar took the hookah out of its mouth, and yawned once or twice, and shook itself. Then it got down off the mushroom, and crawled away into the grass, merely remarking, as it went, "One side will make you grow taller, and the other side will make you grow shorter."

"One side of *what*? The other side of *what*?" thought Alice to herself.

"Of the mushroom," said the Caterpillar, just as if she had asked it aloud; and in another moment it was out of sight.

Alice remained looking thoughtfully at the mushroom for a minute, trying to make out which were the two sides of it; and, as it was perfectly round, she found this a very difficult question. However, at last she stretched her arms round it as far as they would go, and broke off a bit of the edge with each hand.

"And now which is which?" she said to herself, and nibbled a little of the right-hand bit to try the effect. The next moment she felt a violent blow underneath her chin: it had struck her foot!

She was a good deal frightened by this very sudden change, but she felt that there was no time to be lost, as she was sinking rapidly: so she set to work at once to eat some of the other bit. Her chin was pressed so closely against her foot, that there was hardly room to open her mouth; but she did it at last, and managed to swallow a morsel of the left-hand bit.

* * * * * * * * * * * * * *

"Come, my head's free at last!" said Alice in a tone of delight, which changed into alarm in another moment, when she found that her shoulders were nowhere to be found: all she could see, when she looked down, was an immense length of neck, which seemed to rise like a stalk out of a sea of green leaves that lay far below her.

"What *can* all that green stuff be?" said Alice. "And where *have* my shoulders got to? And oh, my poor hands, how is it I ca'n't see you?" She was moving them about, as she spoke, but no result seemed to follow, except a little shaking among the distant green leaves.

As there seemed to be no chance of getting her hands up to her head, she tried to get her head down to *them,* and was delighted to find that her neck would bend about easily in any direction, like a serpent. She had just succeeded in curving it down into a graceful zigzag, and was going to dive in among the leaves, which she found to be nothing but the tops of the trees under which she had been wandering, when a sharp hiss made her draw back in a hurry: a large pigeon had flown into her face, and was beating her violently with its wings.

"Serpent!" screamed the Pigeon.

"I'm *not* a serpent!" said Alice indignantly. "Let me alone!"

"Serpent, I say again!" repeated the Pigeon, but in a more subdued tone, and added, with a kind of sob, "I've tried every way, but nothing seems to suit them!"

"I haven't the least idea what you're talking about," said Alice.

"I've tried the roots of trees, and I've tried banks, and I've tried hedges," the Pigeon went on, without attending to her; "but those serpents! There's no pleasing them!"

Alice was more and more puzzled, but she thought there was no use in saying anything more till the Pigeon had finished.

"As if it wasn't trouble enough hatching the eggs," said the Pigeon; "but I must be on the look-out for serpents, night and day! Why, I haven't had a wink of sleep these three weeks!"

"I'm very sorry you've been annoyed," said Alice, who was beginning to see its meaning.

"And just as I'd taken the highest tree in the wood," continued the Pigeon, raising its voice to a shriek, "and just as I was thinking I should be free of them at last, they must needs come wriggling down from the sky! Ugh, Serpent!"

"But I'm *not* a serpent, I tell you!" said Alice. "I'm a——I'm a——"

"Well! *What* are you?" said the Pigeon. "I can see you're trying to invent something!"

"I—I'm a little girl," said Alice, rather doubtfully, as she remembered the number of changes she had gone through, that day.

"A likely story indeed!" said the Pigeon, in a tone of the deepest contempt. "I've seen a good many little girls in my time, but never *one* with such a neck as that! No, no! You're a serpent; and there's no use denying it. I suppose you'll be telling me next that you never tasted an egg!"

"I *have* tasted eggs, certainly," said Alice, who was a very truthful child; "but little girls eat eggs quite as much as serpents do, you know."

"I don't believe it," said the Pigeon; "but if they do, why, then they're a kind of serpent: that's all I can say."

This was such a new idea to Alice, that she was quite silent for a minute or two, which gave the Pigeon the opportunity of adding "You're looking for eggs, I know *that* well enough; and what does it matter to me whether you're a little girl or a serpent?"

"It matters a good deal to *me*," said Alice hastily; "but I'm not looking for eggs, as it happens; and, if I was, I shouldn't want *yours:* I don't like them raw."

"Well, be off, then!" said the Pigeon in a sulky tone, as it settled down again into its nest. Alice crouched down among the trees as well as she could, for her neck kept getting entangled among the branches, and every now and then she had to stop and untwist it. After a while she remembered that she still held the pieces of mushroom in her hands, and she set to work very carefully, nibbling first at one and then at the other, and growing sometimes taller, and sometimes shorter, until she had succeeded in bringing herself down to her usual height.

It was so long since she had been anything near the right size, that it felt quite strange at first; but she got used to it in a few minutes, and began talking to herself, as usual, "Come, there's half my plan done now! How puzzling all these changes are! I'm never sure what I'm going to be, from one minute to another! However, I've got back to my right size: the next thing is, to get into that beautiful garden—how *is* that to be done, I wonder?" As she said this, she came suddenly upon an open place, with a little house in it about four feet high. "Whoever lives there," thought Alice, "it'll never do to come upon them *this* size: why, I should frighten them out of their wits!" So she began nibbling at the right-hand bit again, and did not venture to go near the house till she had brought herself down to nine inches high.

VI

Pig & Pepper

For a minute or two she stood looking at the house, and wondering what to do next, when suddenly a footman in livery came running out of the wood—(she considered him to be a footman because he was in livery: otherwise, judging by his face only, she would have called him a fish)—and rapped loudly at the door with his knuckles. It was opened by another footman in livery, with a round face, and large eyes like a frog; and both footmen, Alice noticed, had powdered hair that curled all over their heads. She felt very curious to know what it was all about, and crept a little way out of the wood to listen.

The Fish-Footman began by producing from under his arm a great letter, nearly as large as himself, and this he handed over to the other, saying, in a solemn tone, "For the Duchess. An invitation from the Queen to play croquet." The Frog-Footman repeated, in the same solemn tone, only changing the order of the words a little, "From the Queen. An invitation for the Duchess to play croquet."

Then they both bowed low, and their curls got entangled together.

Alice laughed so much at this, that she had to run back into the wood for fear of their hearing her; and, when she next peeped out, the Fish-Footman was gone, and the other was sitting on the ground near the door, staring stupidly up into the sky.

Alice went timidly up to the door, and knocked.

"There's no sort of use in knocking," said the Footman, "and that for two reasons. First, because I'm on the same side of the door as you are: secondly, because they're making such a noise inside, no one could possibly hear you." And certainly there *was* a most extraordinary noise going on within—a constant howling and sneezing, and every now and then a great crash, as if a dish or kettle had been broken to pieces.

"Please, then," said Alice, "how am I to get in?"

"There might be some sense in your knocking," the Footman went on, without attending to her, "if we had the door between us. For instance, if you were *inside*, you might knock, and I could let you out, you know." He was looking up into the sky all the time he was speaking, and this Alice thought decidedly uncivil. "But perhaps he ca'n't help it," she said to herself; "his eyes are so *very* nearly at the top of his head. But at any rate he might answer questions.—How am I to get in?" she repeated, aloud.

"I shall sit here," the Footman remarked, "till to-morrow——"

At this moment the door of the house opened, and a large plate came skimming out, straight at the Footman's head: it just grazed his nose, and broke to pieces against one of the trees behind him.

"——or next day, maybe," the Footman continued in the same tone, exactly as if nothing had happened.

"How am I to get in?" asked Alice again, in a louder tone.

"*Are* you to get in at all?" said the Footman. "That's the first question, you know."

It was, no doubt: only Alice did not like to be told so. "It's really dreadful," she muttered to herself, "the way all the creatures argue. It's enough to drive one crazy!"

The Footman seemed to think this a good opportunity for repeating his remark, with variations. "I shall sit here," he said, "on and off, for days and days."

"But what am *I* to do?" said Alice.

"Anything you like," said the Footman, and began whistling.

"Oh, there's no use in talking to him," said Alice desperately: "he's perfectly idiotic!" And she opened the door and went in.

The door led right into a large kitchen, which was full of smoke from one end to the other: the Duchess was sitting on a three-legged stool in the middle, nursing a baby: the cook was leaning over the fire, stirring a large cauldron which seemed to be full of soup.

"There's certainly too much pepper in that soup!" Alice said to herself, as well as she could for sneezing.

There was certainly too much of it in the *air.* Even the Duchess sneezed occasionally; and as for the baby, it was sneezing and howling alternately without a moment's pause. The only two creatures in the kitchen, that did *not* sneeze, were the cook, and a large cat, which was lying on the hearth and grinning from ear to ear.

"Please would you tell me," said Alice, a little timidly, for she was not quite sure whether it was good manners for her to speak first, "why your cat grins like that?"

"It's a Cheshire-Cat," said the Duchess, "and that's why. Pig!"

She said the last word with such sudden violence that Alice quite jumped; but she saw in another moment that it was addressed to the baby, and not to her, so she took courage, and went on again:—

"I didn't know that Cheshire-Cats always grinned; in fact, I didn't know that cats *could* grin."

"They all can," said the Duchess; "and most of 'em do."

"I don't know of any that do," Alice said very politely, feeling quite pleased to have got into a conversation.

"You don't know much," said the Duchess; "and that's a fact."

Alice did not at all like the tone of this remark, and thought it would be as well to introduce some other subject of conversation. While she was trying to fix on one, the cook took the cauldron of soup off the fire, and at once set to work throwing everything within her reach at the Duchess and the baby—the fire-irons came first; then followed a shower of saucepans, plates, and dishes. The Duchess took no notice of them even when they hit her; and the baby was howling so much already, that it was quite impossible to say whether the blows hurt it or not.

"Oh, *please* mind what you're doing!" cried Alice, jumping up and down in an agony of terror. "Oh, there goes his *precious*

nose!", as an unusually large saucepan flew close by it, and very nearly carried it off.

"If everybody minded their own business," the Duchess said, in a hoarse growl, "the world would go round a deal faster than it does."

"Which would *not* be an advantage," said Alice, who felt very glad to get an opportunity of showing off a little of her knowledge. "Just think what work it would make with the day and night! You see the earth takes twenty-four hours to turn round on its axis——"

"Talking of axes," said the Duchess, "chop off her head!"

Alice glanced rather anxiously at the cook, to see if she meant to take the hint; but the cook was busily stirring the soup, and seemed not to be listening, so she went on again: "Twenty-four hours, I *think;* or is it twelve? I——"

"Oh, don't bother *me!*" said the Duchess. "I never could abide figures!" And with that she began nursing her child again, singing a sort of lullaby to it as she did so, and giving it a violent shake at the end of every line:—

> *"Speak roughly to your little boy,*
> *And beat him when he sneezes:*
> *He only does it to annoy,*
> *Because he knows it teases."*
>   CHORUS.

(in which the cook and the baby joined):—

> *"Wow! Wow! Wow!"*

While the Duchess sang the second verse of the song, she kept tossing the baby violently up and down, and the poor little thing howled so, that Alice could hardly hear the words:—

> *"I speak severely to my boy,*
> *I beat him when he sneezes;*
> *For he can thoroughly enjoy*
> *The pepper when he pleases!"*
>   CHORUS.

> *"Wow! Wow! Wow!"*

"Here! You may nurse it a bit, if you like!" the Duchess said to Alice, flinging the baby at her as she spoke. "I must go and get ready to play croquet with the Queen," and she hurried out of the room. The cook threw a frying-pan after her as she went, but it just missed her.

Alice caught the baby with some difficulty, as it was a queer-shaped little creature, and held out its arms and legs in all directions, "just like a star-fish," thought Alice. The poor little thing was snorting like a steam-engine when she caught it, and kept doubling itself up and straightening itself out again, so that altogether, for the first minute or two, it was as much as she could do to hold it.

As soon as she had made out the proper way of nursing it (which was to twist it up into a sort of knot, and then keep tight hold of its right ear and left foot, so as to prevent its undoing itself), she carried it out into the open air. "If I don't take this child away with me," thought Alice, "they're sure to kill it in a day or two. Wouldn't it be murder to leave it behind?" She said the last words out loud, and the little thing grunted in reply (it had left off sneezing by this time). "Don't grunt," said Alice; "that's not at all a proper way of expressing yourself."

The baby grunted again, and Alice looked very anxiously into its face to see what was the matter with it. There could be no doubt that it had a *very* turn-up nose, much more like a snout than a real nose: also its eyes were getting extremely small for a baby: altogether Alice did not like the look of the thing at all. "But perhaps it was only sobbing," she thought, and looked into its eyes again, to see if there were any tears.

No, there were no tears. "If you're going to turn into a pig, my dear," said Alice, seriously, "I'll have nothing more to do with you. Mind now!" The poor little thing sobbed again (or grunted, it was impossible to say which), and they went on for some while in silence.

Alice was just beginning to think to herself, "Now, what am I to do with this creature, when I get it home?" when it grunted again, so violently, that she looked down into its face in some alarm. This time there could be *no* mistake about it: it was neither more nor less than a pig, and she felt that it would be quite absurd for her to carry it any further.

So she set the little creature down and felt quite relieved to see it trot away quietly into the wood. "If it had grown up," she said to herself, "it would have made a dreadfully ugly child: but it makes rather a handsome pig, I think." And she began thinking over other children she knew, who might do very well as pigs, and was just saying to herself "if one only knew the right way to change them——" when she was a little startled by seeing the Cheshire-Cat sitting on a bough of a tree a few yards off.

The Cat only grinned when it saw Alice. It looked good-natured, she thought: still it had *very* long claws and a great many teeth, so she felt that it ought to be treated with respect.

"Cheshire-Puss," she began, rather timidly, as she did not at all know whether it would like the name: however, it only grinned a little wider. "Come, it's pleased so far," thought Alice, and she went on. "Would you tell me, please, which way I ought to go from here?"

"That depends a good deal on where you want to get to," said the Cat.

"I don't much care where——" said Alice.

"Then it doesn't matter which way you go," said the Cat.

"——so long as I get *somewhere,*" Alice added as an explanation.

"Oh, you're sure to do that," said the Cat, "if you only walk long enough."

Alice felt that this could not be denied, so she tried another question. "What sort of people live about here?"

"In *that* direction," the Cat said, waving its right paw round, "lives a Hatter: and in *that* direction," waving the other paw, "lives a March Hare. Visit either you like: they're both mad."

"But I don't want to go among mad people," Alice remarked.

"Oh, you ca'n't help that," said the Cat: "we're all mad here. I'm mad. You're mad."

"How do you know I'm mad?" said Alice.

"You must be," said the Cat, "or you wouldn't have come here."

Alice didn't think that proved it at all: however, she went on: "And how do you know that you're mad?"

"To begin with," said the Cat, "a dog's not mad. You grant that?"

"I suppose so," Alice.

"Well, then," the Cat went on, "you see a dog growls when it's angry, and wags its tail when it's pleased. Now *I* growl when I'm pleased, and wag my tail when I'm angry. Therefore I'm mad."

"*I* call it purring, not growling," said Alice.

"Call it what you like," said the Cat. "Do you play croquet with the Queen to-day?"

"I should like it very much," said Alice, "but I haven't been invited yet."

"You'll see me there," said the Cat, and vanished.

Alice was not much surprised at this, she was getting so well used to queer things happening. While she was still looking at the place where it had been, it suddenly appeared again.

"By-the-bye, what became of the baby?" said the Cat. "I'd nearly forgotten to ask."

"It turned into a pig," Alice answered very quietly, just as if the Cat had come back in a natural way.

"I thought it would," said the Cat, and vanished again.

Alice waited a little, half expecting to see it again, but it did not appear, and after a minute or two she walked on in the direction in which the March Hare was said to live. "I've seen hatters before," she said to herself: "the March Hare will be much the most interesting, and perhaps, as this is May, it wo'n't be raving mad—at least not so mad as it was in March." As she said this, she looked up, and there was the Cat again, sitting on a branch of a tree.

"Did you say 'pig', or 'fig'?" said the Cat.

"I said 'pig'," replied Alice; "and I wish you wouldn't keep appearing and vanishing so suddenly: you make one quite giddy!"

"All right," said the Cat; and this time it vanished quite slowly, beginning with the end of the tail, and ending with the grin, which remained some time after the rest of it had gone.

"Well! I've often seen a cat without a grin," thought Alice; "but a grin without a cat! It's the most curious thing I ever saw in all my life!"

She had not gone much farther before she came in sight of the house of the March Hare: she thought it must be the right house, because the chimneys were shaped like ears and the roof was thatched with fur. It was so large a house, that she did not like to go nearer till she had nibbled some more of the left-hand bit of mushroom, and raised herself to about two feet high: even then she walked up towards it rather timidly, saying to herself "Suppose it should be raving mad after all! I almost wish I'd gone to see the Hatter instead!"

VII

A Mad Tea Party

There was a table set out under a tree in front of the house, and the March Hare and the Hatter were having tea at it: a Dormouse was sitting between them, fast asleep, and the other two were using it as a cushion, resting their elbows on it, and talking over its head. "Very uncomfortable for the Dormouse," thought Alice; "only as it's asleep, I suppose it doesn't mind."

The table was a large one, but the three were all crowded together at one corner of it. "No room! No room!" they cried out when they saw Alice coming. "There's *plenty* of room!" said Alice indignantly, and she sat down in a large arm-chair at one end of the table.

"Have some wine," the March Hare said in an encouraging tone.

Alice looked all round the table, but there was nothing on it but tea. "I don't see any wine," she remarked.

"There isn't any," said the March Hare.

"Then it wasn't very civil of you to offer it," said Alice angrily.

"It wasn't very civil of you to sit down without being invited," said the March Hare.

"I didn't know it was *your* table," said Alice: "it's laid for a great many more than three."

"Your hair wants cutting," said the Hatter. He had been looking at Alice for some time with great curiosity, and this was his first speech.

"You should learn not to make personal remarks," Alice said with some severity: "it's very rude."

The Hatter opened his eyes very wide on hearing this; but all he *said* was "Why is a raven like a writing-desk?"[4]

"Come, we shall have some fun now!" thought Alice. "I'm

glad they've begun asking riddles—I believe I can guess that," she added aloud.

"Do you mean that you think you can find out the answer to it?" said the March Hare.

"Exactly so," said Alice.

"Then you should say what you mean," the March Hare went on.

"I do," Alice hastily replied; "at least—at least I mean what I say—that's the same thing, you know."

"Not the same thing a bit!" said the Hatter. "Why, you might just as well say that 'I see what I eat' is the same thing as 'I eat what I see'!"

"You might just as well say," added the March Hare, "that 'I like what I get' is the same thing as 'I get what I like'!"

"You might just as well say," added the Dormouse, which seemed to be talking in its sleep, "that 'I breathe when I sleep' is the same thing as 'I sleep when I breathe'!"

"It *is* the same thing with you," said the Hatter, and here the conversation dropped, and the party sat silent for a minute, while Alice thought over all she could remember about ravens and writing-desks, which wasn't much.

The Hatter was the first to break the silence. "What day of the month is it?" he said, turning to Alice: he had taken his watch out of his pocket, and was looking at it uneasily, shaking it every now and then, and holding it to his ear.

Alice considered a little, and then said "The fourth."*

"Two days wrong!" sighed the Hatter. "I told you butter wouldn't suit the works!" he added, looking angrily at the March Hare.

"It was the *best* butter," the March Hare meekly replied.

"Yes, but some crumbs must have got in as well," the Hatter grumbled: "you shouldn't have put it in with the breadknife."

The March Hare took the watch and looked at it gloomily: then he dipped it into his cup of tea, and looked at it again: but he could think of nothing better to say than his first remark, "It was the *best* butter, you know."

Alice had been looking over his shoulder with some curiosity. "What a funny watch!" she remarked. "It tells the day of the month, and doesn't tell what o'clock it is!"

"Why should it?" muttered the Hatter. "Does *your* watch tell you what year it is?"

"Of course not," Alice replied very readily: "but that's because it stays the same year for such a long time together."

"Which is just the case with *mine*," said the Hatter.

Alice felt dreadfully puzzled. The Hatter's remark seemed to her to have no sort of meaning in it, and yet it was certainly English. "I don't quite understand you," she said, as politely as she could.

"The Dormouse is asleep again," said the Hatter, and he poured a little hot tea upon its nose.

The Dormouse shook its head impatiently, and said, without opening its eyes, "Of course, of course: just what I was going to remark myself."

"Have you guessed the riddle yet?" the Hatter said, turning to Alice again.

"No, I give it up," Alice replied. "What's the answer?"

---

*Alice Liddell's birthday was the fourth of March.

"I haven't the slightest idea," said the Hatter.

"Nor I," said the March Hare.

Alice sighed wearily. "I think you might do something better with the time," she said, "than wasting it in asking riddles that have no answers."

"If you knew Time as well as I do," said the Hatter, "you wouldn't talk about wasting *it*. It's *him*."

"I don't know what you mean," said Alice.

"Of course you don't!" the Hatter said, tossing his head contemptuously. "I dare say you never even spoke to Time!"

"Perhaps not;" Alice cautiously replied; "but I know I have to beat time when I learn music."

"Ah! That accounts for it," said the Hatter. "He wo'n't stand beating. Now, if you only kept on good terms with him, he'd do almost anything you liked with the clock. For instance, suppose it were nine o'clock in the morning, just time to begin lessons: you'd only have to whisper a hint to Time, and round goes the clock in a twinkling! Half-past one, time for dinner!"

("I only wish it was," the March Hare said to itself in a whisper.)

"That would be grand, certainly," said Alice thoughtfully; "but then—I shouldn't be hungry for it, you know."

"Not at first, perhaps," said the Hatter: "but you could keep it to half-past one as long as you liked."

"Is that the way *you* manage?" Alice asked.

The Hatter shook his head mournfully. "Not I!" he replied. "We quarreled last March——just before *he* went mad, you know——" (pointing with his teaspoon at the March Hare,) "——it was at the great concert given by the Queen of Hearts, and I had to sing

> *'Twinkle, twinkle, little bat!*
> *How I wonder what you're at!'*

You know the song, perhaps?"

"I've heard something like it," said Alice.

"It goes on, you know," the Hatter continued, "in this way:

> 'Up above the world you fly
> Like a tea-tray in the sky.
>   Twinkle, twinkle——' "

Here the Dormouse shook itself, and began singing in its sleep "*Twinkle, twinkle, winkle, twinkle*——" and went on so long that they had to pinch it to make it stop.

"Well, I'd hardly finished the first verse," said the Hatter, "when the Queen bawled out 'He's murdering the time! Off with his head!'"

"How dreadfully savage!" exclaimed Alice.

"And ever since that" the Hatter went on in a mournful tone, "he wo'n't do a thing I ask! It's always six o'clock now."

A bright idea came into Alice's head. "Is that the reason so many tea-things are put out here?" she asked.

"Yes, that's it," said the Hatter with a sigh: "it's always tea-time, and we've no time to wash the things between whiles."

"Then you keep moving round, I suppose?" said Alice.

"Exactly so," said the Hatter: "as the things get used up."

"But what happens when you come to the beginning again?" Alice ventured to ask.

"Suppose we change the subject," the March Hare interrupted, yawning. "I'm getting tired of this. I vote the young lady tells us a story."

"I'm afraid I don't know one," said Alice, rather alarmed at the proposal.

"Then the Dormouse shall!" they both cried. "Wake up, Dormouse!" And they pinched it on both sides at once.

The Dormouse slowly opened its eyes. "I wasn't asleep," it said in a hoarse, feeble voice, "I heard every word you fellows were saying."

"Tell us a story!" said the March Hare.

"Yes, please do!" pleaded Alice.

"And be quick about it," added the Hatter, "or you'll be asleep again before it's done."

"Once upon a time there were three little sisters," the Dormouse began in a great hurry; "and their names were Elsie, Lacie, and Tillie; and they lived at the bottom of a well——"

"What did they live on?" said Alice, who always took a great interest in questions of eating and drinking.

"They lived on treacle,"* said the Dormouse, after thinking a minute or two.

"They couldn't have done that, you know," Alice gently remarked. "They'd have been ill."

"So they were," said the Dormouse; "*very* ill."

Alice tried a little to fancy to herself what such an extraordinary way of living would be like, but it puzzled her too much: so she went on: "But why did they live at the bottom of a well?"

"Take some more tea," the March Hare said to Alice, very earnestly.

"I've had nothing yet," Alice replied in an offended tone: "so I ca'n't take more."

"You mean you ca'n't take *less*," said the Hatter: "it's very easy to take *more* than nothing."

"Nobody asked *your* opinion," said Alice.

"Who's making personal remarks now?" the Hatter asked triumphantly.

---

*A kind of molasses.

Alice did not quite know what to say to this: so she helped herself to some tea and bread-and-butter, and then turned to the Dormouse, and repeated her question. "Why did they live at the bottom of a well?"

The Dormouse again took a minute or two to think about it, and then said "It was a treacle-well."

"There's no such thing!" Alice was beginning very angrily, but the Hatter and the March Hare went "Sh! Sh!" and the Dormouse sulkily remarked "If you ca'n't be civil, you'd better finish the story for yourself."

"No, please go on!" Alice said very humbly. "I wo'n't interrupt you again. I dare say there may be *one*."

"One, indeed!" said the Dormouse indignantly. However, he consented to go on. "And so these three little sisters—they were learning to draw, you know——"

"What did they draw?" said Alice, quite forgetting her promise.

"Treacle," said the Dormouse, without considering at all, this time.

"I want a clean cup," interrupted the Hatter: "let's all move one place on."

He moved on as he spoke, and the Dormouse followed him: the March Hare moved into the Dormouse's place, and Alice rather unwillingly took the place of the March Hare. The Hatter was the only one who got any advantage from the change; and Alice was a good deal worse off than before, as the March Hare had just upset the milk-jug into his plate.

Alice did not wish to offend the Dormouse again, so she began very cautiously: "But I don't understand. Where did they draw the treacle from?"

"You can draw water out of a water-well," said the Hatter; "so I should think you could draw treacle out of a treacle-well—eh, stupid?

"But they were *in* the well," Alice said to the Dormouse, not choosing to notice this last remark.

"Of course they were," said the Dormouse: "well in."

This answer so confused poor Alice, that she let the Dormouse go on for some time without interrupting it.

"They were learning to draw," the Dormouse went on, yawning and rubbing its eyes, for it was getting very sleepy; "and they drew all manner of things—everything that begins with an M——"

"Why with an M?" said Alice.

"Why not?" said the March Hare.

Alice was silent.

The Dormouse had closed its eyes by this time, and was going off into a doze; but, on being pinched by the Hatter, it woke up again with a little shriek, and went on: "——that begins with an M, such as mouse-traps, and the moon, and memory, and muchness—you know you say things are 'much of a muchness'—did you ever see such a thing as a drawing of a muchness!"

"Really, now you ask me," said Alice, very much confused, "I don't think——"

"Then you shouldn't talk," said the Hatter.

This piece of rudeness was more than Alice could bear: she got up in great disgust, and walked off: the Dormouse fell asleep instantly, and neither of the others took the least notice of her going, though she looked back once or twice, half hoping that they would call after her: the last time she saw them, they were trying to put the Dormouse into the teapot.

"At any rate I'll never go *there* again!" said Alice, as she picked her way through the wood. "It's the stupidest tea-party I ever was at in all my life!"

Just as she said this, she noticed that one of the trees had a door leading right into it. "That's very curious!" she thought. "But everything's curious today. I think I may as well go in at once." And in she went.

Once more she found herself in the long hall, and close to the little glass table. "Now, I'll manage better this time," she said to herself, and began by taking the little golden key, and unlocking the door that led into the garden. Then she set to work nibbling at the mushroom (she had kept a piece of it in her pocket) till she was about a foot high: then she walked down the little passage: and *then*—she found herself at last in the beautiful garden, among the bright flowerbeds and the cool fountains.

VIII

The Queen's Croquet Ground

A large rose-tree stood near the entrance of the garden: the roses growing on it were white, but there were three gardeners at it, busily painting them red. Alice thought this a very curious thing, and she went nearer to watch them, and, just as she came up to them, she heard one of them say "Look out now, Five! Don't go splashing paint over me like that!"

"I couldn't help it," said Five, in a sulky tone. "Seven jogged my elbow."

On which Seven looked up and said "That's right, Five! Always lay the blame on others!"

"*You'd* better not talk!" said Five. "I heard the Queen say only yesterday you deserved to be beheaded."

"What for?" said the one who had spoken first.

"That's none of *your* business, Two!" said Seven.

"Yes, it *is* his business!" said Five. "And I'll tell him—it was for bringing the cook tulip-roots instead of onions."

Seven flung down his brush, and had just begun "Well, of all the unjust things—" when his eye chanced to fall upon Alice, as she stood watching them, and he checked himself suddenly: the others looked round also, and all of them bowed low.

"Would you tell me, please," said Alice, a little timidly, "why you are painting those roses?"

Five and Seven said nothing, but looked at Two. Two began, in a low voice, "Why, the fact is, you see, Miss, this here ought to have been a *red* rose-tree, and we put a white one in by mistake; and, if the Queen was to find it out, we should all have our heads cut off, you know. So you see, Miss, we're doing our best, afore she comes, to—" At this moment, Five, who had been anxiously looking across the garden, called out "The Queen! The

91

Queen!", and the three gardeners instantly threw themselves flat upon their faces. There was a sound of many footsteps, and Alice looked round, eager to see the Queen.

First came ten soldiers carrying clubs: these were all shaped like the three gardeners, oblong and flat, with their hands and feet at the corners: next the ten courtiers: these were orna-mented all over with diamonds, and walked two and two, as the sol-diers did. After these came the royal chil-dren: there were ten of them, and the little dears came jump-ing merrily along, hand in hand, in couples: they were all ornamented with hearts. Next came the guests, mostly Kings and Queens, and among them Alice recognised the White Rab-bit: it was talking in a hurried nervous manner, smiling at every-thing that was said, and went by without noticing her. Then followed the Knave of Hearts, carrying the King's crown on a crimson velvet cushion; and, last of all this grand procession, came THE KING AND THE QUEEN OF HEARTS.

Alice was rather doubtful whether she ought not to lie down on her face like the three gardeners, but she could not remem-ber ever having heard of such a rule at processions; "and besides, what would be the use of a procession," thought she, "if people had all to lie down on their faces, so that they couldn't see it?" So she stood where she was, and waited.

When the procession came opposite to Alice, they all stopped and looked at her, and the Queen said, severely, "Who is this?" She said it to the Knave of Hearts, who only bowed and smiled in reply.

"Idiot!" said the Queen, tossing her head impatiently; and, turning to Alice, she went on: "What's your name, child?"

"My name is Alice, so please your Majesty," said Alice very politely; but she added, to herself, "Why, they're only a pack of cards, after all. I needn't be afraid of them!"

"And who are *these*?" said the Queen, pointing to the three gardeners who were lying round the rose-tree; for, you see, as they were lying on their faces, and the pattern on their backs was the same as the rest of the pack, she could not tell whether they were gardeners, or soldiers, or courtiers, or three of her own children.

"How should *I* know?" said Alice, surprised at her own courage. "It's no business of *mine*."

The Queen turned crimson with fury, and, after glaring at her for a moment like a wild beast, began screaming "Off with her head! Off with——"

"Nonsense!" said Alice, very loudly and decidedly, and the Queen was silent.

The King laid his hand upon her arm, and timidly said "Consider, my dear: she is only a child!"

The Queen turned angrily away from him, and said to the Knave "Turn them over!"

The Knave did so, very carefully, with one foot.

"Get up!" said the Queen in a shrill, loud voice, and the three gardeners instantly jumped up, and began bowing to the King, the Queen, the royal children, and everybody else.

"Leave off that!" screamed the Queen. "You make me giddy." And then, turning to the rose-tree, she went on "What *have* you been doing here?"

"May it please your Majesty," said Two, in a very humble tone, going down on one knee as he spoke, "we were trying—"

"*I* see!" said the Queen, who had meanwhile been examining the roses. "Off with their heads!" and the procession moved on, three of the soldiers remaining behind to execute the unfortunate gardeners, who ran to Alice for protection.

"You sha'n't be beheaded!" said Alice, and she put them into a large flowerpot that stood near. The three soldiers wandered about for a minute or two, looking for them, and then quietly marched off after the others.

"Are their heads off?" shouted the Queen.

"Their heads are gone, if it please your Majesty!" the soldiers shouted in reply.

"That's right!" shouted the Queen. "Can you play croquet?"

The soldiers were silent, and looked at Alice, as the question was evidently meant for her.

"Yes!" shouted Alice.

"Come on, then!" roared the Queen, and Alice joined the procession, wondering very much what would happen next.

"It's—it's a very fine day!" said a timid voice at her side. She was walking by the White Rabbit, who was peeping anxiously into her face.

"Very," said Alice. "Where's the Duchess?"

"Hush! Hush!" said the Rabbit in a low hurried tone. He looked anxiously over his shoulder as he spoke, and then raised himself upon tiptoe, put his mouth close to her ear, and whispered "She's under sentence of execution."

"What for?" said Alice.

"Did you say 'What a pity!'?" the Rabbit asked.

"No, I didn't," said Alice. "I don't think it's at all a pity. I said 'What for?'"

"She boxed the Queen's ears—" the Rabbit began. Alice gave a little scream of laughter. "Oh, hush!" the Rabbit whispered in a frightened tone. "The Queen will hear you! You see she came rather late, and the Queen said—"

"Get to your places!" shouted the Queen in a voice of thunder, and people began running about in all directions, tumbling up against each other: however, they got settled down in a minute or two, and the game began.

Alice thought she had never seen such a curious croquet-ground in her life: it was all ridges and furrows: the croquet balls were live hedgehogs, and the mallets live flamingoes, and the soldiers had to double themselves up and stand on their hands and feet, to make the arches.

The chief difficulty Alice found at first was in managing her flamingo: she succeeded in getting its body tucked away, comfortably enough, under her arm, with its legs hanging down, but generally, just as she had got its neck nicely straightened out, and was going to give the hedgehog a blow with its head, it *would* twist itself round and look up in her face, with such a puzzled expression that she could not help bursting out laughing; and, when she had got its head down, and was going to begin again, it was very provoking to find that the hedgehog had unrolled itself, and was in the act of crawling away: besides all this, there was generally a ridge or a furrow in the way wherever she wanted to send the hedgehog to, and, as the doubled-up soldiers were always getting up and walking off to other parts of the ground, Alice soon came to the conclusion that it was a very difficult game indeed.

The players all played at once, without waiting for turns, quarreling all the while, and fighting for the hedgehogs; and in a very short time the Queen was in a furious passion, and went stamping about, and shouting "Off with his head!" or "Off with her head!" about once in a minute. Alice began to feel very uneasy: to be sure, she had not as yet had any dispute with the Queen, but she knew that it might happen any minute, "and then," thought she, "what would become of me? They're dreadfully fond of beheading people here: the great wonder is, that there's any one left alive!"

She was looking about for some way of escape, and wondering whether she could get away without being seen, when she noticed a curious appearance in the air: it puzzled her very much at first, but after watching it a minute or two she made it out to be a grin, and she said to herself "It's the Cheshire-Cat: now I shall have somebody to talk to."

"How are you getting on?" said the Cat, as soon as there was mouth enough for it to speak with.

Alice waited till the eyes appeared, and then nodded. "It's no use speaking to it," she thought, "till its ears have come, or at least one of them." In another minute the whole head appeared, and then Alice put down her flamingo, and began an account of the game, feeling very glad she had some one to listen to her. The Cat seemed to think that there was enough of it now in sight, and no more of it appeared.

"I don't think they play at all fairly," Alice began, in rather a complaining tone, "and they all quarrel so dreadfully one ca'n't hear oneself speak—and they don't seem to have any rules in particular: at least, if there are, nobody attends to them—and you've no idea how confusing it is all the things being alive: for instance, there's the arch I've got to go through next walking about at the other end of the ground—and I should have croqueted the Queen's hedgehog just now, only it ran away when it saw mine coming!"

"How do you like the Queen?" said the Cat in a low voice.

"Not at all," said Alice: "she's so extremely—" Just then she noticed that the Queen was close behind her, listening: so she went on "—likely to win, that it's hardly worth while finishing the game."

The Queen smiled and passed on.

"Who *are* you talking to?" said the King, coming up to Alice, and looking at the Cat's head with great curiosity.

"It's a friend of mine—a Cheshire-Cat," said Alice: "allow me to introduce it."

"I don't like the look of it at all," said the King: "however, it may kiss my hand, if it likes."

"I'd rather not," the Cat remarked.

"Don't be impertinent," said the King, "and don't look at me like that!" He got behind Alice as he spoke.

"A cat may look at a king," said Alice. "I've read that in some book, but I don't remember where."

"Well, it must be removed," said the King very decidedly; and he called to the Queen, who was passing at the moment, "My dear! I wish you would have this cat removed!"

The Queen had only one way of settling all difficulties, great or small. "Off with his head!" she said without even looking round.

"I'll fetch the executioner myself," said the King eagerly, and he hurried off.

Alice thought she might as well go back and see how the game was going on, as she heard the Queen's voice in the distance, screaming with passion. She had already heard her sentence three of the players to be executed for having missed their turns, and she did not like the look of things at all, as the game was in such confusion that she never knew whether it was her turn or not. So she went off in search of her hedgehog.

The hedgehog was engaged in a fight with another hedgehog, which seemed to Alice an excellent opportunity for croqueting one of them with the other: the only difficulty was, that her flamingo was gone across to the other side of the garden, where Alice could see it trying in a helpless sort of way to fly up into a tree.

By the time she had caught the flamingo and brought it back, the fight was over, and both the hedgehogs were out of sight: "but it doesn't matter much," thought Alice, "as all the arches are gone from this side of the ground." So she tucked it away under her arm, that it might not escape again, and went back to have a little more conversation with her friend.

When she got back to the Cheshire-Cat, she was surprised to find quite a large crowd collected round it: there was a dispute going on between the executioner, the King, and the Queen, who were all talking at once, while all the rest were quite silent, and looked very uncomfortable.

The moment Alice appeared, she was appealed to by all three to settle the question, and they repeated their arguments to her, though, as they all spoke at once, she found it very hard to make out exactly what they said.

The executioner's argument was, that you couldn't cut off a head unless there was a body to cut it off from: that he had never had to do such a thing before, and he wasn't going to begin at *his* time of life.

The King's argument was that anything that had a head could be beheaded, and that you weren't to talk nonsense.

The Queen's argument was that, if something wasn't done about it in less than no time, she'd have everybody executed, all round. (It was this last remark that had made the whole party look so grave and anxious.)

Alice could think of nothing else to say but "It belongs to the Duchess: you'd better ask *her* about it."

"She's in prison," the Queen said to the executioner: "fetch her here." And the executioner went off like an arrow.

The Cat's head began fading away the moment he was gone, and, by the time he had come back with the Duchess, it had entirely disappeared: so the King and the executioner ran wildly up and down, looking for it, while the rest of the party went back to the game.

IX

The Mock Turtle's Story

Y ou ca'n't think how glad I am to see you again, you dear old thing!" said the Duchess, as she tucked her arm affectionately into Alice's, and they walked off together.

Alice was very glad to find her in such a pleasant temper, and thought to herself that perhaps it was only the pepper that had made her so savage when they met in the kitchen.

"When *I'm* a Duchess," she said to herself (not in a very hopeful tone, though), "I wo'n't have any pepper in my kitchen *at all.* Soup does very well without—Maybe it's always pepper that makes people hot-tempered," she went on, very much pleased at having found out a new kind of rule, "and vinegar that makes them sour—and camomile that makes them bitter—and—and barley-sugar and such things that make children sweet-tempered. I only wish people knew *that:* then they wouldn't be so stingy about it, you know——"

She had quite forgotten the Duchess by this time, and was a little startled when she heard her voice close to her ear. "You're thinking about something, my dear, and that makes you forget to talk. I ca'n't tell you just now what the moral of that is, but I shall remember it in a bit."

"Perhaps it hasn't one," Alice ventured to remark.

"Tut, tut, child!" said the Duchess. "Every thing's got a moral, if only you can find it." And she squeezed herself up closer to Alice's side as she spoke.

Alice did not much like her keeping so close to her: first, because the Duchess was *very* ugly; and secondly, because she was exactly the right height to rest her chin on Alice's shoulder, and it was an uncomfortably sharp chin. However, she did not like to be rude: so she bore it as well as she could.

103

"The game's going on rather better now," she said, by way of keeping up the conversation a little.

"'Tis so," said the Duchess: "and the moral of that is—'Oh, 'tis love, 'tis love, that makes the world go round!'"

"Somebody said," Alice whispered, "that it's done by everybody minding their own business!"

"Ah, well! It means much the same thing," said the Duchess, digging her sharp little chin into Alice's shoulder as she added "and the moral of *that* is—'Take care of the sense, and the sounds will take care of themselves.'"

"How fond she is of finding morals in things!" Alice thought to herself.

"I dare say you're wondering why I don't put my arm round your waist," the Duchess said, after a pause: "the reason is, that I'm doubtful about the temper of your flamingo. Shall I try the experiment?"

"He might bite," Alice cautiously replied, not feeling at all anxious to have the experiment tried.

"Very true," said the Duchess: "flamingoes and mustard both bite. And the moral of that is—'Birds of a feather flock together.'"

"Only mustard isn't a bird," Alice remarked.

"Right, as usual," said the Duchess: "what a clear way you have of putting things!"

"It's a mineral, I *think*," said Alice.

"Of course it is," said the Duchess, who seemed ready to agree to everything that Alice said: "there's a large mustard-mine near here. And the moral of that is—'The more there is of mine, the less there is of yours.'"

"Oh, I know!" exclaimed Alice, who had not attended to this last remark. "It's a vegetable. It doesn't look like one, but it is."

"I quite agree with you," said the Duchess; "and the moral of that is—'Be what you would seem to be'—or, if you'd like it put more simply—'Never imagine yourself not to be otherwise than what it might appear to others that what you were or might have been was not otherwise than what you had been would have appeared to them to be otherwise.'"

"I think I should understand that better," Alice said very politely, "if I had it written down: but I ca'n't quite follow it as you say it."

"That's nothing to what I could say if I chose," the Duchess replied, in a pleased tone.

"Pray don't trouble yourself to say it any longer than that," said Alice.

"Oh, don't talk about trouble!" said the Duchess. "I make you a present of everything I've said as yet."

"A cheap sort of present!" thought Alice. "I'm glad people don't give birthday-presents like that!" But she did not venture to say it out loud.

"Thinking again?" the Duchess asked, with another dig of her sharp little chin.

"I've a right to think," said Alice sharply, for she was beginning to feel a little worried.

"Just about as much right," said the Duchess, "as pigs have to fly; and the m——"

But here, to Alice's great surprise, the Duchess's voice died away, even in the middle of her favourite word 'moral,' and the arm that was linked into hers began to tremble. Alice looked up, and there stood the Queen in front of them, with her arms folded, frowning like a thunderstorm.

"A fine day, your Majesty!" the Duchess began in a low, weak voice.

"Now, I give you fair warning," shouted the Queen, stamping on the ground as she spoke; "either you or your head must be off, and that in about half no time! Take your choice!"

The Duchess took her choice, and was gone in a moment.

"Let's go on with the game," the Queen said to Alice; and Alice was too much frightened to say a word, but slowly followed her back to the croquet-ground.

The other guests had taken advantage of the Queen's absence, and were resting in the shade: however, the moment they saw her, they hurried back to the game, the Queen merely remarking that a moment's delay would cost them their lives.

All the time they were playing the Queen never left off quarreling with the other players, and shouting "Off with his head!" or "Off with her head!" Those whom she sentenced were taken into custody by the soldiers, who of course had to leave off being arches to do this, so that, by the end of half an hour or so, there were no arches left, and all the players, except the King, the Queen, and Alice, were in custody and under sentence of execution.

Then the Queen left off, quite out of breath, and said to Alice "Have you seen the Mock Turtle yet?"

"No," said Alice. "I don't even know what a Mock Turtle is."

"It's the thing Mock Turtle Soup is made from," said the Queen.

"I never saw one, or heard of one," said Alice.

"Come on, then," said the Queen, "and he shall tell you his history."

As they walked off together, Alice heard the King say in a low voice, to the company generally, "You are all pardoned." "Come, *that's* a good thing!" she said to herself, for she had felt quite unhappy at the number of executions the Queen had ordered.

They very soon came upon a Gryphon,* lying fast asleep in the sun. (If you don't know what a Gryphon is, look at the picture.) "Up, lazy thing!" said the Queen, "and take this young lady to see the Mock Turtle, and to hear his history. I must go back and see after some executions I have ordered;" and she walked off, leaving Alice alone with the Gryphon. Alice did not quite like the look of the creature, but on the whole she thought it would be quite as safe to stay with it as to go after that savage Queen: so she waited.

---

*Mythical creature with an eagle's head and wings and a lion's body; also spelled "griffin."

The Gryphon sat up and rubbed its eyes: then it watched the Queen till she was out of sight: then it chuckled. "What fun!" said the Gryphon, half to itself, half to Alice.

"What *is* the fun?" said Alice.

"Why, *she*," said the Gryphon. "It's all her fancy, that: they never executes nobody you know. Come on!"

"Everybody says 'come on!' here," thought Alice, as she went slowly after it: "I never was so ordered about before, in all my life, never!"

They had not gone far before they saw the Mock Turtle in the distance, sitting sad and lonely on a little ledge of rock, and, as they came nearer, Alice could hear him sighing as if his heart would break. She pitied him deeply. "What is his sorrow?" she asked the Gryphon. And the Gryphon answered, very nearly in the same words as before, "It's all his fancy, that: he hasn't got no sorrow, you know. Come on!"

So they went up to the Mock Turtle, who looked at them with large eyes full of tears, but said nothing.

"This here young lady," said the Gryphon, "she wants for to know your history, she do."

"I'll tell it her," said the Mock Turtle in a deep, hollow tone. "Sit down, both of you, and don't speak a word till I've finished."

So they sat down, and nobody spoke for some minutes. Alice thought to herself "I don't see how he can *ever* finish, if he doesn't begin." But she waited patiently.

"Once," said the Mock Turtle at last, with a deep sigh, "I was a real Turtle."

These words were followed by a very long silence, broken only by an occasional exclamation of "Hjckrrh!" from the Gryphon, and the constant heavy sobbing of the Mock Turtle. Alice was very nearly getting up and saying "Thank you, Sir, for your interesting story," but she could not help thinking there *must* be more to come, so she sat still and said nothing.

"When we were little," the Mock Turtle went on at last, more calmly, though still sobbing a little now and then, "we went to school in the sea. The master was an old Turtle—we used to call him Tortoise——"

"Why did you call him Tortoise, if he wasn't one?" Alice asked.

"We called him Tortoise because he taught us," said the Mock Turtle angrily. "Really you are very dull!"

"You ought to be ashamed of yourself for asking such a simple question," added the Gryphon; and then they both sat silent and looked at poor Alice, who felt ready to sink into the earth. At last the Gryphon said to the Mock Turtle "Drive on, old fellow! Don't be all day about it!", and he went on in these words:—

"Yes, we went to school in the sea, though you mayn't believe it——"

"I never said I didn't!" interrupted Alice.

"You did," said the Mock Turtle.

"Hold your tongue!" added the Gryphon, before Alice could speak again. The Mock Turtle went on.

"We had the best of educations—in fact, we went to school every day——"

"*I've* been to a day-school, too," said Alice. "You needn't be so proud as all that."

"With extras?" asked the Mock Turtle, a little anxiously.

"Yes," said Alice: "we learned French and music."

"And washing?" said the Mock Turtle.

"Certainly not!" said Alice indignantly.

"Ah! Then yours wasn't a really good school," said the Mock Turtle in a tone of great relief. "Now, at *ours,* they had, at the end of the bill, 'French, music, *and washing*—extra.'"

"You couldn't have wanted it much," said Alice; "living at the bottom of the sea."

"I couldn't afford to learn it," said the Mock Turtle with a sigh. "I only took the regular course."

"What was that?" inquired Alice.

"Reeling and Writhing, of course, to begin with," the Mock Turtle replied; "and then the different branches of Arithmetic—Ambition, Distraction, Uglification, and Derision."

"I never heard of 'Uglification,'" Alice ventured to say. "What is it?"

The Gryphon lifted up both its paws in surprise. "Never heard of uglifying!" it exclaimed. "You know what to beautify is, I suppose?"

"Yes," said Alice doubtfully: "it means—to—make—anything—prettier."

"Well, then," the Gryphon went on, "if you don't know what to uglify is, you *are* a simpleton."

Alice did not feel encouraged to ask any more questions about it: so she turned to the Mock Turtle, and said "What else had you to learn?"

"Well, there was Mystery," the Mock Turtle replied, counting off the subjects on his flappers,—"Mystery, ancient and modern, with Seaography: then Drawling—the Drawling-master was an old conger-eel, that used to come once a week: *he* taught us Drawling, Stretching, and Fainting in Coils."

"What was *that* like?" said Alice.

"Well, I ca'n't show it you, myself," the Mock Turtle said: "I'm too stiff. And the Gryphon never learnt it."

"Hadn't time," said the Gryphon: "I went to the Classical master, though. He was an old crab, *he* was."

"I never went to him," the Mock Turtle said with a sigh. "He taught Laughing and Grief, they used to say."

"So he did, so he did," said the Gryphon, sighing in his turn; and both creatures hid their faces in their paws.

"And how many hours a day did you do lessons?" said Alice, in a hurry to change the subject.

"Ten hours the first day," said the Mock Turtle: "nine the next, and so on."

"What a curious plan!" exclaimed Alice.

"That's the reason they're called lessons," the Gryphon remarked: "because they lessen from day to day."

This was quite a new idea to Alice, and she thought it over a little before she made her next remark. "Then the eleventh day must have been a holiday?"

"Of course it was," said the Mock Turtle.

"And how did you manage on the twelfth?" Alice went on eagerly.

"That's enough about lessons," the Gryphon interrupted in a very decided tone. "Tell her something about the games now."

X

The Lobster Quadrille

The Mock Turtle sighed deeply, and drew the back of one flapper across his eyes. He looked at Alice and tried to speak, but, for a minute or two, sobs choked his voice. "Same as if he had a bone in his throat," said the Gryphon; and it set to work shaking him and punching him in the back. At last the Mock Turtle recovered his voice, and, with tears running down his cheeks, he went on again:—

"You may not have lived much under the sea—" ("I haven't," said Alice)—"and perhaps you were never even introduced to a lobster—" (Alice began to say "I once tasted——" but checked herself hastily, and said "No, never") "——so you can have no idea what a delightful thing a Lobster-Quadrille is!"

"No, indeed," said Alice. "What sort of a dance is it?"

"Why," said the Gryphon, "you first form into a line along the sea-shore——"

"Two lines!" cried the Mock Turtle. "Seals, turtles, salmon, and so on: then, when you've cleared all the jelly-fish out of the way——"

"*That* generally takes some time," interrupted the Gryphon.

"—you advance twice——"

"Each with a lobster as a partner!" cried the Gryphon.

"Of course," the Mock Turtle said: "advance twice, set to partners——"

"—change lobsters, and retire in same order," continued the Gryphon.

"Then, you know," the Mock Turtle went on, "you throw the——"

"The lobsters!" shouted the Gryphon, with a bound into the air.

"—as far out to sea as you can——"

"Swim after them!" screamed the Gryphon.

"Turn a somersault in the sea!" cried the Mock Turtle, capering wildly about.

"Change lobsters again!" yelled the Gryphon at the top of its voice.

"Back to land again, and—that's all the first figure," said the Mock Turtle, suddenly dropping his voice; and the two creatures, who had been jumping about like mad things all this time, sat down again very sadly and quietly, and looked at Alice.

"It must be a very pretty dance," said Alice timidly.

"Would you like to see a little of it?" said the Mock Turtle.

"Very much indeed," said Alice.

"Come, let's try the first figure!" said the Mock Turtle to the Gryphon. "We can do it without lobsters, you know. Which shall sing?"

"Oh, *you* sing," said the Gryphon. "I've forgotten the words."

So they began solemnly dancing round and round Alice, every now and then treading on her toes when they passed too close, and waving their fore-paws to mark the time, while the Mock Turtle sang this, very slowly and sadly:—

> *"Will you walk a little faster?" said a whiting*
> *to a snail,*
> *"There's a porpoise close behind us, and he's*
> *treading on my tail.*
> *See how eagerly the lobsters and the turtles all*
> *advance!*
> *They are waiting on the shingle—will you come*
> *and join the dance?*
> *Will you, wo'n't you, will you, wo'n't you,*
> *will you join the dance?*
> *Will you, wo'n't you, will you, wo'n't you,*
> *wo'n't you join the dance?*
>
> *"You can really have no notion how delightful*
> *it will be*
> *When they take us up and throw us, with the*
> *lobsters, out to sea!"*

But the snail replied "Too far, too far!", and
    gave a look askance—
Said he thanked the whiting kindly, but he
    would not join the dance.
Would not, could not, would not, could not,
    would not join the dance.
Would not, could not, would not, could not,
    could not join the dance.

"What matters it how far we go?" his scaly
    friend replied.
"There is another shore, you know, upon the
    other side.

The further off from England the nearer is to
    France—
Then turn not pale, beloved snail, but come and
    join the dance.
Will you, wo'n't you, will you, wo'n't you,
    will you join the dance?
Will you, wo'n't you, will you, wo'n't you,
    wo'n't you join the dance?"

"Thank you, it's a very interesting dance to watch," said Alice, feeling very glad that it was over at last: "and I do so like that curious song about the whiting!"

"Oh, as to the whiting," said the Mock Turtle, "they—you've seen them, of course?"

"Yes," said Alice, "I've often seen them at dinn——" she checked herself hastily.

"I don't know where Dinn may be," said the Mock Turtle; "but, if you've seen them so often, of course you know what they're like?"

"I believe so," Alice replied thoughtfully. "They have their tails in their mouths—and they're all over crumbs."

"You're wrong about the crumbs," said the Mock Turtle: "crumbs would all wash off in the sea. But they *have* their tails in their mouths; and the reason is—" here the Mock Turtle yawned and shut his eyes. "Tell her about the reason and all that," he said to the Gryphon.

"The reason is," said the Gryphon, "that they *would* go with the lobsters to the dance. So they got thrown out to sea. So they had to fall a long way. So they got their tails fast in their mouths. So they couldn't get them out again. That's all."

"Thank you," said Alice, "it's very interesting. I never knew so much about a whiting before."

"I can tell you more than that, if you like," said the Gryphon. "Do you know why it's called a whiting?"*

"I never thought about it," said Alice. "Why?"

"*It does the boots and shoes,*" the Gryphon replied very solemnly.

---

*A common fish, often served in England with the tail tucked into the mouth.

Alice was thoroughly puzzled. "Does the boots and shoes!" she repeated in a wondering tone.

"Why, what are *your* shoes done with?" said the Gryphon. "I mean, what makes them so shiny?"

Alice looked down at them, and considered a little before she gave her answer. "They're done with blacking, I believe."

"Boots and shoes under the sea," the Gryphon went on in a deep voice, "are done with whiting. Now you know."

"And what are they made of?" Alice asked in a tone of great curiosity.

"Soles and eels, of course," the Gryphon replied, rather impatiently: "any shrimp could have told you that."

"If I'd been the whiting," said Alice, whose thoughts were still running on the song, "I'd have said to the porpoise 'Keep back, please! We don't want *you* with us!'"

"They were obliged to have him with them," the Mock Turtle said. "No wise fish would go anywhere without a porpoise."

"Wouldn't it, really?" said Alice, in a tone of great surprise.

"Of course not," said the Mock Turtle. "Why, if a fish came to *me,* and told me he was going a journey, I should say 'With what porpoise?'"

"Don't you mean 'purpose'?" said Alice.

"I mean what I say," the Mock Turtle replied, in an offended tone. And the Gryphon added "Come, let's hear some of *your* adventures."

"I could tell you my adventures—beginning from this morning," said Alice a little timidly; "but it's no use going back to yesterday, because I was a different person then."

"Explain all that," said the Mock Turtle.

"No, no! The adventures first," said the Gryphon in an impatient tone: "explanations take such a dreadful time."

So Alice began telling them her adventures from the time when she first saw the White Rabbit. She was a little nervous about it, just at first, the two creatures got so close to her, one on each side, and opened their eyes and mouths so *very* wide; but she gained courage as she went on. Her listeners were perfectly quiet till she got to the part about her repeating *"You are old, Father William,"* to the Caterpillar, and the words all coming different, and then the Mock Turtle drew a long breath, and said "That's very curious!"

"It's all about as curious as it can be," said the Gryphon.

"It all came different!" the Mock Turtle repeated thoughtfully. "I should like to hear her try and repeat something now. Tell her to begin." He looked at the Gryphon as if he thought it had some kind of authority over Alice.

"Stand up and repeat *''Tis the voice of the sluggard,'*" said the Gryphon.

"How the creatures order one about, and make one repeat lessons!" thought Alice. "I might just as well be at school at once."

However, she got up, and began to repeat it, but her head was so full of the Lobster-Quadrille, that she hardly knew what she was saying; and the words came very queer indeed:—

"'Tis the voice of the Lobster: I heard him declare
'You have baked me too brown, I must sugar my hair.'
As a duck with its eyelids, so he with his nose
Trims his belt and his buttons, and turns out his toes.
When the sands are all dry, he is gay as a lark,
And will talk in contemptuous tones of the Shark:
But, when the tide rises and sharks are around,
His voice has a timid and tremulous sound."

"That's different from what *I* used to say when I was a child," said the Gryphon.

"Well, *I* never heard it before," said the Mock Turtle; "but it sounds uncommon nonsense."

Alice said nothing: she had sat down with her face in her hands, wondering if anything would *ever* happen in a natural way again.

"I should like to have it explained," said the Mock Turtle.

"She ca'n't explain it," said the Gryphon hastily. "Go on with the next verse."

"But about his toes?" the Mock Turtle persisted. "How *could* he turn them out with his nose, you know?"

"It's the first position in dancing," Alice said; but she was dreadfully puzzled by the whole thing, and longed to change the subject.

"Go on with the next verse," the Gryphon repeated: "it begins *'I passed by his garden.'*"

Alice did not dare to disobey, though she felt sure it would all come wrong, and she went on in a trembling voice:—

"I passed by his garden, and marked, with one eye,
How the Owl and the Panther were sharing a pie:
The Panther took pie-crust, and gravy, and meat,
While the Owl had the dish as its share of the treat.
When the pie was all finished, the Owl, as a boon,
Was kindly permitted to pocket the spoon:
While the Panther received knife and fork with a growl,
And concluded the banquet by——"

"What *is* the use of repeating all that stuff?" the Mock Turtle interrupted, "if you don't explain it as you go on? It's by far the most confusing thing *I* ever heard!"

"Yes, I think you'd better leave off," said the Gryphon, and Alice was only too glad to do so.

"Shall we try another figure of the Lobster-Quadrille?" the Gryphon went on. "Or would you like the Mock Turtle to sing you another song?"

"Oh, a song, please, if the Mock Turtle would be so kind,"

Alice replied, so eagerly that the Gryphon said, in a rather
offended tone, "Hm! No accounting for tastes! Sing her *'Turtle
Soup,'* will you, old fellow?"

The Mock Turtle sighed deeply, and began, in a voice
choked with sobs, to sing this :—

> *"Beautiful Soup, so rich and green,*
> *Waiting in a hot tureen!*
> *Who for such dainties would not stoop?*
> *Soup of the evening, beautiful Soup!*
> *Soup of the evening, beautiful Soup!*
>   *Beau—ootiful Soo—oop!*
>   *Beau—ootiful Soo—oop!*
> *Soo—oop of the e—e—evening,*
>   *Beautiful, beautiful Soup!*
>
> *"Beautiful Soup! Who cares for fish,*
> *Game, or any other dish?*
> *Who would not give all else for two*
>   *Pennyworth only of beautiful Soup?*
> *Pennyworth only of beautiful Soup?*
>   *Beau—ootiful Soo—oop!*
>   *Beau—ootiful Soo—oop!*
> *Soo —oop of the e—e—evening,*
>   *Beautiful, beauti—FUL SOUP!"*

"Chorus again!" cried the Gryphon, and the Mock Turtle
had just begun to repeat it, when a cry of "The trial's beginning!" was heard in the distance.

"Come on!" cried the Gryphon, and, taking Alice by the
hand, it hurried off, without waiting for the end of the song.

"What trial is it?" Alice panted as she ran; but the Gryphon
only answered "Come on!" and ran the faster, while more and
more faintly came, carried on the breeze that followed them,
the melancholy words:—

> *"Soo—oop of the e—e—evening,*
>   *Beautiful, beautiful Soup!"*

XI

Who Stole the Tarts?

The King and Queen of Hearts were seated on their throne when they arrived, with a great crowd assembled about them—all sorts of little birds and beasts, as well as the whole pack of cards: the Knave was standing before them, in chains, with a soldier on each side to guard him; and near the King was the White Rabbit, with a trumpet in one hand, and a scroll of parchment in the other. In the very middle of the court was a table, with a large dish of tarts upon it: they looked so good, that it made Alice quite hungry to look at them—"I wish they'd get the trial done," she thought, "and hand round the refreshments!" But there seemed to be no chance of this; so she began looking at everything about her to pass away the time.

Alice had never been in a court of justice before, but she had read about them in books, and she was quite pleased to find that she knew the name of nearly everything there. "That's the judge," she said to herself, "because of his great wig."

The judge, by the way, was the King; and, as he wore his crown over the wig (look at the frontispiece if you want to see how he did it), he did not look at all comfortable, and it was certainly not becoming.

"And that's the jury-box," thought Alice; "and those twelve creatures," (she was obliged to say "creatures," you see, because some of them were animals, and some were birds,) "I suppose they are the jurors." She said this last word two or three times over to herself, being rather proud of it: for she thought, and rightly too, that very few little girls of her age knew the meaning of it at all. However, "jurymen" would have done just as well.

The twelve jurors were all writing very busily on slates. "What are they doing?" Alice whispered to the Gryphon. "They ca'n't have anything to put down yet, before the trial's begun."

"They're putting down their names," the Gryphon whispered in reply, "for fear they should forget them before the end of the trial."

"Stupid things!" Alice began in a loud indignant voice; but she stopped herself hastily, for the White Rabbit cried out, "Silence in the court!", and the King put on his spectacles and looked anxiously round, to make out who was talking.

Alice could see, as well as if she were looking over their shoulders, that all the jurors were writing down "Stupid things!" on their slates, and she could even make out that one of them didn't know how to spell "stupid," and that he had to ask his neighbour to tell him. "A nice muddle their slates'll be in, before the trial's over!" thought Alice.

One of the jurors had a pencil that squeaked. This, of course, Alice could *not* stand, and she went round the court and got behind him, and very soon found an opportunity of taking it away. She did it so quickly that the poor little juror (it was Bill, the Lizard) could not make out at all what had become of it; so, after hunting all about for it, he was obliged to write with one finger for the rest of the day; and this was of very little use, as it left no mark on the slate.

"Herald, read the accusation!" said the King.

On this the White Rabbit blew three blasts on the trumpet, and then unrolled the parchment-scroll, and read as follows:—

> "The Queen of Hearts, she made some tarts,
>   All on a summer day:
> The Knave of Hearts, he stole those tarts
>   And took them quite away!"

"Consider your verdict," the King said to the jury.

"Not yet, not yet!" the Rabbit hastily interrupted. "There's a great deal to come before that!"

"Call the first witness," said the King; and the White Rabbit blew three blasts on the trumpet, and called out "First witness!"

The first witness was the Hatter. He came in with a teacup in one hand and a piece of bread-and-butter in the other. "I beg pardon, your Majesty," he began, "for bringing these in; but I hadn't quite finished my tea when I was sent for."

"You ought to have finished," said the King. "When did you begin?"

The Hatter looked at the March Hare, who had followed him into the court, arm-in-arm with the Dormouse. "Fourteenth of March, I *think* it was," he said.

"Fifteenth," said the March Hare.

"Sixteenth," said the Dormouse.

"Write that down," the King said to the jury; and the jury eagerly wrote down all three dates on their slates, and then added them up, and reduced the answer to shillings and pence.

"Take off your hat," the King said to the Hatter.

"It isn't mine," said the Hatter.

"Stolen!" the King exclaimed, turning to the jury, who instantly made a memorandum of the fact.

"I keep them to sell," the Hatter added as an explanation. "I've none of my own. I'm a hatter."

Here the Queen put on her spectacles, and began staring hard at the Hatter, who turned pale and fidgeted.

"Give your evidence," said the King; "and don't be nervous, or I'll have you executed on the spot."

This did not seem to encourage the witness at all: he kept shifting from one foot to the other, looking uneasily at the Queen, and in his confusion he bit a large piece out of his teacup instead of the bread-and-butter.

Just at this moment Alice felt a very curious sensation, which puzzled her a good deal until she made out what it was: she was beginning to grow larger again, and she thought at first she would get up and leave the court; but on second thoughts she decided to remain where she was as long as there was room for her.

"I wish you wouldn't squeeze so," said the Dormouse, who was sitting next to her. "I can hardly breathe."

"I ca'n't help it," said Alice very meekly: "I'm growing."

"You've no right to grow *here*," said the Dormouse.

"Don't talk nonsense," said Alice more boldly: "you know you're growing too."

"Yes, but *I* grow at a reasonable pace," said the Dormouse: "not in that ridiculous fashion." And he got up very sulkily and crossed over to the other side of the court.

All this time the Queen had never left off staring at the Hatter, and, just as the Dormouse crossed the court, she said, to one of the officers of the court, "Bring me the list of the singers in the last concert!" on which the wretched Hatter trembled so, that he shook off both his shoes.

"Give your evidence," the King repeated angrily, "or I'll have you executed, whether you're nervous or not."

"I'm a poor man, your Majesty," the Hatter began, in a trembling voice, "and I hadn't begun my tea—not above a week or so—and what with the bread-and-butter getting so thin—and the twinkling of the tea——"

"The twinkling of *what*?" said the King.

"It *began* with the tea," the Hatter replied.

"Of course twinkling *begins* with a T!" said the King sharply. "Do you take me for a dunce? Go on!"

"I'm a poor man," the Hatter went on, "and most things twinkled after that—only the March Hare said——"

"I didn't!" the March Hare interrupted in a great hurry.

"You did!" said the Hatter.

"I deny it!" said the March Hare.

"He denies it," said the King: "leave out that part."

"Well, at any rate, the Dormouse said——" the Hatter went on, looking anxiously round to see if he would deny it too; but the Dormouse denied nothing, being fast asleep.

"After that," continued the Hatter, "I cut some more bread-and-butter——"

"But what did the Dormouse say?" one of the jury asked.

"That I ca'n't remember," said the Hatter.

"You *must* remember," remarked the King, "or I'll have you executed."

The miserable Hatter dropped his teacup and bread-and-butter, and went down on one knee. "I'm a poor man, your Majesty," he began.

"You're a *very* poor *speaker*," said the King.

Here one of the guinea-pigs cheered, and was immediately suppressed by the officers of the court. (As that is rather a hard word, I will just explain to you how it was done. They had a large canvas bag, which tied up at the mouth with strings: into this they slipped the guinea-pig, head first, and then sat upon it.)

"I'm glad I've seen that done," thought Alice. "I've so often read in the newspapers, at the end of trials, 'There was some attempt at applause, which was immediately suppressed by the officers of the court,' and I never understood what it meant till now."

"If that's all you know about it, you may stand down," continued the King.

"I ca'n't go no lower," said the Hatter: "I'm on the floor, as it is."

"Then you may *sit* down," the King replied.

Here the other guinea-pig cheered, and was suppressed.

"Come, that finishes the guinea-pigs!" thought Alice. "Now we shall get on better."

"I'd rather finish my tea," said the Hatter, with an anxious look at the Queen, who was reading the list of singers.

"You may go," said the King, and the Hatter hurriedly left the court, without even waiting to put his shoes on.

"——and just take his head off outside," the Queen added to one of the officers; but the Hatter was out of sight before the officer could get to the door.

"Call the next witness!" said the King.

The next witness was the Duchess's cook. She carried the pepper-box in her hand, and Alice guessed who it was, even before she got into the court, by the way the people near the door began sneezing all at once.

"Give your evidence," said the King.

"Sha'n't," said the cook.

The King looked anxiously at the White Rabbit, who said, in a low voice, "Your Majesty must cross-examine *this* witness."

"Well, if I must, I must," the King said with a melancholy air, and, after folding his arms and frowning at the cook till his eyes were nearly out of sight, he said, in a deep voice, "What are tarts made of?"

"Pepper, mostly," said the cook.

"Treacle," said a sleepy voice behind her.

"Collar that Dormouse!" the Queen shrieked out. "Behead that Dormouse! Turn that Dormouse out of court! Suppress him! Pinch him! Off with his whiskers!"

For some minutes the whole court was in confusion, getting the Dormouse turned out, and, by the time they had settled down again, the cook had disappeared.

"Never mind!" said the King, with an air of great relief. "Call the next witness." And, he added, in an undertone to the Queen, "Really, my dear, *you* must cross-examine the next witness. It quite makes my forehead ache!"

Alice watched the White Rabbit as he fumbled over the list, feeling very curious to see what the next witness would be like, "—for they haven't got much evidence *yet*," she said to herself. Imagine her surprise, when the White Rabbit read out, at the top of his shrill little voice, the name "Alice!"

XII

Alice's Evidence

H ere!" cried Alice, quite forgetting in the flurry of the moment how large she had grown in the last few minutes, and she jumped up in such a hurry that she tipped over the jury-box with the edge of her skirt, upsetting all the jurymen on to the heads of the crowd below, and there they lay sprawling about, reminding her very much of a globe of gold-fish she had accidentally upset the week before.

"Oh, I *beg* your pardon!" she exclaimed in a tone of great dismay, and began picking them up again as quickly as she could, for the accident of the gold-fish kept running in her head, and she had a vague sort of idea that they must be collected at once and put back into the jury-box, or they would die.

"The trial cannot proceed," said the King, in a very grave voice, "until all the jurymen are back in their proper places—*all*," he repeated with great emphasis, looking hard at Alice as he said so.

Alice looked at the jury-box, and saw that, in her haste, she had put the Lizard in head downwards, and the poor little thing was waving its tail about in a melancholy way, being quite unable to move. She soon got it out again, and put it right; "not that it signifies much," she said to herself; "I should think it would be *quite* as much use in the trial one way up as the other."

As soon as the jury had a little recovered from the shock of being upset, and their slates and pencils had been found and handed back to them, they set to work very diligently to write out a history of the accident, all except the Lizard, who seemed too much overcome to do anything but sit with its mouth open, gazing up into the roof of the court.

"What do you know about this business?" the King said to Alice.

"Nothing," said Alice.

"Nothing *whatever?*" persisted the King.

"Nothing whatever," said Alice.

"That's very important," the King said, turning to the jury. They were just beginning to write this down on their slates, when the White Rabbit interrupted: "*Un*important, your Majesty means, of course," he said, in a very respectful tone, but frowning and making faces at him as he spoke.

"*Un*important, of course, I meant," the King hastily said, and went on to himself in an undertone, "important—

unimportant—unimportant—important——" as if he were trying which word sounded best.

Some of the jury wrote it down "important," and some "unimportant." Alice could see this, as she was near enough to look over their slates; "but it doesn't matter a bit," she thought to herself.

At this moment the King, who had been for some time busily writing in his note-book, called out "Silence!", and read out from his book, "Rule Forty-two. *All persons more than a mile high to leave the court.*"

Everybody looked at Alice.

"*I'm* not a mile high," said Alice.

"You are," said the King.

"Nearly two miles high," added the Queen.

"Well, I sha'n't go, at any rate," said Alice: "besides, that's not a regular rule: you invented it just now."

"It's the oldest rule in the book," said the King.

"Then it ought to be Number One," said Alice.

The King turned pale, and shut his note-book hastily. "Consider your verdict," he said to the jury, in a low trembling voice.

"There's more evidence to come yet, please your Majesty," said the White Rabbit, jumping up in a great hurry: "this paper has just been picked up."

"What's in it?" said the Queen.

"I haven't opened it yet," said the White Rabbit; "but it seems to be a letter, written by the prisoner to—to somebody."

"It must have been that," said the King, "unless it was written to nobody, which isn't usual, you know."

"Who is it directed to?" said one of the jurymen.

"It isn't directed at all," said the White Rabbit: "in fact, there's nothing written on the *outside.*" He unfolded the paper as he spoke, and added "It isn't a letter, after all: it's a set of verses."

"Are they in the prisoner's handwriting?" asked another of the jurymen.

"No, they're not," said the White Rabbit, "and that's the queerest thing about it." (The jury all looked puzzled.)

"He must have imitated somebody else's hand," said the King. (The jury all brightened up again.)

"Please your Majesty," said the Knave, "I didn't write it, and they ca'n't prove that I did: there's no name signed at the end."

"If you didn't sign it," said the King, "that only makes the matter worse. You *must* have meant some mischief, or else you'd have signed your name like an honest man."

There was a general clapping of hands at this: it was the first really clever thing the King had said that day.

"That *proves* his guilt, of course," said the Queen: "so, off with——."

"It doesn't prove anything of the sort!" said Alice. "Why, you don't even know what they're about!"

"Read them," said the King.

The White Rabbit put on his spectacles. "Where shall I begin, please your Majesty?" he asked.

"Begin at the beginning," the King said, very gravely, "and go on till you come to the end: then stop."

There was dead silence in the court, whilst the White Rabbit read out these verses:—

> *"They told me you had been to her,*
>   *And mentioned me to him:*
> *She gave me a good character,*
>   *But said I could not swim.*
>
> *He sent them word I had not gone*
>   *(We know it to be true):*
> *If she should push the matter on,*
>   *What would become of you?*
>
> *I gave her one, they gave him two,*
>   *You gave us three or more;*
> *They all returned from him to you,*
>   *Though they were mine before.*
>
> *If I or she should chance to be*
>   *Involved in this affair,*
> *He trusts to you to set them free,*
>   *Exactly as we were.*

My notion was that you had been
   (Before she had this fit)
An obstacle that came between
   Him, and ourselves, and it.

Don't let him know she liked them best,
   For this must ever be
A secret, kept from all the rest,
   Between yourself and me."

"That's the most important piece of evidence we've heard yet," said the King, rubbing his hands; "so now let the jury——"

"If any one of them can explain it," said Alice, (she had grown so large in the last few minutes that she wasn't a bit afraid of interrupting him,) "I'll give him sixpence. *I* don't believe there's an atom of meaning in it."

The jury all wrote down, on their slates, "*She* doesn't believe there's an atom of meaning in it," but none of them attempted to explain the paper.

"If there's no meaning in it," said the King, "that saves a world of trouble, you know, as we needn't try to find any. And yet I don't know," he went on, spreading out the verses on his knee, and looking at them with one eye; "I seem to see some meaning in them, after all. '—*said I could not swim*—' you ca'n't swim, can you?" he added, turning to the Knave.

The Knave shook his head sadly. "Do I look like it?" he said. (Which he certainly did *not*, being made entirely of cardboard.)

"All right, so far," said the King; and he went on muttering over the verses to himself: " *'We know it to be true'*—that's the jury, of course—*'If she should push the matter on'*—that must be the Queen—*'What would become of you?'*—What, indeed!—*'I gave her one, they gave him two'*—why, that must be what he did with the tarts, you know——"

"But it goes on *'they all returned from him to you',*" said Alice.

"Why, there they are!" said the King triumphantly, pointing to the tarts on the table. "Nothing can be clearer than *that.* Then again—*'before she had this fit'*—you never had *fits,* my dear, I think?" he said to the Queen.

"Never!" said the Queen, furiously, throwing an inkstand at the Lizard as she spoke. (The unfortunate little Bill had left off writing on his slate with one finger, as he found it made no mark; but he now hastily began again, using the ink, that was trickling down his face, as long as it lasted.)

"Then the words don't *fit* you," said the King, looking round the court with a smile. There was a dead silence.

"It's a pun!" the King added in an angry tone, and everybody laughed. "Let the jury consider their verdict," the King said, for about the twentieth time that day.

"No, no!" said the Queen. "Sentence first—verdict afterwards."

"Stuff and nonsense!" said Alice loudly. "The idea of having the sentence first!"

"Hold your tongue!" said the Queen turning purple.

"I wo'n't!" said Alice.

"Off with her head!" the Queen shouted at the top of her voice. Nobody moved.

"Who cares for *you?*" said Alice (she had grown to her full size by this time). "You're nothing but a pack of cards!"

At this the whole pack rose up into the air, and came flying down upon her; she gave a little

scream, half of fright and half of anger, and tried to beat
them off, and found herself lying on the bank, with her head
in the lap of her sister, who was gently brushing away some
dead leaves that had fluttered down from the trees upon her
face.

"Wake up, Alice dear!" said her sister. "Why, what a long sleep
you've had!"

"Oh, I've had such a curious dream!" said Alice. And she told
her sister, as well as she could remember them, all these strange

Adventures of hers that you have just been reading about; and, when she had finished, her sister kissed her, and said "It *was* a curious dream, dear, certainly; but now run in to your tea: it's getting late." So Alice got up and ran off, thinking while she ran, as well she might, what a wonderful dream it had been.

But her sister sat still just as she left her, leaning her head on her hand, watching the setting sun, and thinking of little Alice and all her wonderful Adventures, till she too began dreaming after a fashion, and this was her dream:—

First, she dreamed about little Alice herself: once again the tiny hands were clasped upon her knee, and the bright eager eyes were looking up into hers—she could hear the very tones of her voice, and see that queer little toss of her head to keep back the wandering hair that *would* always get into her eyes—and still as she listened, or seemed to listen, the whole place around her became alive with the strange creatures of her little sister's dream.

The long grass rustled at her feet as the White Rabbit hurried by—the frightened Mouse splashed his way through the neighbouring pool—she could hear the rattle of the teacups as the March Hare and his friends shared their never-ending meal, and the shrill voice of the Queen ordering off her unfortunate guests to execution—once more the pig-baby was sneezing on the Duchess' knee, while plates and dishes crashed around it—once more the shriek of the Gryphon, the squeaking of the Lizard's slate-pencil, and the choking of the suppressed guinea-pigs, filled the air, mixed up with the distant sob of the miserable Mock Turtle.

So she sat on, with closed eyes, and half believed herself in Wonderland, though she knew she had but to open them again, and all would change to dull reality—the grass would be only rustling in the wind, and the pool rippling to the waving of the reeds—the rattling teacups would change to tinkling sheep-bells, and the Queen's shrill cries to the voice of the shepherd-boy—and the sneeze of the baby, the shriek of the

Gryphon, and all the other queer noises, would change (she knew) to the confused clamour of the busy farm-yard—while the lowing of the cattle in the distance would take the place of the Mock Turtle's heavy sobs.

Lastly, she pictured to herself how this same little sister of hers would, in the after-time, be herself a grown woman; and how she would keep, through all her riper years, the simple and loving heart of her childhood; and how she would gather about her other little children, and make *their* eyes bright and eager with many a strange tale, perhaps even with the dream of Wonderland of long ago; and how she would feel with all their simple sorrows, and find a pleasure in all their simple joys, remembering her own child-life, and the happy summer days.

Through the Looking-Glass
and What Alice Found There

PREFACE TO 1896 EDITION

As the chess-problem, given on the previous page, has puzzled some of my readers, it may be well to explain that it is correctly worked out, so far as the *moves* are concerned. The *alternation* of Red and White is perhaps not so strictly observed as it might be, and the "castling" of the three Queens is merely a way of saying that they entered the palace; but the "check" of the White King at move 6, the capture of the Red Knight at move 7, and the final "checkmate" of the Red King, will be found, by any one who will take the trouble to set the pieces and play the moves as directed, to be strictly in accordance with the laws of the game.

The new words, in the poem "Jabberwocky" (see p. 164), have given rise to some differences of opinion as to their pronunciation; so it may be well to give instructions on *that* point also. Pronounce "slithy" as if it were the two words "sly, the": make the "g" *hard* in "gyre" and "gimble": and pronounce "rath" to rhyme with "bath."

For this sixty-first thousand, fresh electrotypes have been taken from the wood-blocks (which, never having been used for printing from, are in as good condition as when first cut in 1871), and the whole book has been set up afresh with new type. If the artistic qualities of this reissue fall short, in any particular, of those possessed by the original issue, it will not be for want of painstaking on the part of author, publisher, or printer.

I take this opportunity of announcing that the Nursery "Alice," hitherto priced at four shillings, net, is now to be had on the same terms as the ordinary shilling picture-books— although I feel sure that it is, in every quality (except the *text* itself, in which I am not qualified to pronounce), greatly superior to them. Four shillings was a perfectly reasonable price to charge, considering the very heavy initial outlay I had incurred: still, as the Public have practically said, "We will *not* give more than a shilling for a picture-book, however artistically got-up," I am content to reckon my outlay on the book as so much dead loss, and, rather than let the little ones, for whom it was written, go without it, I am selling it at a price which is, to me, much the same thing as *giving* it away.

Christmas, 1896

Contents

RED

WHITE

INTRODUCTION.

Child of the pure unclouded brow
And dreaming eyes of wonder!
Though time be fleet, and I and thou
Are half a life asunder,
Thy loving smile will surely hail
The love-gift of a fairy-tale.

I have not seen thy sunny face,
Nor heard thy silver laughter;
No thought of me shall find a place
In thy young life's hereafter—
Enough that now thou wilt not fail
To listen to my fairy-tale.

A tale begun in other days,
When summer suns were glowing—
A simple chime, that served to time
The rhythm of our rowing—
Whose echoes live in memory yet,
Though envious years would say "forget."

Come, hearken then, ere voice of dread,
With bitter tidings laden,
Shall summon to unwelcome bed
A melancholy maiden!
We are but older children, dear,
Who fret to find our bedtime near.

Without, the frost, the blinding snow,
The storm-wind's moody madness—
Within, the firelight's ruddy glow
And childhood's nest of gladness,
The magic words shall hold thee fast:
Thou shalt not heed the raving blast.

And though the shadow of a sigh
May tremble through the story,
For "happy summer days" gone by,
And vanish'd summer glory—
It shall not touch with breath of bale,
The pleasance of our fairy-tale.

CHAPTER I.

LOOKING-GLASS HOUSE.

One thing was certain, that the *white* kitten had had nothing to do with it:—it was the black kitten's fault entirely. For the white kitten had been having its face washed by the old cat for the last quarter of an hour (and bearing it pretty well, considering); so you see that it *couldn't* have had any hand in the mischief.

The way Dinah washed her children's faces was this: first she held the poor thing down by its ear with one paw, and then with the other paw she rubbed its face all over, the wrong way, beginning at the nose: and just now, as I said, she was hard at work on the white kitten, which was lying quite still and trying to purr—no doubt feeling that it was all meant for its good.

But the black kitten had been finished with earlier in the afternoon, and so, while Alice was sitting curled up in a corner of the great arm-chair, half talking to herself and half asleep, the kitten had been having a grand game of romps with the ball of worsted Alice had been trying to wind up, and had been rolling it up and down till it had all come undone again, and there it was, spread over the hearth-rug, all knots and tangles, with the kitten running after its own tail in the middle.

"Oh, you wicked, wicked little thing!" cried Alice, catching up the kitten and giving it a little kiss to make it understand that it was in disgrace. "Really, Dinah ought to have taught you better manners! You *ought,* Dinah, you know you ought!" she added, looking reproachfully at the old cat, and speaking in as cross a voice as she could manage—and then she scrambled back into the arm-chair, taking the kitten and the worsted with her, and began winding up the ball again. But she didn't get on very fast, as she was talking all the time, sometimes to the kitten, and sometimes to herself. Kitty sat very demurely on her knee, pretending to watch the progress of the winding, and now and then putting out one paw and gently touching the ball, as if it would be glad to help if it might.

"Do you know what to-morrow is, Kitty?" Alice began. "You'd have guessed if you'd been up in the window with me—only Dinah was making you tidy, so you couldn't. I was watching the boys getting in sticks for the bonfire—and it wants plenty of sticks, Kitty! Only it got so cold, and it snowed so, they had to leave off. Never mind, Kitty, we'll go and see the bonfire to-morrow." Here Alice wound two or three turns of the worsted round the kitten's neck, just to see how it would look: this led to a scramble, in which the ball rolled down upon the floor, and yards and yards of it got unwound again.

"Do you know, I was so angry, Kitty," Alice went on, as soon as they were comfortably settled again, "when I saw all the mischief you had been doing, I was very nearly opening the window and putting you out into the snow! And you'd have deserved it, you little mischievous darling! What have you got to say for yourself? Now don't interrupt me!" she went on, holding up one finger. "I'm going to tell you all your faults. Number one: you squeaked twice while Dinah was washing your face this morning. Now you can't deny it, Kitty: I heard you! What's that you say?" (pretending that the kitten was speaking.) "Her paw went into your eye? Well, that's *your* fault, for keeping your eyes open—if you'd shut them tight up, it wouldn't have happened. Now don't make any more excuses, but listen! Number two: you pulled Snowdrop away by the tail just as I had put down the saucer of milk before her! What, you were thirsty, were you? How do you know she wasn't thirsty too? Now for number three: you unwound every bit of the worsted while I wasn't looking!

"That's three faults, Kitty, and you've not been punished for any of them yet. You know I'm saving up all your punishments for Wednesday week.* Suppose they had saved up all *my* punishments!" she went on, talking more to herself than the kitten.

---

*Exactly one week from Wednesday.

"What *would* they do at the end of a year? I should be sent to prison, I suppose, when the day came. Or—let me see—suppose each punishment was to be going without a dinner; then, when the miserable day came, I should have to go without fifty dinners at once! Well, I shouldn't mind *that* much! I'd far rather go without them than eat them!

"Do you hear the snow against the window-panes, Kitty? How nice and soft it sounds! Just as if some one was kissing the window all over outside. I wonder if the snow *loves* the trees and fields, that it kisses them so gently? And then it covers them up snug, you know, with a white quilt; and perhaps it says, 'Go to sleep, darlings, till the summer comes again.' And when they wake up in the summer, Kitty, they dress themselves all in green, and dance about—whenever the wind blows—oh, that's very pretty!" cried Alice, dropping the ball of worsted to clap her hands. "And I do so *wish* it was true! I'm sure the woods look sleepy in the autumn, when the leaves are getting brown.

"Kitty, can you play chess? Now, don't smile, my dear, I'm asking it seriously. Because, when we were playing just now, you watched just as if you understood it: and when I said 'Check!' you purred! Well, it *was* a nice check, Kitty, and really, I might have won, if it hadn't been for that nasty Knight, that came wriggling down among my pieces. Kitty, dear, let's pretend——" And here I wish I could tell you half the things Alice used to say, beginning with her favorite phrase "Let's pretend." She had had quite a long argument with her sister only the day before—all because Alice had begun with "Let's pretend we're kings and queens;" and her sister, who liked being very exact, had argued that they couldn't, because there were only two of them, and Alice had been reduced at last to say, "Well, *you* can be one of them then, and *I'll* be all the rest." And once she had really frightened her old nurse by shouting suddenly in her ear, "Nurse! Do let's pretend that I'm a hungry hyæna, and you're a bone!"

But this is taking us away from Alice's speech to the kitten. "Let's pretend that you're the Red Queen, Kitty! Do you know, I think if you sat up and folded your arms, you'd look exactly like her. Now do try, there's a dear!" And Alice got the Red Queen off the table, and set it up before the kitten as a model for it to imitate: however, the thing didn't succeed, principally, Alice said, because the kitten wouldn't fold its arms properly. So, to punish it, she held it up to the Looking-glass that it might see how sulky it was—"and if you're not good directly," she added, "I'll put you through into Looking-glass House. How would you like *that*?

"Now, if you'll only attend, Kitty, and not talk so much, I'll tell you all my ideas about Looking-glass House. First, there's the room you can see through the glass—that's just the same as our drawing-room, only the things go the other way. I can see all of it when I get upon a chair—all but the bit just behind the fireplace. Oh! I do so wish I could see *that* bit! I want so much to know whether they've a fire in the winter: you never *can* tell, you know, unless our fire smokes, and then smoke comes up in that room too—but that may be only pretence, just to make it look as if they had a fire. Well then, the books are something like our books, only the words go the wrong way; I know that, because I've held up one of our books to the glass, and then they hold up one in the other room.

"How would you like to live in Looking-glass House, Kitty? I wonder if they'd give you milk in there? Perhaps Looking-glass milk isn't good to drink—But oh, Kitty! now we come to the passage. You can just see a little *peep* of the passage in Looking-glass House, if you leave the door of our drawing-room wide open: and it's very like our passage as far as you can see, only you know it may be quite different on beyond. Oh, Kitty! how nice it would be if we could only get through into Looking-glass House! I'm sure it's got, oh! such beautiful things in it! Let's pretend there's a way of getting through into it, some-how, Kitty. Let's pretend the glass has got all soft like gauze, so that we can get through. Why, it's turning into a sort of mist now, I declare! It'll be easy enough to get through——" She was up on the chimney-piece while she said this, though she hardly knew how she had got there. And certainly the glass *was* beginning to melt away, just like a bright silvery mist.

In another moment Alice was through the glass, and had jumped lightly down into the Looking-glass room. The very first thing she did was to look whether there was a fire in the fireplace, and she was quite pleased to find that there was a real one, blazing away as brightly as the one she had left behind. "So I shall be as warm here as I was in the old room," thought Alice: "warmer, in fact, because there'll be no one here to scold me away from the fire. Oh, what fun it'll be, when they see me through the glass in here, and can't get at me!"

Then she began looking about, and noticed that what could be seen from the old room was quite common and uninteresting, but that all the rest was as different as possible. For instance, the pictures on the wall next the fire seemed to be all alive, and the very clock on the chimney-piece (you know you can only see the back of it in the Looking-glass) had got the face of a little old man and grinned at her.

"They don't keep this room so tidy as the other," Alice thought to herself, as she noticed several of the chessmen down in the hearth among the cinders: but in another moment, with a little "Oh!" of surprise, she was down on her hands and knees watching them. The chessmen were walking about two and two!

"Here are the Red King and the Red Queen," Alice said (in a whisper, for fear of frightening them), "and there are the

White King and the White Queen sitting on the edge of the shovel—and here are two Castles walking arm in arm—I don't think they can hear me," she went on as she put her head closer down, "and I'm nearly sure they can't see me. I feel somehow as if I were invisible——"

Here something began squeaking on the table behind Alice, and made her turn her head just in time to see one of the White Pawns roll over and begin kicking: she watched it with great curiosity to see what would happen next.

"It is the voice of my child!" the White Queen cried out, as she rushed past the King, so violently that she knocked him over among the cinders. "My precious Lily! My imperial kitten!" and she began scrambling wildly up the side of the fender.

"Imperial fiddlestick!" said the King, rubbing his nose, which had been hurt by the fall. He had a right to be a *little* annoyed with the Queen, for he was covered with ashes from head to foot.

Alice was very anxious to be of use, and, as the poor little Lily was nearly screaming herself into a fit, she hastily picked up the Queen and set her on the table by the side of her noisy little daughter.

The Queen gasped, and sat down: the rapid journey through the air had quite taken away her breath, and for a minute or two she could do nothing but hug the little Lily in silence. As soon as she had recovered her breath a little, she called out to the White King, who was sitting sulkily among the ashes, "Mind the volcano!"

"What volcano?" said the King, looking up anxiously into the fire, as if he thought that was the most likely place to find one.

"Blew—me—up," panted the Queen, who was still a little out of breath. "Mind you come up—the regular way—don't get blown up!"

Alice watched the White King as he slowly struggled up from bar to bar, till at last she said, "Why, you'll be hours and hours getting to the table, at that rate. I'd far better help you, hadn't I?" But the King took no notice of the question: it was quite clear that he could neither hear her nor see her.

So Alice picked him up very gently, and lifted him across

more slowly than she had lifted the Queen, that she mightn't take his breath away: but, before she put him on the table, she thought she might as well dust him a little, he was so covered with ashes.

She said afterwards that she had never seen in all her life such a face as the King made, when he found himself held in the air by an invisible hand, and being dusted: he was far too much astonished to cry out, but his eyes and his mouth went on getting larger and larger, and rounder and rounder, till her hand shook so with laughing that she nearly let him drop upon the floor.

"Oh! *please* don't make such faces, my dear!" she cried out, quite forgetting that the King couldn't hear her. "You make me laugh so that I can hardly hold you! And don't keep your mouth so wide open! All the ashes will get into it—there, now I think you're tidy enough!" she added, as she smoothed his hair, and set him upon the table near the Queen.

The King immediately fell flat on his back, and lay perfectly still: and Alice was a little alarmed at what she had done, and went round the room to see if she could find any water to throw over him. However, she could find nothing but a bottle of ink, and when she got back with it she found he had recovered, and he and the Queen were talking together in a frightened whisper—so low, that Alice could hardly hear what they said.

The King was saying, "I assure you, my dear, I turned cold to the very ends of my whiskers!"

To which the Queen replied: "You haven't got any whiskers."

"The horror of that moment," the King went on, "I shall never, *never* forget!"

"You will though," the Queen said, "if you don't make a memorandum of it."

Alice looked on with great interest as the King took an enormous memorandum-book out of his pocket, and began writing. A sudden thought struck her, and she took hold of the end of the pencil, which came some way over his shoulder, and began writing for him.

The poor King looked puzzled and unhappy, and struggled with the pencil for some time without saying anything; but

Alice was too strong for him, and at last he panted out, "My dear! I really *must* get a thinner pencil. I can't manage this one a bit; it writes all manner of things that I don't intend——"

"What manner of things?" said the Queen, looking over the book (in which Alice had put *'The White Knight is sliding down the poker. He balances very badly.'*) "That's not a memorandum of *your* feelings!"

There was a book lying near Alice on the table, and while she sat watching the White King (for she was still a little anxious about him, and had the ink all ready to throw over him, in case he fainted again), she turned over the leaves to find some part that she could read, "—for it's all in some language I don't know," she said to herself.

It was like this:

JABBERWOCKY.

'Twas brillig, and the slithy toves
Did gyre and gimble in the wabe;
All mimsy were the borogoves,
And the mome raths outgrabe.

She puzzled over this for some time, but at last a bright thought struck her. "Why, it's a Looking-glass book, of course! And if I hold it up to a glass, the words will all go the right way again."

This was the poem that Alice read:

JABBERWOCKY.[1]

'Twas brillig, and the slithy toves
Did gyre and gimble in the wabe;
All mimsy were the borogoves,
And the mome raths outgrabe.

"Beware the Jabberwock, my son!
The jaws that bite, the claws that catch!
Beware the Jubjub bird, and shun
The frumious Bandersnatch!"

He took his vorpal sword in hand:
Long time the manxome foe he sought—
So rested he by the Tumtum tree,
And stood awhile in thought.

And as in uffish thought he stood,
The Jabberwock, with eyes of flame,
Came whiffling through the tulgey wood,
And burbled as it came!

One, two! One, two! And through and through
The vorpal blade went snicker-snack!
He left it dead, and with its head
He went galumphing back.

"And hast thou slain the Jabberwock?
Come to my arms, my beamish boy!
O frabjous day! Callooh! Callay!"
He chortled in his joy.

'Twas brillig, and the slithy toves
    Did gyre and gimble in the wabe;
All mimsy were the borogoves,
    And the mome raths outgrabe.

"It seems very pretty," she said when she had finished it, "but it's *rather* hard to understand!" (You see she didn't like to confess, even to herself, that she couldn't make it out at all.) "Somehow it seems to fill my head with ideas—only I don't exactly know what they are! However, *somebody* killed *something:* that's clear, at any rate——"

"But oh!" thought Alice, suddenly jumping up, "if I don't make haste I shall have to go back through the Looking-glass, before I've seen what the rest of the house is like! Let's have a look at the garden first!" She was out of the room in a moment, and ran down stairs—or, at least, it wasn't exactly running, but a new invention for getting down stairs quickly and easily, as Alice said to herself. She just kept the tips of her fingers on the hand-rail, and floated gently down without even touching the stairs with her feet; then she floated on through the hall, and would have gone straight out at the door in the same way, if she hadn't caught hold of the door-post. She was getting a little giddy too with so much floating in the air, and was rather glad to find herself walking again in the natural way.

CHAPTER II.

THE GARDEN OF LIVE FLOWERS.

I should see the garden far better," said Alice to herself, "if I
could get to the top of that hill: and here's a path that leads
straight to it—at least, no it doesn't do that—" (after going
a few yards along the path, and turning several sharp corners),
"but I suppose it will at last. But how curiously it twists! It's
more like a corkscrew than a path! Well, *this* turn goes to the
hill, I suppose—no, it doesn't! This goes straight back to the
house! Well then, I'll try it the other way."

And so she did: wandering up and down, and trying turn
after turn, but always coming back to the house, do what she
would. Indeed, once, when she turned a corner rather more
quickly than usual, she ran against it before she could stop herself.

"It's no use talking about it," Alice said, looking up at the
house and pretending it was arguing with her. "I'm *not* going
in again yet. I know I should have to get through the Looking-
glass again—back into the old room—and there'd be an end
of all my adventures!"

So, resolutely turning her back upon the house, she set out
once more down the path, determined to keep straight on till
she got to the hill. For a few minutes all went on well, and she
was just saying, "I really *shall* do it this time——" when the path
gave a sudden twist and shook itself (as she described it afterwards), and the next moment she found herself actually walking in at the door.

"Oh, it's too bad!" she cried. "I never saw such a house for
getting in the way! Never!"

However, there was the hill full in sight, so there was nothing
to be done but start again. This time she came upon a large

flowerbed,[2] with a border of daisies, and a willow-tree growing in the middle.

"O Tiger-lily," said Alice, addressing herself to one that was waving gracefully about in the wind, "I *wish* you could talk!"

"We *can* talk," said the Tiger-lily: "When there's anybody worth talking to."

Alice was so astonished that she couldn't speak for a minute: it quite seemed to take her breath away. At length, as the Tiger-lily only went on waving about, she spoke again, in a timid voice—almost in a whisper. "And can *all* the flowers talk?"

"As well as *you* can," said the Tiger-lily. "And a great deal louder."

"It isn't manners for us to begin, you know," said the Rose, "and I really was wondering when you'd speak! Said I to myself, 'Her face has got *some* sense in it, though it's not a clever one!' Still, you're the right color, and that goes a long way."

"I don't care about the color," the Tiger-lily remarked. "If only her petals curled up a little more, she'd be all right."

Alice didn't like being criticised, so she began asking questions. "Aren't you sometimes frightened at being planted out here, with nobody to take care of you?"

"There's the tree in the middle," said the Rose: "what else is it good for?"

"But what could it do, if any danger came?" Alice asked.

"It could bark," said the Rose.

"It says 'Bough-wough!'"[3] cried a Daisy, "that's why its branches are called boughs!"

"Didn't you know *that*?" cried another Daisy, and here they all began shouting together, till the air seemed quite full of little shrill voices. "Silence, every one of you!" cried the Tiger-lily, waving itself passionately from side to side, and trembling with excitement. "They know I can't get at them!" it panted, bending its quivering head towards Alice, "or they wouldn't dare to do it!"

"Never mind!" Alice said in a soothing tone, and stooping down to the daisies, who were just beginning again, she whispered, "If you don't hold your tongues, I'll pick you!"

There was silence in a moment, and several of the pink daisies turned white.

"That's right!" said the Tiger-lily. "The daisies are worst of all. When one speaks, they all begin together, and it's enough to make one wither to hear the way they go on!"

"How is it you can all talk so nicely?" Alice said, hoping to get it into a better temper by a compliment. "I've been in many gardens before, but none of the flowers could talk."

"Put your hand down, and feel the ground," said the Tiger-lily. "Then you'll know why."

Alice did so. "Its very hard," she said, "but I don't see what that has to do with it."

"In most gardens," the Tiger-lily said, "they make the beds too soft—so that the flowers are always asleep."

This sounded a very good reason, and Alice was quite pleased to know it. "I never thought of that before!" she said.

"It's *my* opinion that you never think *at all*," the Rose said in a rather severe tone.

"I never saw anybody that looked stupider," a Violet said, so suddenly, that Alice quite jumped; for it hadn't spoken before.

"Hold *your* tongue!" cried the Tiger-lily. "As if *you* ever saw anybody! You keep your head under the leaves, and snore away there, till you know no more what's going on in the world, than if you were a bud!"

"Are there any more people in the garden besides me?" Alice said, not choosing to notice the Rose's last remark.

"There's one other flower in the garden that can move about like you," said the Rose. "I wonder how you do it——" ("You're always wondering," said the Tiger-lily), "but she's more bushy than you are."

"Is she like me?" Alice asked eagerly, for the thought crossed her mind, "There's another little girl in the garden somewhere!"

"Well, she has the same awkward shape as you," the Rose said, "but she's redder—and her petals are shorter, I think."

"Her petals are done up close, almost like a dahlia," the Tiger-lily interrupted: "not tumbled about anyhow, like yours."

"But that's not *your* fault," the Rose added kindly: "you're beginning to fade, you know—and then one can't help one's petals getting a little untidy."

Alice didn't like this idea at all: so, to change the subject, she asked, "Does she ever come out here?"

"I daresay you'll see her soon," said the Rose. "She's one of the thorny kind."

"Where does she wear the thorns?" Alice asked with some curiosity.

"Why, all round her head, of course," the Rose replied. "I was wondering *you* hadn't got some too. I thought it was the regular rule."

"She's coming!" cried the Larkspur. "I hear her footstep, thump, thump, along the gravel-walk!"

Alice looked round eagerly, and found that it was the Red

Queen. "She's grown a good deal!" was her first remark. She had indeed: when Alice first found her in the ashes, she had been only three inches high—and here she was, half a head taller than Alice herself.

"It's the fresh air that does it," said the Rose: "wonderfully fine air it is out here."

"I think I'll go and meet her," said Alice, for, though the flowers were interesting enough, she felt that it would be far grander to have a talk with a real Queen.

"You can't possibly do that," said the Rose: "*I* should advise you to walk the other way."

This sounded nonsense to Alice, so she said nothing, but set off at once towards the Red Queen. To her surprise, she lost sight of her in a moment, and found herself walking in at the front-door again.

A little provoked, she drew back and after looking every-where for the Queen (whom she spied out at last a long way off), she thought she would try the plan, this time, of walking in the opposite direction.

It succeeded beautifully. She had not been walking a minute before she found herself face to face with the Red Queen, and full in sight of the hill she had been so long aiming at.

"Where do you come from?" said the Red Queen. "And where are you going? Look up, speak nicely, and don't twiddle your fingers all the time."

Alice attended to all these directions, and explained, as well as she could, that she had lost her way.

"I don't know what you mean by *your* way," said the Queen: "all the ways about here belong to *me*—but why did you come out here at all?" she added in a kinder tone. "Curtsey while you're thinking what to say. It saves time."

Alice wondered a little at this, but she was too much in awe of the Queen to disbelieve it. "I'll try it when I go home," she thought to herself, "the next time I'm a little late for dinner."

"It's time for you to answer now," the Queen said, looking at her watch: "open your mouth a *little* wider when you speak, and always say, 'your Majesty.'"

"I only wanted to see what the garden was like, your Majesty——"

"That's right," said the Queen, patting her on the head, which Alice didn't like at all; "though, when you say 'garden,'— *I've* seen gardens, compared with which this would be a wilderness."

Alice didn't dare to argue the point, but went on: "—and I thought I'd try and find my way to the top of that hill——"

"When you say 'hill,'" the Queen interrupted, "*I* could show you hills, in comparison with which you'd call that a valley."

"No, I shouldn't," said Alice, surprised into contradicting

her at last: "a hill *can't* be a valley, you know. That would be nonsense——"

The Red Queen shook her head. "You may call it 'nonsense' if you like," she said, "but *I've* heard nonsense, compared with which that would be as sensible as a dictionary!"

Alice curtseyed again, as she was afraid from the Queen's tone that she was a *little* offended and they walked on in silence till they got to the top of the hill.

For some minutes Alice stood without speaking, looking out in all directions over the country—and a most curious country it was. There were a number of tiny little brooks running straight across it from side to side, and the ground between was divided up into squares by a number of little green hedges, that reached from brook to brook.

"I declare it's marked out just like a large chess-board!" Alice said at last. "There ought to be some men moving about somewhere—and so there are!" she added in a tone of delight, and her heart began to beat quick with excitement as she went on. "It's a great huge game of chess that's being played—all over the world—if this *is* the world at all, you know. Oh, what fun it is! How I *wish* I was one of them! I wouldn't mind being a Pawn, if only I might join—though of course I should *like* to be a Queen, best."

She glanced rather shyly at the real Queen as she said this, but her companion only smiled pleasantly, and said, "That's easily managed. You can be the White Queen's Pawn, if you like, as Lily's too young to play; and you're in the Second Square to begin with: when you get to the Eighth Square you'll be a Queen——" Just at this moment, somehow or other, they began to run.

Alice never could quite make out, in thinking it over afterwards, how it was that they began: all she remembers is, that they were running hand in hand, and the Queen went so fast that it was all she could do to keep up with her: and still the Queen kept crying "Faster! Faster!" but Alice felt she *could not* go faster, though she had no breath left to say so.

The most curious part of the thing was, that the trees and other things round them never changed their places at all: however fast they went, they never seemed to pass anything. "I wonder if all the things move along with us?" thought poor puzzled Alice.

And the Queen seemed to guess her thoughts, for she cried, "Faster! Don't try to talk!"

Not that Alice had any idea of doing *that*. She felt as if she would never be able to talk again, she was getting so much out of breath: and still the Queen cried "Faster! Faster!" and dragged her along. "Are we nearly there?" Alice managed to pant out at last.

"Nearly there?" the Queen repeated. "Why, we passed it ten minutes ago! Faster!" And they ran on for a time in silence, with the wind whistling in Alice's ears, and almost blowing her hair off her head, she fancied.

"Now! Now!" cried the Queen. "Faster! Faster!" And they went so fast that at last they seemed to skim through the air, hardly touching the ground with their feet, till suddenly, just as Alice was getting quite exhausted, they stopped, and she found herself sitting on the ground, breathless and giddy.

The Queen propped her up against a tree and said kindly, "You may rest a little now."

Alice looked round her in great surprise. "Why, I do believe we've been under this tree the whole time! Everything's just as it was!"

"Of course it is," said the Queen: "what would you have it?"

"Well, in *our* country," said Alice, still panting a little, "you'd generally get to somewhere else—if you ran very fast for a long time, as we've been doing."

"A slow sort of country!" said the Queen. "Now, *here* you see, it takes all the running *you* can do, to keep in the same place. If you want to get somewhere else, you must run at least twice as fast as that!"

"I'd rather not try, please!" said Alice. "I'm quite content to stay here—only I *am* so hot and thirsty!"

"I know what *you'd* like!" the Queen said good-naturedly, taking a little box out of her pocket. "Have a biscuit?"

Alice thought it would not be civil to say "No," though it wasn't at all what she wanted. So she took it, and ate it as well as she could: and it was *very* dry: and she thought she had never been so nearly choked in all her life.

"While you're refreshing yourself," said the Queen, "I'll just take the measurements." And she took a ribbon out of her pocket, marked in inches, and began measuring the ground, and sticking little pegs in here and there.

"At the end of two yards," she said putting in a peg to mark the distance, "I shall give you your directions—have another biscuit?"

"No, thank you," said Alice: "one's *quite* enough!"

"Thirst quenched, I hope?" said the Queen.

Alice did not know what to say to this, but luckily the Queen did not wait for an answer, but went on. "At the end of *three* yards I shall repeat them—for fear of your forgetting them. At the end of *four*, I shall say good-bye. And at the end of *five*, I shall go!"

She had got all the pegs put in by this time, and Alice looked on with great interest as she returned to the tree, and then began slowly walking down the row.

At the two-yard peg she faced round, and said, "A pawn goes two squares in its first move, you know. So you'll go *very* quickly through the Third Square—by railway, I should think—and you'll find yourself in the Fourth Square in no time. Well, *that* square belongs to Tweedledum and Tweedledee—the Fifth is mostly water—the Sixth belongs to Humpty Dumpty. But you make no remark?"

"I—I didn't know I had to make one—just then," Alice faltered out.

"You *should* have said," the Queen went on in a tone of grave reproof, " 'It's extremely kind of you to tell me all this'—however, we'll suppose it said—the Seventh Square is all forest—however, one of the Knights will show you the way—and in the Eighth Square we shall be Queens together, and it's all feasting and fun!" Alice got up and curtseyed, and sat down again.

At the next peg the Queen turned again, and this time she said, "Speak in French when you can't think of the English for a thing—turn out your toes when you walk—and remember who you are!" She did not wait for Alice to curtsey this time, but walked on quickly to the next peg, where she turned for a moment to say "good-bye," and then hurried on to the last.

How it happened, Alice never knew, but exactly as she came to the last peg, she was gone. Whether she vanished into the air, or whether she ran quickly into the wood ("and she *can* run very fast!" thought Alice), there was no way of guessing, but she was gone, and Alice began to remember that she was a Pawn, and that it would soon be time for her to move.

CHAPTER III.

LOOKING-GLASS INSECTS.

Of course the first thing to do was to make a grand survey of the country she was going to travel through. "It's something very like learning geography," thought Alice, as she stood on tiptoe in hopes of being able to see a little further. "Principal rivers—there *are* none. Principal mountains—I'm on the only one, but I don't think it's got any name. Principal towns—why, what *are* those creatures, making honey down there? They can't be bees—nobody ever saw bees a mile off, you know——" and for some time she stood silent, watching one of them that was bustling about among the flowers, poking its proboscis into them, "just as if it was a regular bee," thought Alice.

However, this was anything but a regular bee: in fact, it was an elephant—as Alice soon found out, though the idea quite took her breath away at first. "And what enormous flowers they must be!" was her next idea. "Something like cottages with the roofs taken off, and stalks put to them—and what quantities of honey they must make! I think I'll go down and—no, I won't go *just* yet," she went on, checking herself just as she was beginning to run down the hill, and trying to find some excuse for turning shy so suddenly. "It'll never do to go down among them without a good long branch to brush them away—and what fun it'll be when they ask me how I liked my walk. I shall say—'Oh, I liked it well enough—' (here came the favorite little toss of the head), 'only it was so dusty and hot, and the elephants did tease so!' "

"I think I'll go down the other way," she said after a pause: "and perhaps I may visit the elephants later on. Besides, I do so want to get into the Third Square!"

So with this excuse she ran down the hill and jumped over
the first of the six little brooks.

"Tickets, please!" said the Guard, putting his head in at the
window. In a moment everybody was holding out a ticket: they
were about the same size as the people, and quite seemed to
fill the carriage.

"Now then! Show your ticket, child!" the Guard went on, looking angrily at Alice. And a great many voices all said together
("like the chorus of a song," thought Alice), "Don't keep him
waiting, child! Why, his time is worth a thousand pounds a
minute!"

"I'm afraid I haven't got one," Alice said in a frightened
tone: "there wasn't a ticket-office where I came from." And again
the chorus of voices went on: "There wasn't room for one where
she came from. The land there is worth a thousand pounds an
inch!"

"Don't make excuses," said the Guard: "you should have bought one from the engine-driver." And once more the chorus of voices went on with "The man that drives the engine. Why, the smoke alone is worth a thousand pounds a puff!"

Alice thought to herself, "Then there's no use in speaking." The voices didn't join in this time, as she hadn't spoken, but, to her great surprise, they all *thought* in chorus (I hope you understand what *thinking in chorus* means—for I must confess that *I* don't), "Better say nothing at all. Language is worth a thousand pounds a word!"

"I shall dream about a thousand pounds to-night, I know I shall!" thought Alice.

All this time the Guard was looking at her, first through a telescope, then through a microscope, and then through an opera-glass. At last he said, "You're traveling the wrong way," and shut up the window and went away.

"So young a child," said the gentleman sitting opposite to her, (he was dressed in white paper,) "ought to know which way she's going, even if she doesn't know her own name!"

A Goat, that was sitting next to the gentleman in white, shut his eyes and said in a loud voice, "She ought to know her way to the ticket-office, even if she doesn't know her alphabet!"

There was a Beetle sitting next the Goat (it was a very queer carriage-full of passengers altogether), and, as the rule seemed to be that they should all speak in turn, *he* went on with "She'll have to go back from here as luggage!"

Alice couldn't see who was sitting beyond the Beetle, but a hoarse voice spoke next. "Change engines——" it said, and there it choked and was obliged to leave off.

"It sounds like a horse," Alice thought to herself. And an extremely small voice, close to her ear, said, "You might make a joke on that—something about 'horse' and 'hoarse,' you know."

Then a very gentle voice in the distance said, "She must be labelled 'Lass, with care,' you know."

And after that other voices went on ("What a number of people there are in the carriage!" thought Alice), saying "She must go by post, as she's got a head* on her." "She must be sent as a message by the telegraph." "She must draw the train herself the rest of the way," and so on.

But the gentleman dressed in white paper leaned forwards and whispered in her ear, "Never mind what they all say, my dear, but take a return-ticket every time the train stops."

"Indeed I shan't!" Alice said rather impatiently. "I don't belong to this railway journey at all—I was in a wood just now— and I wish I could get back there!"

"You might make a joke on *that*," said the little voice close to her ear: "something about 'you *would* if you could,' you know."

"Don't tease so," said Alice, looking about in vain to see where the voice came from: "if you're so anxious to have a joke made, why don't you make one yourself?"

The little voice sighed deeply: it was *very* unhappy, evidently, and Alice would have said something pitying to comfort it, "if it would only sigh like other people!" she thought. But this was such a wonderfully small sigh, that she wouldn't have heard it at all, if it hadn't come *quite* close to her ear. The consequence of this was that it tickled her ear very much, and quite took off her thoughts from the unhappiness of the poor little creature.

"I know you are a friend," the little voice went on; "a dear friend, and an old friend. And you won't hurt me, though I *am* an insect."

"What kind of insect?" Alice inquired a little anxiously. What she really wanted to know was, whether it could sting or not, but she thought this wouldn't be quite a civil question to ask.

"What, then you don't—" the little voice began, when it was drowned by a shrill scream from the engine, and everybody jumped up in alarm, Alice among the rest.

The Horse, who had put his head out of the window, quietly drew it in and said, "It's only a brook we have to jump over." Everybody seemed satisfied with this, though Alice felt a little nervous at the idea of trains jumping at all. "However, it'll take us into the Fourth Square, that's some comfort!" she said to herself. In another moment she felt the carriage rise straight

*Reference to the head of Queen Victoria, whose portrait appeared on postage stamps.

up into the air, and in her fright she caught at the thing near-
est to her hand, which happened to be the Goat's beard.

      *   *   *   *   *

          *   *   *   *

      *   *   *   *   *

But the beard seemed to melt away as she touched it, and
she found herself sitting quietly under some tree—while the
Gnat (for that was the insect she had been talking to) was bal-
ancing itself on a twig just over her head, and fanning her with
its wings.

It certainly was a *very* large Gnat: "about the size of a chicken,"
Alice thought. Still, she couldn't feel nervous with it, after they
had been talking together so long.

"——then you don't like all insects?" the Gnat went on, as
quietly as if nothing had happened.

"I like them when they can talk," Alice said. "None of them
ever talk, where *I* come from."

"What sort of insects do you rejoice in, where *you* come
from?" the Gnat inquired.

"I don't *rejoice* in insects at all," Alice explained, "because
I'm rather afraid of them—at least the large kinds. But I can tell
you the names of some of them."

"Of course they answer to their names?" the Gnat remarked
carelessly.

"I never knew them do it."

"What's the use of their having names," the Gnat said, "if
they won't answer to them?"

"No use to *them*," said Alice; "but it's useful to the people that
name them, I suppose. If not, why do things have names at all?"

"I can't say," the Gnat replied. "Further on, in the wood
down there, they've got no names—however, go on with your
list of insects; you're wasting time."

"Well, there's the Horse-fly," Alice began, counting off the
names on her fingers.

"All right," said the Gnat: "half way up that bush, you'll see a
Rocking-horse-fly, if you look. It's made entirely of wood, and
gets about by swinging itself from branch to branch."

"What does it live on?" Alice asked, with great curiosity.

"Sap and sawdust," said the Gnat. "Go on with the list."

Alice looked at the Rocking-horse-fly with great interest, and made up her mind that it must have been just repainted, it looked so bright and sticky; and then she went on.

"And there's the Dragon-fly."

"Look on the branch above your head," said the Gnat, "and there you'll find a Snap-dragon-fly. Its body is made of plum-pudding, its wings of holly-leaves, and its head is a raisin burning in brandy."

"And what does it live on?" Alice asked, as before.

"Frumenty* and mince-pie," the Gnat replied; "and it makes its nest in a Christmas-box."

"And then there's the Butterfly," Alice went on, after she had taken a good look at the insect with its head on fire, and had thought to herself, "I wonder if that's the reason insects are so fond of flying into candles—because they want to turn into Snap-dragon-flies!"

"Crawling at your feet," said the Gnat (Alice drew her feet back in some alarm), "you may observe a Bread-and-butter-fly. Its wings are thin slices of bread-and-butter, its body is a crust, and its head is a lump of sugar."

---

*Dessert made with sugar, raisins, and boiled wheat.

"And what does *it* live on?"

"Weak tea with cream in it."

A new difficulty came into Alice's head, "Supposing it couldn't find any?" she suggested.

"Then it would die, of course."

"But that must happen very often," Alice remarked thoughtfully.

"It always happens," said the Gnat.

After this, Alice was silent for a minute or two, pondering. The Gnat amused itself meanwhile by humming round and round her head: at last it settled again and remarked, "I suppose you don't want to lose your name?"

"No, indeed," Alice said, a little anxiously.

"And yet I don't know," the Gnat went on in a careless tone: "only think how convenient it would be if you could manage to go home without it! For instance, if the governess wanted to call you to your lessons, she would call out 'Come here——,' and there she would have to leave off, because there wouldn't be any name for her to call, and of course you wouldn't have to go, you know."

"That would never do, I'm sure," said Alice: "the governess would never think of excusing me lessons for that. If she couldn't remember my name, she'd call me 'Miss!' as the servants do."

"Well, if she said 'Miss,' and didn't say anything more," the Gnat remarked, "of course you'd miss your lessons. That's a joke. I wish *you* had made it."

"Why do you wish *I* had made it?" Alice asked. "It's a very bad one."

But the Gnat only sighed deeply, while two large tears came rolling down its cheeks.

"You shouldn't make jokes," Alice said, "if it makes you so unhappy."

Then came another of those melancholy little sighs, and this time the poor Gnat really seemed to have sighed itself away, for, when Alice looked up, there was nothing whatever to be seen on the twig, and, as she was getting quite chilly with sitting still so long, she got up and walked on.

She very soon came to an open field, with a wood on the other side of it: it looked much darker than the last wood, and Alice felt a *little* timid about going into it. However, on second thoughts, she made up her mind to go on: "for I certainly won't go *back*," she thought to herself, and this was the only way to the Eighth Square.

"This must be the wood," she said thoughtfully to herself, "where things have no names. I wonder what'll become of *my* name when I go in? I shouldn't like to lose it at all—because they'd have to give me another and it would be almost certain to be an ugly one. But then the fun would be, trying to find the creature that had got my old name! That's just like the advertisements, you know, when people lose dogs—*'answers to the name of "Dash:" had on a brass collar'*—just fancy calling everything you met 'Alice,' till one of them answered! Only they wouldn't answer at all, if they were wise."

She was rambling on in this way when she reached the wood: it looked very cool and shady. "Well, at any rate it's a great comfort," she said as she stepped under the trees, "after being so hot, to get into the—into the—into *what?*" she went on, rather surprised at not being able to think of the word. "I mean to get under the—under the—under *this,* you know!" putting her hand on the trunk of the tree. "What *does* it call itself, I wonder? I do believe it's got no name—why, to be sure it hasn't!"

She stood silent for a minute, thinking: then she suddenly began again. "Then it really *has* happened, after all! And now, who am I? I *will* remember, if I can! I'm determined to do it!" But being determined didn't help her much, and all she could say, after a great deal of puzzling, was, "L, I *know* it begins with L!"

Just then a Fawn came wandering by: it looked at Alice with its large gentle eyes but didn't seem at all frightened. "Here then! Here then!" Alice said as she held out her hand and tried to stroke it; but it only started back a little, and then stood looking at her again.

"What do you call yourself?" the Fawn said at last. Such a soft sweet voice it had!

"I wish I knew!" thought poor Alice. She answered, rather sadly, "Nothing, just now."

"Think again," it said: "that won't do."

Alice thought, but nothing came of it. "Please, would you tell me what *you* call yourself?" she said timidly. "I think that might help a little."

"I'll tell you, if you'll come a little further on," the Fawn said. "I can't remember here."

So they walked on together through the wood, Alice with her arms clasped lovingly round the soft neck of the Fawn, till

they came out into another open field, and here the Fawn gave
a sudden bound into the air, and shook itself free from Alice's
arms. "I'm a Fawn!" it cried out in a voice of delight, "and, dear
me! you're a human child!" A sudden look of alarm came into
its beautiful brown eyes, and in another moment it had darted
away at full speed.

Alice stood looking after it, almost ready to cry with vexation at having lost her dear little fellow-traveller so suddenly.
"However, I know my name now," she said, "that's *some* comfort. Alice—Alice—I won't forget it again. And now, which of
these finger-posts ought I to follow, I wonder?"

It was not a very difficult question to answer, as there was
only one road through the wood, and the two finger-posts both
pointed along it. "I'll settle it," Alice said to herself, "when the
road divides and they point different ways."

But this did not seem likely to happen. She went on and on,

a long way, but wherever the road divided there were sure to be two finger-posts pointing the same way, one marked 'TO TWEEDLEDUM'S HOUSE,' and the other 'TO THE HOUSE OF TWEEDLEDEE.'

"I do believe," said Alice at last, "that they live in the same house! I wonder I never thought of that before—But I can't stay there long. I'll just call and say 'How d'ye do?' and ask them the way out of the wood. If I could only get to the Eighth Square before it gets dark!" So she wandered on, talking to herself as she went, till, on turning a sharp corner, she came upon two fat little men, so suddenly that she could not help starting back, but in another moment she recovered herself, feeling sure that they must be

```
  *         *         *         *         *         *
       *         *         *         *         *
  *         *         *         *         *         *
       *         *         *         *         *
  *         *         *         *         *         *
       *         *         *         *         *
  *         *         *         *         *         *
```

CHAPTER IV.

TWEEDLEDUM AND TWEEDLEDEE.

They were standing under a tree, each with an arm round the other's neck, and Alice knew which was which in a moment, because one of them had 'DUM' embroidered on his collar, and the other 'DEE.' "I suppose they've each got 'TWEEDLE' round at the back of the collar," she said to herself.

They stood so still that she quite forgot they were alive, and she was just looking round to see if the word 'TWEEDLE' was written at the back of each collar, when she was startled by a voice coming from the one marked 'DUM.'

"If you think we're wax-works," he said, "you ought to pay, you know. Wax-works weren't made to be looked at for nothing. Nohow!"

"Contrariwise," added the one marked 'DEE,' "if you think we're alive, you ought to speak."

"I'm sure I'm very sorry," was all Alice could say; for the words of the old song kept ringing through her head like the ticking of a clock, and she could hardly help saying them out loud:

> "Tweedledum and Tweedledee
>   Agreed to have a battle;
> For Tweedledum said Tweedledee
>   Had spoiled his nice new rattle.
>
> Just then flew down a monstrous crow,
>   As black as a tar barrel
> Which frightened both the heroes so,
>   They quite forgot their quarrel."

"I know what you're thinking about," said Tweedledum: "but it isn't so, nohow."

"Contrariwise," continued Tweedledee, "if it was so, it might be; and if it were so, it would be; but as it isn't, it ain't. That's logic."

"I was thinking," Alice said very politely, "which is the best way out of this wood: it's getting so dark. Would you tell me please?"

But the fat little men only looked at each other and grinned.

They looked so exactly like a couple of great school boys, that Alice couldn't help pointing her finger at Tweedledum, and saying "First Boy!"

"Nohow!" Tweedledum cried out briskly, and shut his mouth up again with a snap.

"Next Boy!" said Alice, passing on to Tweedledee, though she felt quite certain he would only shout out, "Contrariwise!" and so he did.

"You've begun wrong!" cried Tweedledum. "The first thing in a visit is to say 'How d'ye do?' and shake hands!" And here the two brothers gave each other a hug, and then they held out the two hands that were free, to shake hands with her.

Alice did not like shaking hands with either of them first, for fear of hurting the other one's feelings; so, as the best way out of the difficulty, she took hold of both hands at once: the next moment they were dancing round in a ring. This seemed quite natural (she remembered afterwards), and she was not even surprised to hear music playing: it seemed to come from the tree under which they were dancing, and it was done (as well as she could make it out) by the branches rubbing one across the other, like fiddles and fiddle-sticks.

"But it certainly *was* funny," (Alice said afterwards, when she was telling her sister the history of all this,) "to find myself singing *'Here we go round the mulberry bush.'* I don't know when I began it, but somehow I felt as if I'd been singing it a long long time!"

The other two dancers were fat, and very soon out of breath. "Four times round is enough for one dance," Tweedledum panted out, and they left off dancing as suddenly as they had begun: the music stopped at the same moment.

Then they let go of Alice's hands, and stood looking at her for a minute: there was a rather awkward pause, as Alice didn't know how to begin a conversation with people she had just been dancing with. "It would never do to say 'How d'ye do?' *now*," she said to herself: "we seem to have got beyond that, somehow!"

"I hope you're not much tired?" she said at last.

"Nohow. And thank you *very* much for asking," said Tweedledum.

"So *much* obliged!" added Tweedledee. "You like poetry?"

"Ye-es pretty well—*some* poetry," Alice said doubtfully. "Would you tell me which road leads out of the wood?"

"What shall I repeat to her?" said Tweedledee, looking round at Tweedledum with great solemn eyes, and not noticing Alice's question.

"*'The Walrus and the Carpenter'* is the longest," Tweedledum replied, giving his brother an affectionate hug.

Tweedledee began instantly:

> *"The sun was shining—"*

Here Alice ventured to interrupt him. "If it's *very* long," she said, as politely as she could, "would you please tell me first which road—"

Tweedledee smiled gently, and began again:

> *"The sun was shining on the sea,*[4]
>> *Shining with all his might:*
> *He did his very best to make*
>> *The billows smooth and bright—*
> *And this was odd, because it was*
>> *The middle of the night.*
>
> *The moon was shining sulkily,*
>> *Because she thought the sun*
> *Had got no business to be there*
>> *After the day was done—*
> *'It's very rude of him,' she said,*
>> *'To come and spoil the fun!'*
>
> *The sea was wet as wet could be,*
>> *The sands were dry as dry.*
> *You could not see a cloud, because*
>> *No cloud was in the sky:*
> *No birds were flying overhead—*
>> *There were no birds to fly.*
>
> *The Walrus and the Carpenter*
>> *Were walking close at hand;*
> *They wept like anything to see*
>> *Such quantities of sand:*
> *'If this were only cleared away,'*
>> *They said, 'it would be grand!'*

'If seven maids with seven mops
    Swept it for half a year,
Do you suppose,' the Walrus said,
    'That they could get it clear?'
'I doubt it,' said the Carpenter,
    And shed a bitter tear.

'O Oysters, come and walk with us!'
    The Walrus did beseech.
'A pleasant walk, a pleasant talk
    Along the briny beach:
We cannot do with more than four,
    To give a hand to each.'

The eldest Oyster looked at him,
    But never a word he said:
The eldest Oyster winked his eye,
    And shook his heavy head—
Meaning to say he did not choose
    To leave the oyster-bed.

But four young Oysters hurried up,
    All eager for the treat:

Their coats were brushed, their faces washed,
*   Their shoes were clean and neat—*
And this was odd, because, you know,
*   They hadn't any feet.*

Four other Oysters followed them,
*   And yet another four;*
And thick and fast they came at last,
*   And more, and more, and more—*
All hopping through the frothy waves,
*   And scrambling to the shore.*

The Walrus and the Carpenter
*   Walked on a mile or so,*
And then they rested on a rock
*   Conveniently low:*
And all the little Oysters stood
*   And waited in a row.*

'The time has come,' the Walrus said,
*   'To talk of many things:*
Of shoes—and ships—and sealing wax—
*   Of cabbages—and kings—*
And why the sea is boiling hot—
*   And whether pigs have wings.'*

'But wait a bit,' the Oysters cried,
*   'Before we have our chat;*
For some of us are out of breath,
*   And all of us are fat!'*
'No hurry!' said the Carpenter.
*   They thanked him much for that.*

'A loaf of bread,' the Walrus said,
*   'Is what we chiefly need:*
Pepper and vinegar besides
*   Are very good indeed—*
Now if you're ready, Oysters dear
*   We can begin to feed.'*

'But not on us!' the Oysters cried,
   Turning a little blue.
'After such kindness, that would be
   A dismal thing to do!'
'The night is fine,' the Walrus said,
   'Do you admire the view?'

'It was so kind of you to come!
   And you are very nice!'
The Carpenter said nothing but
   'Cut us another slice:
I wish you were not quite so deaf—
   I've had to ask you twice!'

'It seems a shame,' the Walrus said,
   'To play them such a trick,
After we've brought them out so far,
   And made them trot so quick!'
The Carpenter said nothing but
   'The butter's spread too thick!'

'I weep for you,' the Walrus said:
  'I deeply sympathize.'
With sobs and tears he sorted out
  Those of the largest size,
Holding his pocket-handkerchief
  Before his streaming eyes.

'O Oysters,' said the Carpenter,
  'You've had a pleasant run!
Shall we be trotting home again?'
  But answer came there none—
And this was scarcely odd, because
  They'd eaten every one."

"I like the Walrus best," said Alice: "because you see he was a *little* sorry for the poor oysters."

"He ate more than the Carpenter, though," said Tweedledee. "You see he held his handkerchief in front, so that the Carpenter couldn't count how many he took: contrariwise."

"That was mean!" Alice said indignantly. "Then I like the Carpenter best—if he didn't eat so many as the Walrus."

"But he ate as many as he could get," said Tweedledum.

This was a puzzler. After a pause, Alice began, "Well! They

were *both* very unpleasant characters—" Here she checked herself in some alarm, at hearing something that sounded to her like the puffing of a large steam-engine in the wood near them, though she feared it was more likely to be a wild beast. "Are there any lions or tigers about here?" she asked timidly.

"It's only the Red King snoring," said Tweedledee.

"Come and look at him!" the brothers cried, and they each took one of Alice's hands, and led her up to where the King was sleeping.

"Isn't he a *lovely* sight?" said Tweedledum.

Alice couldn't say honestly that he was. He had a tall red night-cap on, with a tassel, and he was lying crumpled up into a sort of untidy heap, and snoring loud—"fit to snore his head off!" as Tweedledum remarked.

"I'm afraid he'll catch cold with lying on the damp grass," said Alice, who was a very thoughtful little girl.

"He's dreaming now," said Tweedledee: "and what do you think he's dreaming about?"

Alice said "Nobody can guess that."

"Why, about *you!*" Tweedledee exclaimed, clapping his hands triumphantly. "And if he left off dreaming about you, where do you suppose you'd be?"

"Where I am now, of course," said Alice.

"Not you!" Tweedledee retorted contemptuously. "You'd be nowhere. Why, you're only a sort of thing in his dream!"

"If that there King was to wake," added Tweedledum, "you'd go out—bang!—just like a candle!"

"I shouldn't!" Alice exclaimed indignantly. "Besides, if *I'm* only a sort of thing in his dream, what are *you*, I should like to know?"

"Ditto," said Tweedledum.

"Ditto, ditto!" cried Tweedledee.

He shouted this so loud that Alice couldn't help saying, "Hush! You'll be waking him, I'm afraid, if you make so much noise."

"Well, it's no use *your* talking about waking him," said Tweedledum, "when you're only one of the things in his dream. You know very well you're not real."

"I *am* real!" said Alice, and began to cry.

"You won't make yourself a bit realler by crying," Tweedledee remarked: "there's nothing to cry about."

"If I wasn't real," Alice said—half-laughing through her tears, it all seemed so ridiculous—"I shouldn't be able to cry."

"I hope you don't suppose those are real tears?" Tweedledum interrupted in a tone of great contempt.

"I know they're talking nonsense," Alice thought to herself:

"and it's foolish to cry about it." So she brushed away her tears, and went on as cheerfully as she could, "At any rate I'd better be getting out of the wood, for really it's coming on very dark. Do you think it's going to rain?"

Tweedledum spread a large umbrella over himself and his brother, and looked up into it. "No, I don't think it is," he said: "at least—not under *here*. Nohow."

"But it may rain *outside*?"

"It may—if it chooses," said Tweedledee: "we've no objection. Contrariwise."

"Selfish things!" thought Alice, and she was just going to say "Good-night" and leave them, when Tweedledum sprang out from under the umbrella, and seized her by the wrist.

"Do you see *that*?" he said, in a voice choking with passion, and his eyes grew large and yellow all in a moment, as he pointed with a trembling finger at a small white thing lying under the tree.

"It's only a rattle," Alice said, after a careful examination of the little white thing. "Not a rattle-*snake*, you know," she added hastily, thinking that he was frightened: "only an old rattle— quite old and broken."

"I knew it was!" cried Tweedledum, beginning to stamp about wildly and tear his hair. "It's spoilt, of course!" Here he looked at Tweedledee, who immediately sat down on the ground and tried to hide himself under the umbrella.

Alice laid her hand upon his arm, and said in a soothing tone, "You needn't be so angry about an old rattle."

"But it isn't old!" Tweedledum cried, in a greater fury than ever. "It's new, I tell you—I bought it yesterday—my nice NEW RATTLE!" and his voice rose to a perfect scream.

All this time Tweedledee was trying his best to fold up the umbrella, with himself in it: which was such an extraordinary thing to do, that it quite took off Alice's attention from the angry brother. But he couldn't quite succeed, and it ended in his rolling over, bundled up in the umbrella, with only his head out: and there he lay, opening and shutting his mouth and his large eyes—"looking more like a fish than anything else," Alice thought.

"Of course you agree to have a battle?" Tweedledum said in a calmer tone.

"I suppose so," the other sulkily replied, as he crawled out of the umbrella: "only *she* must help us to dress up, you know."

So the two brothers went off hand-in-hand into the wood, and returned in a minute with their arms full of things—such as bolster, blankets, hearth-rugs, table-cloths, dish-covers, and coal-scuttles. "I hope you're a good hand at pinning and tying strings?" Tweedledum remarked. "Every one of these things has got to go on, somehow or other."

Alice said afterwards she had never seen such a fuss made about anything in all her life—the way those two bustled about—and the quantity of things they put on—and the trouble they gave her in tying strings and fastening buttons—"Really they'll be more like bundles of old clothes than anything else, by the time they're ready!" she said to herself, as she arranged a bolster round the neck of Tweedledee, "to keep his head from being cut off," as he said.

"You know," he added very gravely, "it's one of the most serious things that can possibly happen to one in a battle—to get one's head cut off."

Alice laughed loud: but she managed to turn it into a cough, for fear of hurting his feelings.

"Do I look very pale?" said Tweedledum, coming up to have his helmet tied on. (He *called* it a helmet, though it certainly looked much more like a saucepan.)

"Well—yes—a *little*," Alice replied gently.

"I'm very brave generally," he went on in a low voice: "only to-day I happen to have a headache."

"And *I've* got a toothache!" said Tweedledee, who had over-heard the remark. "I'm far worse than you!"

"Then you'd better not fight to-day," said Alice, thinking it a good opportunity to make peace.

"We *must* have a bit of a fight, but I don't care about going on long," said Tweedledum. "What's the time now?"

Tweedledee looked at his watch, and said "Half-past four."

"Let's fight till six, and then have dinner," said Tweedledum.

"Very well," the other said, rather sadly: "and *she* can watch us—only you'd better not come *very* close," he added: "I generally hit everything I can see—when I get really excited."

"And *I* hit everything within reach," cried Tweedledum, "whether I can see it or not!"

Alice laughed. "You must hit the *trees* pretty often, I should think," she said.

Tweedledum looked round him with a satisfied smile. "I don't suppose," he said, "there'll be a tree left standing, for ever so far round, by the time we've finished!"

"And all about a rattle!" said Alice, still hoping to make them a *little* ashamed of fighting for such a trifle.

"I shouldn't have minded it so much," said Tweedledum, "if it hadn't been a new one."

"I wish the monstrous crow would come!" thought Alice.

"There's only one sword, you know," Tweedledum said to his brother: "but you can have the umbrella—it's quite as sharp. Only we must begin quick. It's getting as dark as it can."

"And darker," said Tweedledee.

It was getting dark so suddenly that Alice thought there must be a thunderstorm coming on. "What a thick black cloud that is!" she said. "And how fast it comes! Why, I do believe it's got wings!"

"It's the crow!" Tweedledum cried out in a shrill voice of alarm: and the two brothers took to their heels and were out of sight in a moment.

Alice ran a little way into the wood, and stopped under a large tree. "It can never get at me *here*," she thought: "its far too large to squeeze itself in among the trees. But I wish it wouldn't flap its wings so—it makes quite a hurricane in the wood—here's somebody's shawl being blown away!"

CHAPTER V.

WOOL AND WATER.

She caught the shawl as she spoke, and looked about for the owner: in another moment the White Queen came running wildly through the wood, with both arms stretched out wide, as if she were flying, and Alice very civilly went to meet her with the shawl.

"I'm very glad I happened to be in the way," Alice said, as she helped her to put on her shawl again.

The White Queen only looked at her in a helpless frightened sort of way, and kept repeating something in a whisper to herself that sounded like "Bread-and-butter, bread-and-butter," and Alice felt that if there was to be any conversation at all, she must manage it herself. So she began rather timidly: "Am I addressing the White Queen?"

"Well, yes, if you call that a-dressing," the Queen said. "It isn't *my* notion of the thing, at all."

Alice thought it would never do to have an argument at the very beginning of their conversation, so she smiled and said, "If your Majesty will only tell me the right way to begin, I'll do it as well as I can."

"But I don't want it done at all!" groaned the poor Queen. "I've been a-dressing myself for the last two hours."

It would have been all the better, as it seemed to Alice, if she had got some one else to dress her, she was so dreadfully untidy. "Every single thing's crooked," Alice thought to herself, "and she's all over pins!—May I put your shawl straight for you?" she added aloud.

"I don't know what's the matter with it!" the Queen said in a melancholy voice. "It's out of temper, I think. I've pinned it here, and I've pinned it there, but there's no pleasing it!"

"It *can't* go straight, you know, if you pin it all on one side," Alice said, as she gently put it right for her; "and, dear me, what a state your hair is in!"

"The brush has got entangled in it!" the Queen said with a sigh. "And I lost the comb yesterday."

Alice carefully released the brush, and did her best to get the hair into order. "Come, you look rather better now!" she said, after altering most of the pins. "But really you should have a lady's-maid!"

"I'm sure I'll take you with pleasure!" the Queen said. "Twopence a week, and jam every other day."

Alice couldn't help laughing, as she said, "I don't want you to hire *me*—and I don't care for jam."

"It's very good jam," said the Queen.

"Well, I don't want any *to-day*, at any rate."

"You couldn't have it if you *did* want it," the Queen said. "The rule is, jam to-morrow and jam yesterday—but never jam to-day."

"It *must* come sometimes to 'jam to-day,'" Alice objected.

"No it can't," said the Queen. "It's jam every *other* day: to-day isn't any *other* day, you know."

"I don't understand you," said Alice. "It's dreadfully confusing!"

"That's the effect of living backwards," the Queen said kindly: "it always makes one a little giddy first—"

"Living backwards!" Alice repeated in great astonishment. "I never heard of such a thing!"

"—but there's one great advantage in it, that one's memory works both ways."

"I'm sure *mine* only works one way," Alice remarked. "I can't remember things before they happen."

"It's a poor sort of memory that only works backwards," the Queen remarked.

"What sort of things do *you* remember best?" Alice ventured to ask.

"Oh, things that happen the week after next," the Queen replied in a careless tone. "For instance, now," she went on, sticking a large piece of plaster* on her finger as she spoke, "there's the King's Messenger. He's in prison now, being punished: and the trial doesn't even begin till next Wednesday: and of course the crime comes last of all."

"Suppose he never commits the crime?" said Alice.

"That would be all the better, wouldn't it?" the Queen said, as she bound the plaster round her finger with a bit of ribbon.

Alice felt there was no denying *that.* "Of course it would be all the better," she said: "but it wouldn't be all the better his being punished."

"You're wrong *there,* at any rate," said the Queen: "were *you* ever punished?"

"Only for faults," said Alice.

---

*A bandage.

"And you were all the better for it, I know!" the Queen said triumphantly.

"Yes, but then I *had* done the things I was punished for," said Alice: "that makes all the difference."

"But if you *hadn't* done them," the Queen said, "that would have been better still; better, and better, and better!" Her voice went higher with each "better," till it got quite to a squeak at last.

Alice was just beginning to say "There's a mistake somewhere—," when the Queen began screaming, so loud that she had to leave the sentence unfinished. "Oh, oh, oh!" shouted the Queen, shaking her hand about as if she wanted to shake it off. "My finger's bleeding! Oh, oh, oh, oh!"

Her screams were so exactly like the whistle of a steam-engine, that Alice had to hold both her hands over her ears.

"What *is* the matter?" she said, as soon as there was a chance of making herself heard, "Have you pricked your finger?"

"I haven't pricked it *yet*," the Queen said, "but I soon shall— oh, oh, oh!"

"When do you expect to do it?" Alice asked, feeling very much inclined to laugh.

"When I fasten my shawl again," the poor Queen groaned out: "the brooch will come undone directly. Oh, oh!" As she said the words the brooch flew open, and the Queen clutched wildly at it, and tried to clasp it again.

"Take care!" cried Alice. "You're holding it all crooked!" And she caught at the brooch; but it was too late: the pin had slipped, and the Queen had pricked her finger.

"That accounts for the bleeding, you see," she said to Alice with a smile. "Now you understand the way things happen here."

"But why don't you scream now?" Alice asked, holding her hands ready to put over her ears again.

"Why, I've done all the screaming already," said the Queen. "What would be the good of having it all over again?"

By this time it was getting light. "The crow must have flown away, I think," said Alice: "I'm so glad it's gone. I thought it was the night coming on."

"I wish *I* could manage to be glad!" the Queen said. "Only I never can remember the rule. You must be very happy, living in this wood, and being glad whenever you like!"

"Only it is so *very* lonely here!" Alice said in a melancholy voice; and at the thought of her loneliness two large tears came rolling down her cheeks.

"Oh, don't go on like that!" cried the poor Queen, wringing her hands in despair. "Consider what a great girl you are. Consider what a long way you've come to-day. Consider what o'clock it is. Consider anything, only don't cry!"

Alice could not help laughing at this, even in the midst of her tears. "Can *you* keep from crying by considering things?" she asked.

"That's the way it's done," the Queen said with great decision: "nobody can do two things at once, you know. Let's consider your age to begin with—how old are you?"

"I'm seven and a half exactly."

"You needn't say 'exactly,' " the Queen remarked: "I can believe it without that. Now I'll give *you* something to believe. I'm just one hundred and one, five months and a day."

"I can't believe *that!*" said Alice.

"Can't you?" the Queen said in a pitying tone. "Try again: draw a long breath, and shut your eyes."

Alice laughed. "There's no use trying," she said: "one *can't* believe impossible things."

"I daresay you haven't had much practice," said the Queen. "When I was your age, I always did it for half-an-hour a day. Why, sometimes I've believed as many as six impossible things before breakfast. There goes the shawl again!"

The brooch had come undone as she spoke, and a sudden gust of wind blew the Queen's shawl across a little brook. The Queen spread out her arms again, and went flying after it, and this time she succeeded in catching it for herself. "I've got it!" she cried in a triumphant tone. "Now you shall see me pin it on again, all by myself!"

"Then I hope your finger is better now?" Alice said very politely, as she crossed the little brook after the Queen.

     *   *   *   *   *

        *   *   *   *

     *   *   *   *   *

"Oh, much better!" cried the Queen, her voice rising into a squeak as she went on. "Much be-etter! Be-etter! Be-e-e-etter! Be-e-ehh!" The last word ended in a long bleat, so like a sheep that Alice quite started.

She looked at the Queen, who seemed to have suddenly wrapped herself up in wool. Alice rubbed her eyes, and looked again. She couldn't make out what had happened at all. Was she in a shop? And was that really—was it really a *sheep* that was sitting on the other side of the counter? Rub as she would, she could make nothing more of it: she was in a little dark shop, leaning with her elbows on the counter, and opposite to her was an old Sheep, sitting in an armchair knitting, and every now and then leaving off to look at her through a great pair of spectacles.

"What is it you want to buy?" the Sheep said at last, looking up for a moment from her knitting.

"I don't *quite* know yet," Alice said very gently. "I should like to look all round me first, if I might."

"You may look in front of you, and on both sides, if you like," said the Sheep; "but you can't look *all* round you—unless you've got eyes at the back of your head."

But these, as it happened, Alice had. *not* got: so she contented herself with turning round, looking at the shelves as she came to them.

The shop seemed to be full of all manner of curious things—but the oddest part of it all was, that whenever she looked hard at any shelf, to make out exactly what it had on it, that particular shelf was always quite empty: though the others round it were crowded as full as they could hold.

"Things flow about so here!" she said at last in a plaintive tone, after she had spent a minute or so in vainly pursuing a large bright thing, that looked sometimes like a doll and sometimes like a work-box, and was always in the shelf next above the one she was looking at. "And this one is the most provoking of all—but I'll tell you what—" she added, as a sudden thought struck her, "I'll follow it up to the very top shelf of all. It'll puzzle it to go through the ceiling, I expect!"

But even this plan failed: the 'thing' went through the ceiling as quietly as possible, as if it were quite used to it.

"Are you a child or a teetotum?"* the Sheep said, as she took up another pair of needles. "You'll make me giddy soon, if you go on turning round like that." She was now working with fourteen pairs at once, and Alice couldn't help looking at her in great astonishment.

"How *can* she knit with so many?" the puzzled child thought to herself. "She gets more and more like a porcupine every minute!"

"Can you row?" the Sheep asked, handing her a pair of knitting-needles as she spoke.

"Yes, a little—but not on land—and not with needles——" Alice was beginning to say, when suddenly the needles turned into oars in her hands, and she found they were in a little boat, gliding along between banks: so there was nothing for it but to do her best.

"Feather!"† cried the Sheep, as she took up another pair of needles.

This didn't sound like a remark that needed any answer, so Alice said nothing, but pulled away. There was something very queer about the water, she thought, as every now and then the oars got fast in it, and would hardly come out again.

---

*Spinning top with numerals printed on its numerous flat surfaces.
†Feathering is a manner of rowing in which the oar is kept horizontal on the return stroke.

"Feather! Feather!" the Sheep cried again, taking more needles. "You'll be catching a crab directly."

"A dear little crab!" thought Alice. "I should like that."

"Didn't you hear me say 'Feather'?" the Sheep cried angrily, taking up quite a bunch of needles.

"Indeed I did," said Alice: "you've said it very often—and very loud. Please, where *are* the crabs?"

"In the water, of course!" said the Sheep, sticking some of the needles into her hair, as her hands were full. "Feather, I say!"

"*Why* do you say 'Feather' so often?" Alice asked at last, rather vexed. "I'm not a bird!"

"You are," said the Sheep: "you're a little goose."

This offended Alice a little, so there was no more conversation for a minute or two, while the boat glided gently on, sometimes among beds of weeds (which made the oars stick fast in the water, worse than ever), and sometimes under trees, but always with the same tall river-banks frowning over their heads.

"Oh, please! There are some scented rushes!" Alice cried in a sudden transport of delight. "There really are—and *such* beauties!"

"You needn't say 'please' to *me* about 'em," the Sheep said, without looking up from her knitting: "I didn't put 'em there, and I'm not going to take 'em away."

"No, but I meant—please, may we wait and pick some?" Alice pleaded. "If you don't mind stopping the boat for a minute."

"How am *I* to stop it?" said the Sheep. "If you leave off rowing, it'll stop of itself."

So the boat was left to drift down the stream as it would, till it glided gently in among the waving rushes. And then the little sleeves were carefully rolled up, and the little arms were plunged in elbow-deep, to get hold of the rushes a good long way down before breaking them off—and for a while Alice forgot all about the Sheep and the knitting, as she bent over the side of the boat, with just the ends of her tangled hair dipping into the water—while with bright eager eyes she caught at one bunch after another of the darling scented rushes.

"I only hope the boat won't tipple over!" she said to herself. "Oh, *what* a lovely one! Only I couldn't quite reach it." And it certainly *did* seem a little provoking ("almost as if it happened on purpose," she thought) that, though she managed to pick plenty of beautiful rushes as the boat glided by, there was always a more lovely one that she couldn't reach.

"The prettiest are always further!" she said at last, with a sigh at the obstinacy of the rushes in growing so far off, as with flushed cheeks and dripping hair and hands, she scrambled back into her place, and began to arrange her new-found treasures.

What mattered it to her just then that the rushes had begun to fade, and to lose all their scent and beauty, from the very moment that she picked them? Even real scented rushes, you know, last only a very little while—and these, being dream-rushes, melted away almost like snow, as they lay in heaps at her feet—but Alice hardly noticed this, there were so many other curious things to think about.

They hadn't gone much farther before the blade of one of the oars got fast in the water and *wouldn't* come out again (so Alice explained it afterwards), and the consequence was that the handle of it caught her under the chin, and, in spite of a series of shrieks of "Oh, oh, oh!" from poor Alice, it swept her straight off the seat, and down among the heap of rushes.

However, she wasn't a bit hurt, and was soon up again: the Sheep went on with her knitting all the while, just as if nothing had happened. "That was a nice crab you caught!" she remarked, as Alice got back into her place, very much relieved to find herself still in the boat.

"Was it? I didn't see it," said Alice, peeping cautiously over the side of the boat into the dark water. "I wish it hadn't let go—I should so like a little crab to take home with me!" But the sheep only laughed scornfully, and went on with her knitting.

"Are there many crabs here?" said Alice.

"Crabs, and all sorts of things," said the Sheep: "plenty of choice, only make up your mind. Now, what *do* you want to buy?"

"To buy" Alice echoed in a tone that was half astonished and half frightened—for the oars, and the boat, and the river, had vanished all in a moment, and she was back again in the little dark shop.

"I should like to buy an egg, please," she said timidly. "How do you sell them?"

"Fivepence farthing for one—twopence for two," the Sheep replied.

"Then two are cheaper than one?" Alice said in a surprised tone, taking out her purse.

"Only you *must* eat them both, if you buy two," said the Sheep.

"Then I'll have *one*, please," said Alice, as she put the money down on the counter. For she thought to herself, "They mightn't be at all nice, you know."

The Sheep took the money, and put it away in a box: then she said "I never put things into people's hands—that would never do—you must get it for yourself." And so saying, she went off to the other end of the shop, and set the egg upright on a shelf.

"I wonder *why* it wouldn't do?" thought Alice, as she groped her way among the tables and chairs, for the shop was very dark towards the end. "The egg seems to get further away the more I walk towards it. Let me see, is this a chair? Why it's got branches, I declare! How very odd to find trees growing here! And actually here's a little brook! Well, this is the very queerest shop I ever saw!"

*   *   *   *   *

   *   *   *   *

*   *   *   *   *

So she went on, wondering more and more at every step, as everything turned into a tree the moment she came up to it, and she quite expected the egg to do the same.

CHAPTER VI.

HUMPTY DUMPTY.

Howerver, the egg only got larger and larger, and more and more human: when she had come within a few yards of it, she saw that it had eyes and a nose and mouth; and when she had come close to it, she saw clearly that it was HUMPTY DUMPTY himself. "It can't be anybody else!" she said to herself. "I'm as certain of it, as if his name were written all over his face!"

It might have been written a hundred times, easily, on that enormous face. Humpty Dumpty was sitting with his legs crossed, like a Turk, on the top of a high wall—such a narrow one that Alice quite wondered how he could keep his balance— and, as his eyes were steadily fixed in the opposite direction, and he didn't take the least notice of her, she thought he must be a stuffed figure after all.

"And how exactly like an egg he is!" she said aloud, standing with her hands ready to catch him, for she was every moment expecting him to fall.

"It's *very* provoking," Humpty Dumpty said after a long silence, looking away from Alice as he spoke, "to be called an egg—*very!*"

"I said you *looked* like an egg, Sir," Alice gently explained. "And some eggs are very pretty, you know," she added, hoping to turn her remark into a sort of compliment.

"Some people," said Humpty Dumpty, looking away from her as usual, "have no more sense than a baby!"

Alice didn't know what to say to this: it wasn't at all like conversation, she thought, as he never said anything to *her;* in fact, his last remark was evidently addressed to a tree—so she stood and softly repeated to herself:

"Humpty Dumpty sat on a wall:
Humpty Dumpty had a great fall.
All the King's horses and all the King's men
Couldn't put Humpty Dumpty in his place again."

"That last line is much too long for the poetry," she added, almost out loud, forgetting that Humpty Dumpty would hear her.

"Don't stand chattering to yourself like that," Humpty Dumpty said, looking at her for the first time, "but tell me your name and your business."

"My *name* is Alice, but—"

"It's a stupid name enough!" Humpty Dumpty interrupted impatiently. "What does it mean?"

"*Must* a name mean something?" Alice asked doubtfully.

"Of course it must," Humpty Dumpty said with a short laugh: "*my* name means the shape I am—and a good handsome shape it is, too. With a name like yours, you might be any shape almost."[5]

"Why do you sit out here all alone?" said Alice, not wishing to begin an argument.

"Why, because there's nobody with me!" cried Humpty Dumpty. "Did you think I didn't know the answer to *that?* Ask another."

"Don't you think you'd be safer down on the ground?" Alice went on, not with any idea of making another riddle, but simply in her good-natured anxiety for the queer creature. "That wall is so *very* narrow!"

"What tremendously easy riddles you ask!" Humpty Dumpty growled out. "Of course I don't think so! Why, if ever I *did* fall off—which there's no chance of—but *if* I did—" Here he pursed up his lips, and looked so solemn and grand that Alice could hardly help laughing. "*If* I did fall," he went on, "*the King has promised me*—ah, you may turn pale, if you like! You didn't think I was going to say that, did you? *The King has promised me—with his very own mouth—to—to—*"

"To send all his horses and all his men," Alice interrupted, rather unwisely.

"Now I declare that's too bad!" Humpty Dumpty cried, breaking into a sudden passion. "You've been listening at doors—and behind trees—and down chimneys—or you couldn't have known it!"

"I haven't, indeed!" Alice said very gently. "It's in a book."

"Ah, well! They may write such things in a *book*," Humpty Dumpty said in a calmer tone. "That's what you call a History of England, that is. Now, take a good look at me! I'm one that has spoken to a King, *I* am: mayhap you'll never see such another: and to show you I'm not proud, you may shake hands with me!" And he grinned almost from ear to ear, as he leant forwards (and as nearly as possible fell off the wall in doing so) and offered Alice his hand. She watched him a little anxiously as she took it. "If he smiled much more, the ends of his mouth might meet behind," she thought: "and then I don't know what would happen to his head! I'm afraid it would come off!"

"Yes, all his horses and all his men," Humpty Dumpty went on. "They'd pick me up again in a minute, *they* would! However, this conversation is going on a little too fast: let's go back to the last remark but one."

"I'm afraid I can't quite remember it," Alice said very politely.

"In that case we start fresh," said Humpty Dumpty, "and it's my turn to choose a subject—" ("He talks about it just as if it was a game!" thought Alice.) "So here's a question for you. How old did you say you were?"

Alice made a short calculation, and said "Seven years and six months."

"Wrong!" Humpty Dumpty exclaimed triumphantly. "You never said a word like it!"

"I thought you meant 'How old *are* you?'" Alice explained.

"If I'd meant that, I'd have said it," said Humpty Dumpty.

Alice didn't want to begin another argument, so she said nothing.

"Seven years and six months!" Humpty Dumpty repeated thoughtfully. "An uncomfortable sort of age. Now if you'd asked *my* advice, I'd have said 'Leave off at seven'—but it's too late now."

"I never ask advice about growing," Alice said indignantly.

"Too proud?" the other inquired. Alice felt even more indignant at this suggestion. "I mean," she said, "that one can't help growing older."

"*One* can't, perhaps," said Humpty Dumpty, "but *two* can. With proper assistance, you might have left off at seven."

"What a beautiful belt you've got on!" Alice suddenly remarked. (They had had quite enough of the subject of age, she thought: and if they really were to take turns in choosing subjects, it was her turn now.) "At least," she corrected herself on second thoughts, "a beautiful cravat, I should have said—no, a belt, I mean—I beg your pardon!" she added in dismay, for Humpty Dumpty looked thoroughly offended, and she began to wish she hadn't chosen that subject. "If only I knew," she thought to herself, "which was neck and which was waist!"

Evidently Humpty Dumpty was very angry, though he said nothing for a minute or two. When he *did* speak again, it was in a deep growl.

"It is a—*most—provoking*—thing," he said at last, "when a person doesn't know a cravat from a belt!"

"I know it's very ignorant of me," Alice said, in so humble a tone that Humpty Dumpty relented.

"It's a cravat, child, and a beautiful one, as you say. It's a present from the White King and Queen. There now!"

"Is it really?" said Alice, quite pleased to find that she *had* chosen a good subject, after all.

"They gave it me," Humpty Dumpty continued thoughtfully, as he crossed one knee over the other and clasped his hands round it, "they gave it me—for an un-birthday present."

"I beg your pardon?" Alice said with a puzzled air.

"I'm not offended," said Humpty Dumpty.

"I mean, what *is* an un-birthday present?"

"A present given when it isn't your birthday of course."

Alice considered a little. "I like birthday presents best," she said at last.

"You don't know what you're talking about!" cried Humpty Dumpty. "How many days are there in a year?"

"Three hundred and sixty-five," said Alice.

"And how many birthdays have you?"

"One."

"And if you take one from three hundred and sixty-five, what remains?"

"Three hundred and sixty-four, of course."

Humpty Dumpty looked doubtful. "I'd rather see that done on paper," he said.

Alice couldn't help smiling as she took out her memorandum book, and worked the sum for him:

$$365$$
$$\underline{1}$$
$$\underline{364}$$

Humpty Dumpty took the book, and looked at it carefully. "That seems to be done right—" he began.

"You're holding it upside down!" Alice interrupted.

"To be sure I was!" Humpty Dumpty said gaily, as she turned it round for him. "I thought it looked a little queer. As I was saying, that *seems* to be done right—though I haven't time to look it over thoroughly just now—and that shows that there are three hundred and sixty-four days when you might get unbirthday-presents—"

"Certainly," said Alice.

"And only *one* for birthday presents, you know. There's glory for you!"

"I don't know what you mean by 'glory,' " Alice said.

Humpty Dumpty smiled contemptuously. "Of course you don't—till I tell you. I meant 'there's a nice knock-down argument for you!' "

"But 'glory' doesn't mean 'a nice knock-down argument,' " Alice objected.

"When *I* use a word," Humpty Dumpty said in rather a scornful tone, "it means just what I choose it to mean—neither more nor less."

"The question is," said Alice, "whether you *can* make words mean so many different things."

"The question is," said Humpty Dumpty, "which is to be master—that's all."

Alice was too much puzzled to say anything, so after a minute Humpty Dumpty began again. "They've a temper, some of them—particularly verbs, they're the proudest—adjectives you can do anything with, but not verbs—however, *I* can manage the whole lot of them! Impenetrability! That's what *I* say!"

"Would you tell me, please," said Alice, "what that means?"

"Now you talk like a reasonable child," said Humpty Dumpty, looking very much pleased, "I meant by 'impenetrability' that we've had enough of that subject, and it would be just as well if you'd mention what you mean to do next, as I suppose you don't mean to stop here all the rest of your life."

"That's a great deal to make one word mean," Alice said in a thoughtful tone.

"When I make a word do a lot of work like that," said Humpty Dumpty, "I always pay it extra."

"Oh!" said Alice. She was too much puzzled to make any other remark.

"Ah, you should see 'em come round me of a Saturday night," Humpty Dumpty went on, wagging his head gravely from side to side: "for to get their wages, you know."

(Alice didn't venture to ask what he paid them with; and so you see I can't tell *you*.)

"You seem very clever at explaining words, Sir," said Alice. "Would you kindly tell me the meaning of the poem called 'Jabberwocky'?"

"Let's hear it," said Humpty Dumpty. "I can explain all the poems that ever were invented—and a good many that haven't been invented just yet."

This sounded very hopeful, so Alice repeated the first voice:

> " 'Twas brillig, and the slithy toves
> Did gyre and gimble in the wabe:
> All mimsy were the borogoves,
> And she mome raths outgrabe."

"That's enough to begin with," Humpty Dumpty interrupted: "there are plenty of hard words there. '*Brillig*' means four o'clock in the afternoon—the time when you begin *broiling* things for dinner."

"That'll do very well," said Alice: "and '*slithy*'?"

"Well, '*slithy*' means 'lithe and slimy.' 'Lithe' is the same as 'active.' You see it's like a portmanteau*—there are two meanings packed up into one word."

"I see it now," Alice remarked thoughtfully: "and what are '*toves*'?"

"Well, '*toves*' are something like badgers—they're something like Lizards—and they're something like corkscrews."

"They must be very curious-looking creatures."

"They are that," said Humpty Dumpty, "also they make their nests under sun-dials—also they live on cheese."

"And what's to '*gyre*' and to '*gimble*'?"

"To '*gyre*' is to go round and round like a gyroscope. To '*gimble*' is to make holes like a gimblet."

---

*Travel bag that, when opened, reveals two equal compartments.

"And *'the wabe'* is the grass-plot round a sun-dial, I suppose?" said Alice, surprised at her own ingenuity.

"Of course it is. It's called *'wabe,'* you know, because it goes a long way before it, and a long way behind it—"

"And a long way beyond it on each side," Alice added.

"Exactly so. Well then, *'mimsy'* is 'flimsy and miserable' (there's another portmanteau for you). And a *'borogove'* is a thin shabby-looking bird with its feathers sticking out all round— something like a live mop."

"And then *'mome raths'*?" said Alice. "I'm afraid I'm giving you a great deal of trouble."

"Well, a *'rath'* is a sort of green pig: but *'mome'* I'm not certain about. I think it's short for 'from home'—meaning that they'd lost their way, you know."

"And what does *'outgrabe'* mean?"

"Well *'outgribing'* is something between bellowing and whistling, with a kind of sneeze in the middle: however, you'll hear it done, maybe—down in the wood yonder—and when you've once heard it you'll be *quite* content. Who's been repeating all that hard stuff to you?"

"I read it in a book," said Alice. "But I had some poetry repeated to me, much easier than that, by—Tweedledee, I think it was."

"As to poetry, you know," said Humpty Dumpty, stretching out one of his great hands, "*I* can repeat poetry as well as other folk, if it comes to that—"

"Oh, it needn't come to that!" Alice hastily said, hoping to keep him from beginning.

"The piece I'm going to repeat," he went on without noticing her remark, "was written entirely for your amusement."

Alice felt that in that case she really *ought* to listen to it, so she sat down, and said "Thank you" rather sadly.

> "*In winter, when the fields are white,*
> *I sing this song for your delight—*

only I don't sing it," he added, as an explanation.

"I see you don't," said Alice.

"If you can *see* whether I'm singing or not, you've sharper eyes than most," Humpty Dumpty remarked severely. Alice was silent.

> "*In spring, when woods are getting green,*
> *I'll try and tell you what I mean.*"

"Thank you very much," said Alice.

> "*In summer, when the days are long,*
> *Perhaps you'll understand the song:*

In Autumn, when the leaves are brown,
    Take pen and ink, and write it down."

"I will, if I can remember it so long," said Alice.

"You needn't go on making remarks like that," Humpty Dumpty said: "they're not sensible, and they put me out."

"I sent a message to the fish:
    I told them 'This is what I wish.'

The little fishes of the sea,
    They sent an answer back to me.

The little fishes' answer was
    'We cannot do it, Sir, because——'"

"I'm afraid I don't quite understand," said Alice.

"It gets easier further on," Humpty Dumpty replied.

" 'I sent to them again to say
    'It will be better to obey.'

The fishes answered with a grin,
    'Why, what a temper you are in!'

I told them once, I told them twice:
    They would not listen to advice.

I took a kettle large and new,
    Fit for the deed I had to do.

My heart went hop, my heart went thump;
    I filled the kettle at the pump.

Then some one came to me and said,
    'The little fishes are in bed.'

I said to him, I said it plain,
    'Then you must wake them up again.'

I said it very loud and clear;
  I went and shouted in his ear."

Humpty Dumpty raised his voice almost to a scream as he
repeated this verse, and Alice thought with a shudder, "I
wouldn't have been the messenger for *anything!*"

"But he was very stiff and proud;
  He said 'You needn't shout so loud!'

And he was very proud and stiff;
  He said 'I'd go and wake them, if—'

I took a corkscrew from the shelf;
  I went to wake them up myself.

And when I found the door was locked,
  I pulled and pushed and kicked and knocked.

And when I found the door was shut,
  I tried to turn the handle, but—"

There was a long pause.

"Is that all?" Alice timidly asked.

"That's all," said Humpty Dumpty. "Good-bye."

This was rather sudden, Alice thought: but, after such a *very* strong hint that she ought to be going, she felt that it would hardly be civil to stay. So she got up, and held out her hand. "Good-bye, till we meet again!" she said as cheerfully as she could.

"I shouldn't know you again if we *did* meet," Humpty Dumpty replied in a discontented tone, giving her one of his fingers to shake; "you're so exactly like other people."

"The face is what one goes by, generally," Alice remarked in a thoughtful tone.

"That's just what I complain of," said Humpty Dumpty. "Your face is the same as everybody has—the two eyes, so—" (marking their places in the air with his thumb) "nose in the middle, mouth under. It's always the same. Now if you had the two eyes on the same side of the nose, for instance—or the mouth at the top—that would be *some* help."

"It wouldn't look nice," Alice objected. But Humpty Dumpty only shut his eyes and said "Wait till you've tried."

Alice waited a minute to see if he would speak again, but as he never opened his eyes or took any further notice of her, she said "Good-bye!" once more, and, getting no answer to this, she quietly walked away: but she couldn't help saying to herself as she went, "Of all the unsatisfactory—" (she repeated this aloud, as it was a great comfort to have such a long word to say) "of all the unsatisfactory people I *ever* met—" She never finished the sentence, for at this moment a heavy crash shook the forest from end to end.

CHAPTER VII.

THE LION AND THE UNICORN.

The next moment soldiers came running through the wood, at first in twos and threes, then ten or twenty together, and at last in such crowds that they seemed to fill the whole forest. Alice got behind a tree, for fear of being run over, and watched them go by.

She thought that in all her life she had never seen soldiers so uncertain on their feet: they were always tripping over something or other, and whenever one went down, several more always fell over him, so that the ground was soon covered with little heaps of men.

Then came the horses. Having four feet, these managed rather better than the foot-soldiers: but even *they* stumbled now and then; and it seemed to be a regular rule that, whenever a horse stumbled, the rider fell off instantly. The confusion got worse every moment, and Alice was very glad to get out of the wood into an open place, where she found the White King seated on the ground, busily writing in his memorandom-book.

"I've sent them all!" the King cried in a tone of delight, on seeing Alice. "Did you happen to meet any soldiers, my dear, as you came through the wood?"

"Yes, I did," said Alice: "several thousand, I should think."

"Four thousand two hundred and seven, that's the exact number," the King said, referring to his book. "I couldn't send all the horses, you know, because two of them are wanted in the game. And I haven't sent the two Messengers, either. They're both gone to the town. Just look along the road, and tell me if you can see either of them."

"I see nobody on the road," said Alice.

"I only wish *I* had such eyes," the King remarked in a fretful tone. "To be able to see Nobody! And at that distance too! Why, it's as much as *I* can do to see real people, by this light!"

All this was lost on Alice, who was still looking intently along the road, shading her eyes with one hand. "I see somebody now!" she exclaimed at last. "But he's coming very slowly—and what curious attitudes he goes into!" (For the Messenger kept skipping up and down, and wriggling like an eel, as he came along, with his great hands spread out like fans on each side.)

"Not at all," said the King. "He's an Anglo-Saxon Messenger—and those are Anglo-Saxon attitudes. He only does them when he's happy. His name is Haigha." (He pronounced it so as to rhyme with 'mayor.')

"I love my love with an H," Alice couldn't help beginning, "because he is Happy. I hate him with an H, because he is Hideous. I fed him with—with—with Ham sandwiches and Hay. His name is Haigha, and he lives—"

"He lives on the Hill," the King remarked simply, without the least idea that he was joining in the game, while Alice was still hesitating for the name of a town beginning with H. "The other Messenger's called Hatta. I must have *two*, you know—to come and go. One to come, and one to go."

"I beg your pardon?" said Alice.

"It isn't respectable to beg," said the King.

"I only meant that I didn't understand," said Alice. "Why one to come and one to go?"

"Don't I tell you?" the King repeated impatiently. "I must have *two*—to fetch and carry. One to fetch, and one to carry."

At this moment the Messenger arrived: he was far too much out of breath to say a word, and could only wave his hands about, and make the most fearful faces at the poor King.

"This young lady loves you with an H," the King said, introducing Alice in the hope of turning off the Messengers attention from himself—but it was no use—the Anglo-Saxon attitudes only got more extraordinary every moment, while the great eyes rolled wildly from side to side.

"You alarm me!" said the King. "I feel faint—Give me a ham sandwich!"

On which the Messenger, to Alice's great amusement, opened a bag that hung round his neck, and handed a sandwich to the King, who devoured it greedily.

"Another sandwich!" said the King.

"There's nothing but hay left now," the Messenger said, peeping into the bag.

"Hay, then," the King murmured in a faint whisper.

Alice was glad to see that it revived him a good deal. "There's nothing like eating hay when you're faint," he remarked to her, as he munched away.

"I should think throwing cold water over you would be better," Alice suggested: "—or some sal-volatile."*

"I didn't say there was nothing *better*," the King replied. "I said there was nothing *like* it." Which Alice did not venture to deny.

"Who did you pass on the road?" the King went on, holding out his hand to the Messenger for some more hay.

"Nobody," said the Messenger.

"Quite right," said the King: "this young lady saw him too. So of course Nobody walks slower than you."

"I do my best," the Messenger said in a sullen tone. "I'm sure nobody walks much faster than I do!"

"He can't do that," said the King, "or else he'd have been here first. However, now you've got your breath, you may tell us what's happened in the town."

"I'll whisper it," said the Messenger, putting his hands to his mouth in the shape of a trumpet and stooping so as to get close to the King's ear. Alice was sorry for this, as she wanted to

---

*Smelling salts.

hear the news too. However, instead of whispering, he simply shouted at the top of his voice "They're at it again!"

"Do you call *that* a whisper?" cried the poor King, jumping up and shaking himself. "If you do such a thing again, I'll have you buttered! It went through and through my head like an earthquake!"

"It would have to be a very tiny earthquake!" thought Alice. "Who are at it again?" she ventured to ask.

"Why, the Lion and the Unicorn, of course," said the King.

"Fighting for the crown?"

"Yes, to be sure," said the King: "and the best of the joke is, that it's *my* crown all the while! Let's run and see them." And they trotted off, Alice repeating to herself, as she ran, the words of the old song:

> *"The Lion and the Unicorn were fighting for the crown:*
> *The Lion beat the Unicorn all round the town.*
> *Some gave them white bread, some gave them brown;*
> *Some gave them plum-cake and drummed them out of town."*

"Does—the one—that wins—get the crown?" she asked, as well as she could, for the run was putting her quite out of breath.

"Dear me, no!" said the King. "What an idea!"

"Would you—be good enough," Alice panted out, after running a little further, "to stop a minute—just to get—one's breath again?"

"I'm *good* enough," the King said, "only I'm not strong enough. You see, a minute goes by so fearfully quick. You might as well try to stop a Bandersnatch!"

Alice had no more breath for talking, so they trotted on in silence, till they come in sight of a great crowd, in the middle of which the Lion and Unicorn were fighting. They were in such a cloud of dust, that at first Alice could not make out which was which: but she soon managed to distinguish the Unicorn by his horn.

They placed themselves close to where Hatta, the other Messenger, was standing watching the fight, with a cup of tea in one hand and a piece of bread-and-butter in the other.

"He's only just out of prison, and he hadn't finished his tea when he was sent in," Haigha whispered to Alice: "and they only give them oyster-shells in there—so you see he's very hungry and thirsty. How are you, dear child?" he went on, putting his arm affectionately round Hatta's neck.

Hatta looked round and nodded, and went on with his bread-and-butter.

"Were you happy in prison, dear child?" said Haigha.

Hatta looked round once more, and this time a tear or two trickled down his cheek: but not a word would he say.

"Speak, can't you!" Haigha cried impatiently. But Hatta only munched away, and drank some more tea.

"Speak, won't you!" cried the King. "How are they getting on with the fight?"

Hatta made a desperate effort, and swallowed a large piece of bread-and-butter. "They're getting on very well," he said in a choking voice: "each of them has been down about eighty-seven times."

"Then I suppose they'll soon bring the white bread and the brown?" Alice ventured to remark.

"It's waiting for 'em now," said Hatta: "this is a bit of it as I'm eating."

There was a pause in the fight just then, and the Lion and the Unicorn sat down, panting, while the King called out "Ten minutes allowed for refreshments!" Haigha and Hatta set to work at once, carrying round trays of white and brown bread. Alice took a piece to taste, but it was *very* dry.

"I don't think they'll fight any more today," the King said to Hatta: "go and order the drums to begin." And Hatta went bounding away like a grasshopper.

For a minute or two Alice stood silent, watching him. Suddenly she brightened up. "Look, look!" she cried, pointing eagerly. "There's the White Queen running across the country! She came flying out of the wood over yonder—How fast those Queens *can* run!"

"There's some enemy after her, no doubt," the King said, without even looking round. "That wood's full of them."

"But aren't you going to run and help her?" Alice asked, very much surprised at his taking it so quietly.

"No use, no use!" said the King. "She runs so fearfully quick. You might as well try to catch a Bandersnatch! But I'll make a memorandum about her, if you like—She's a dear good creature," he repeated softly to himself, as he opened his memorandum-book. "Do you spell 'creature' with a double 'e'?"

At this moment the Unicorn sauntered by them, with his hands in his pockets. "I had the best of it this time?" he said to the King, just glancing at him as he passed.

"A little—a little," the King replied, rather nervously. "You shouldn't have run him through with your horn, you know."

"It didn't hurt him," the Unicorn said carelessly, and he was going on, when his eye happened to fall upon Alice: he turned round instantly, and stood for some time looking at her with an air of the deepest disgust.

"What—is—this?" he said at last.

"This is a child!" Haigha replied eagerly, coming in front of Alice to introduce her, and spreading out both his hands towards her in an Anglo-Saxon attitude. "We only found it to-day. It's as large as life, and twice as natural!"

"I always thought they were fabulous monsters!" said the Unicorn. "Is it alive?"

"It can talk," said Haigha, solemnly.

The Unicorn looked dreamily at Alice, and said "Talk, child."

Alice could not help her lips curling up into a smile as she began: "Do you know, I always thought Unicorns were fabulous monsters, too! I never saw one alive before!"

"Well, now that we *have* seen each other," said the Unicorn, "if you'll believe in me, I'll believe in you. Is that a bargain?"

"Yes, if you like," said Alice.

"Come, fetch out the plum-cake, old man!" the Unicorn went on, turning from her to the King. "None of your brown bread for me!"

"Certainly—certainly!" the King muttered, and beckoned to Haigha. "Open the bag!" he whispered. "Quick! Not that one—that's full of hay!"

Haigha took a large cake out of the bag, and gave it to Alice to hold, while he got out a dish and carving-knife. How they all came out of it Alice couldn't guess. It was just like a conjuring-trick, she thought.

The Lion had joined them while this was going on: he looked very tired and sleepy, and his eyes were half shut. "What's this!" he said, blinking lazily at Alice, and speaking in a deep hollow tone that sounded like the tolling of a great bell.

"Ah, what *is* it, now?" the Unicorn cried eagerly. "You'll never guess! *I* couldn't."

The Lion looked at Alice wearily. "Are you animal—or vegetable—or mineral?" he said, yawning at every other word.

"It's a fabulous monster!" the Unicorn cried out, before Alice could reply.

"Then hand round the plum-cake, Monster," the Lion said, lying down and putting his chin on his paws. "And sit down, both of you," (to the King and the Unicorn): "fair play with the cake, you know!"

The King was evidently very uncomfortable at having to sit down between the two great creatures; but there was no other place for him.

"What a fight we might have for the crown, *now!*" the Unicorn

said, looking slyly up at the crown, which the poor King was
nearly shaking off his head, he trembled so much.

"I should win easy," said the Lion.

"I'm not so sure of that," said the Unicorn.

"Why, I beat you all round the town, you chicken!" the Lion
replied angrily, half getting up as he spoke.

Here the King interrupted, to prevent the quarrel going on:
he was very nervous, and his voice quite quivered. "All round
the town?" he said. "That's a good long way. Did you go by the
old bridge, or the marketplace? You get the best view by the
old bridge."

"I'm sure I don't know," the Lion growled out as he lay
down again. "There was too much dust to see anything. What a
time the Monster is, cutting up that cake!"

Alice had seated herself on the bank of a little brook, with
the great dish on her knees, and was sawing away diligently
with the knife. "It's very provoking!" she said, in reply to the
Lion (she was getting quite used to being called 'the Monster'). "I've cut several slices already, but they always join on
again!"

"You don't know how to manage Looking-glass cakes," the Unicorn remarked. "Hand it round first, and cut it afterwards."

This sounded nonsense, but Alice very obediently got up, and carried the dish round, and the cake divided itself into three pieces as she did so. "*Now* cut it up," said the Lion, as she returned to her place with the empty dish.

"I say, this isn't fair!" cried the Unicorn, as Alice sat with the knife in her hand, very much puzzled how to begin. "The Monster has given the Lion twice as much as me!"

"She's kept none for herself, anyhow," said the Lion. "Do you like plum-cake, Monster?"

But before Alice could answer him, the drums began.

Where the noise came from she couldn't make out: the air seemed full of it, and it rang through and through her head till she felt quite deafened. She started to her feet and sprang across the little brook in terror,

and had just time to see the Lion and the Unicorn rise to their feet, with angry looks at being interrupted in their feast, before she dropped to her knees, and put her hands over her ears, vainly trying to shut out the dreadful uproar.

"If *that* doesn't 'drum them out of town,'" she thought to herself "nothing ever will!"

CHAPTER VIII.

"IT'S MY OWN INVENTION."

After a while the noise seemed gradually to die away, till all was dead silence, and Alice lifted up her head in some alarm. There was no one to be seen, and her first thought was that she must have been dreaming about the Lion and the Unicorn and those queer Anglo-Saxon Messengers. However, there was the great dish still lying at her feet, on which she had tried to cut the plum-cake. "So I wasn't dreaming, after all," she said to herself, "unless—unless we're all part of the same dream. Only I do hope it's *my* dream, and not the Red King's! I don't like belonging to another person's dream," she went on in a rather complaining tone: "I've a great mind to go and wake him, and see what happens!"

At this moment her thoughts were interrupted by a loud shouting of "Ahoy! Ahoy! Check!" and a Knight dressed in crimson armour, came galloping down upon her, brandishing a great club. Just as he reached her, the horse stopped suddenly: "You're my prisoner!" the Knight cried, as he tumbled off his horse.

Startled as she was, Alice was more frightened for him than for herself at the moment, and watched him with some anxiety as he mounted again. As soon as he was comfortably in the saddle, he began once more "You're my—" but here another voice broke in "Ahoy! Ahoy! Check!" and Alice looked round in some surprise for the new enemy.

This time it was a White Knight.[6] He drew up at Alice's side, and tumbled off his horse just as the Red Knight had done: then he got on again, and the two Knights sat and looked at each other for some time without speaking. Alice looked from one to the other in some bewilderment.

237

"She's *my* prisoner, you know!" the Red Knight said at last.

"Yes, but then *I* came and rescued her!" the White Knight replied.

"Well, we must fight for her, then," said the Red Knight, as he took up his helmet (which hung from the saddle, and was something the shape of a horse's head), and put it on.

"You will observe the rules of Battle, of course?" the White Knight remarked, putting on his helmet too.

"I always do," said the Red Knight, and they began banging away at each other with such fury that Alice got behind a tree to be out of the way of the blows.

"I wonder, now, what the rules of Battle are," she said to herself, as she watched the fight, timidly peeping out from her hiding-place: "one Rule seems to be, that if one Knight hits the other, he knocks him off his horse, and if he misses, he tumbles off himself—and another rule seems to be that they hold their clubs with their arms, as if they were Punch and Judy—What a noise they make when they tumble! Just like a whole set of fire-irons falling into the fender! And how quiet the horses are! They let them get on and off them just as if they were tables!"

Another Rule of Battle, that Alice had not noticed, seemed to be that they always fell on their heads, and the battle ended with their both falling off in this way, side by side: when they got up again, they shook hands, and then the Red Knight mounted and galloped off.

"It was a glorious victory, wasn't it?" said the White Knight, as he came up panting.

"I don't know," Alice said doubtfully. "I don't want to be anybody's prisoner. I want to be a Queen."

"So you will when you've crossed the next brook," said the White Knight. "I'll see you safe to the end of the wood—and then I must go back, you know. That's the end of my move."

"Thank you very much," said Alice. "May I help you off with your helmet?" It was evidently more than he could manage by himself; however she managed to shake him out of it at last.

"Now one can breathe more easily," said the Knight, putting back his shaggy hair with both hands, and turning his gentle face and large mild eyes to Alice. She thought she had never seen such a strange-looking soldier in all her life.

He was dressed in tin armour, which seemed to fit him very badly, and he had a queer-shaped little deal box fastened across his shoulders, upside-down, and with the lid hanging open. Alice looked at it with great curiosity.

"I see you're admiring my little box," the Knight said in a friendly tone. "It's my own invention—to keep clothes and sandwiches in. You see I carry it upside-down, so that the rain can't get in."

"But the things can get *out*," Alice gently remarked. "Do you know the lid's open?"

"I didn't know it," the Knight said, a shade of vexation passing over his face. "Then all the things must have fallen out! And the box is no use without them." He unfastened it as he spoke, and was just going to throw it into the bushes, when a sudden thought seemed to strike him, and he hung it carefully on a tree. "Can you guess why I did that?" he said to Alice.

Alice shook her head.

"In hopes some bees may make a nest in it—then I should get the honey."

"But you've got a bee-hive—or something like one—fastened to the saddle," said Alice.

"Yes, it's a very good bee-hive," the Knight said in a discontented tone, "one of the best kind. But not a single bee has come near it yet. And the other thing is a mouse-trap. I suppose the mice keep the bees out—or the bees keep the mice out, I don't know which."

"I was wondering what the mouse-trap was for," said Alice. "It isn't very likely there would be any mice on the horse's back."

"Not very likely, perhaps," said the Knight; "but, if they *do* come, I don't choose to have them running all about."

"You see," he went on after a pause, "it's as well to be provided for *everything*. That's the reason the horse has all those anklets round his feet."

"But what are they for?" Alice asked in a tone of great curiosity.

"To guard against the bites of sharks," the Knight replied. "It's an invention of my own. And now help me on. I'll go with you to the end of the wood—What's that dish for?"

"It's meant for plum-cake," said Alice.

"We'd better take it with us," the Knight said. "It'll come in handy if we find any plum-cake. Help me to get it into this bag."

This took a long time to manage, though Alice held the bag open very carefully, because the Knight was so *very* awkward in putting in the dish: the first two or three times that he tried he fell in himself instead. "It's rather a tight fit, you see," he said, as they got it in at last; "there are so many candlesticks in the bag." And he hung it to the saddle, which was already loaded with bunches of carrots, and fire-irons, and many other things.

"I hope you've got your hair well fastened on?" he continued, as they set off.

"Only in the usual way," Alice said, smiling.

"That's hardly enough," he said, anxiously. "You see the wind is so *very* strong here. It's as strong as soup."

"Have you invented a plan for keeping the hair from being blown off?" Alice inquired.

"Not yet," said the Knight. "But I've got a plan for keeping it from *falling* off."

"I should like to hear it, very much."

"First you take an upright stick," said the Knight. "Then you make your hair creep up it, like a fruit tree. Now the reason hair falls off is because it hangs *down*—things never fall *upwards*, you know. It's a plan of my own invention. You may try it if you like."

It didn't sound a comfortable plan, Alice thought, and for a few minutes she walked on in silence, puzzling over the idea, and every now and then stopping to help the poor Knight, who certainly was *not* a good rider.

Whenever the horse stopped (which it did very often), he fell off in front; and whenever it went on again (which it generally did rather suddenly), he fell off behind. Otherwise he kept on pretty well, except that he had a habit of now and then falling off sideways; and as he generally did this on the side on which Alice was walking, she soon found that it was the best plan not to walk *quite* close to the horse.

"I'm afraid you've not had much practice in riding," she ventured to say, as she was helping him up from his fifth tumble.

The Knight looked very much surprised, and a little offended at the remark. "What makes you say that?" he asked, as he scrambled back into the saddle, keeping hold of Alice's hair with one hand, to save himself from falling over on the other side.

"Because people don't fall off quite so often, when they've had much practice."

"I've had plenty of practice," the Knight said very gravely: "plenty of practice!"

Alice could think of nothing better to say than "Indeed?" but she said it as heartily as she could. They went on a little way in silence after this, the Knight with his eyes shut, muttering to himself, and Alice watching anxiously for the next tumble.

"The great art of riding," the Knight suddenly began in a loud voice, waving his right arm as he spoke, "is to keep—" Here the sentence ended as suddenly as it had begun, as the Knight fell heavily on the top of his head exactly in the path where Alice was walking. She was quite frightened this time, and said in an anxious tone, as she picked him up, "I hope no bones are broken?"

"None to speak of," the Knight said, as if he didn't mind breaking two or three of them. "The great art of riding, as I was saying, is—to keep your balance properly. Like this, you know—"

He let go the bridle, and stretched out both his arms to show Alice what he meant, and this time he fell flat on his back, right under the horse's feet.

"Plenty of practice!" he went on repeating, all the time that Alice was getting him on his feet again. "Plenty of practice!"

"It's too ridiculous!" cried Alice, losing all her patience this time. "You ought to have a wooden horse on wheels, that you ought!"

"Does that kind go smoothly?" the Knight asked in a tone of great interest, clasping his arms round the horse's neck as he spoke, just in time to save himself from tumbling off again.

"Much more smoothly than a live horse," Alice said, with a little scream of laughter, in spite of all she could do to prevent it.

"I'll get one," the Knight said thoughtfully to himself. "One or two—several."

There was a short silence after this, and then the Knight went on again. "I'm a great hand at inventing things. Now, I daresay you noticed, the last time you picked me up, that I was looking rather thoughtful?"

"You *were* a little grave," said Alice.

"Well, just then I was inventing a new way of getting over a gate—would you like to hear it?"

"Very much indeed," Alice said politely.

"I'll tell you how I came to think of it," said the Knight. "You see, I said to myself, 'The only difficulty is with the feet: the *head* is high enough already.' Now, first I put my head on the top of the gate—then the head's high enough—then I stand on my head—then the feet are high enough, you see—then I'm over, you see."

"Yes, I suppose you'd be over when that was done," Alice said thoughtfully: "but don't you think it would be rather hard?"

"I haven't tried it yet," the Knight said, gravely, "so I can't tell for certain—but I'm afraid it *would* be a little hard."

He looked so vexed at the idea, that Alice changed the subject hastily. "What a curious helmet you've got!" she said cheerfully. "Is that your invention too?"

The Knight looked down proudly at his helmet, which hung from the saddle. "Yes," he said, "but I've invented a better one than that—like a sugar-loaf.* When I used to wear it, if I fell off of the horse, it always touched the ground directly. So I had

---

*Sugarloaf hats, which were cone-shaped, were common in the sixteenth century.

a *very* little way to fall, you see—But there *was* the danger of falling *into* it, to be sure. That happened to me once—and the worst of it was, before I could get out again, the other White Knight came and put it on. He thought it was his own helmet."

The Knight looked so solemn about it that Alice did not dare to laugh. "I'm afraid you must have hurt him," she said in a trembling voice, "being on the top of his head."

"I had to kick him, of course," the Knight said, very seriously. "And then he took the helmet off again—but it took hours and hours to get me out. I was as fast as—as lightning, you know."

"But that's a different kind of fastness," Alice objected.

The Knight shook his head. "It was all kinds of fastness with me, I can assure you!" he said. He raised his hands in some excitement as he said this, and instantly rolled out of the saddle, and fell headlong into a deep ditch.

Alice ran to the side of the ditch to look for him. She was rather startled by the fall, as for some time he had kept on very well, and she was afraid that he really *was* hurt this time. However, though she could see nothing but the soles of his feet, she was much relieved to hear that he was talking on in his usual tone. "All kinds of fastness," he repeated: "but it was careless of him to put another man's helmet on—with the man in it, too."

"How *can* you go on talking so quietly, head downwards?" Alice asked, as she dragged him out by the feet, and laid him in a heap on the bank.

The Knight looked surprised at the question. "What does it matter where my body happens to be?" he said. "My mind goes on working all the same. In fact, the more head downwards I am, the more I keep inventing new things."

"Now the cleverest thing of the sort that I ever did," he went on after a pause, "was inventing a new pudding during the meat-course."

"In time to have it cooked for the next course?" said Alice. "Well, that *was* quick work, certainly!"

"Well, not the *next* course," the Knight said in a slow thoughtful tone: "no, certainly not the next *course*."

"Then it would have to be the next day. I suppose you wouldn't have two pudding-courses in one dinner?"

"Well, not the *next* day," the Knight repeated as before: "not the next *day*. In fact," he went on, holding his head down, and his voice getting lower and lower, "I don't believe that pudding ever *was* cooked! In fact, I don't believe that pudding ever *will* be cooked! And yet it was a very clever pudding to invent."

"What did you mean it to be made of?" Alice asked, hoping to cheer him up, for the poor Knight seemed quite low-spirited about it.

"It began with blotting-paper," the Knight answered with a groan.

"That wouldn't be very nice, I'm afraid—"

"Not very nice *alone*," he interrupted, quite eagerly: "but you've no idea what a difference it makes, mixing it with other things—such as gunpowder and sealing-wax. And here I must leave you." They had just come to the end of the wood.

Alice could only look puzzled: she was thinking of the pudding.

"You are sad," the Knight said in an anxious tone: "let me sing you a song to comfort you."

"Is it very long?" Alice asked, for she had heard a good deal of poetry that day.

"It's long," said the Knight, "but it's very, *very* beautiful.

Everybody that hears me sing it—either it brings the *tears* into their eyes, or else—"

"Or else what?" said Alice, for the Knight had made a sudden pause.

"Or else it doesn't, you know. The name of the song is called 'Haddocks' Eyes.'"

"Oh, that's the name of the song, is it?" Alice said, trying to feel interested.

"No, you don't understand," the Knight said, looking a little vexed. "That's what the name is *called*. The name really *is* 'The Aged Aged Man.'"

"Then I ought to have said 'That's what the *song* is called'?" Alice corrected herself.

"No, you oughtn't: that's quite another thing! The *song* is called 'Ways and Means': but that's only what it's *called,* you know!"

"Well, what *is* the song, then?" said Alice, who was by this time completely bewildered.

"I was coming to that," the Knight said. "The song really *is* 'A-sitting On A Gate': and the tune's my own invention."

So saying, he stopped his horse and let the reins fall on its neck: then, slowly beating time with one hand, and with a faint smile lighting up his gentle foolish face, as if he enjoyed the music of his song, he began.

Of all the strange things that Alice saw in her journey Through the Looking-Glass, this was the one that she always remembered most clearly. Years afterwards she could bring the whole scene back again, as if it had been only yesterday—the mild blue eyes and kindly smile of the Knight—the setting sun gleaming through his hair, and shining on his armour in a blaze of light that quite dazzled her—the horse quietly moving about, with the reins hanging loose on his neck, cropping the grass at her feet—and the black shadows of the forest behind— all this she took in like a picture, as, with one hand shading her eyes, she leant against a tree, watching the strange pair, and listening, in a half dream, to the melancholy music of the song.

"But the tune *isn't* his own invention," she said to herself: "it's 'I give thee all, I can no more.'"[7] She stood and listened very attentively, but no tears came into her eyes.

"I'll tell thee everything I can;
    There's little to relate.
I saw an aged aged man,
    A-sitting on a gate.
'Who are you, aged man?' I said.
    'And how is it you live?'
And his answer trickled through my head
    Like water through a sieve.

He said 'I look for butterflies
    That sleep among the wheat:
I make them into mutton-pies,
    And sell them in the street.
I sell them unto men,' he said,
    'Who sail on stormy seas;
And that's the way I get my bread—
    A trifle, if you please.'

But I was thinking of a plan
    To dye one's whiskers green,
And always use so large a fan
    That they could not be seen.
So, having no reply to give
    To what the old man said,
I cried 'Come, tell me how you live!'
    And thumped him on the head.

His accents mild took up the tale:
    He said 'I go my ways,
And when I find a mountain-rill,
    I set it in a blaze;
And thence they make a stuff they call
    Rowlands' Macassar Oil*—*
Yet twopence-halfpenny is all
    They give me for my toil.'

---

*A hair dressing.

But I was thinking of a way
  To feed oneself on batter,
And so go on from day to day
  Getting a little fatter.
I shook him well from side to side,
  Until his face was blue:
'Come, tell me how you live,' I cried,
  'And what it is you do!'

He said 'I hunt for haddocks' eyes
  Among the heather bright,
And work them into waistcoat-buttons
  In the silent night.
And these I do not sell for gold
  Or coin of silvery shine,
But for a copper halfpenny,
  And that will purchase nine.

'I sometimes dig for buttered rolls,
  Or set limed twigs* for crabs;

*Small branches covered with bird lime; used to trap birds.

I sometimes search the grassy knolls
    For wheels of Hansom-cabs.*
And that's the way' (he gave a wink)
    'By which I get my wealth—
And very gladly will I drink
    Your Honor's noble health.'

I heard him then, for I had just
    Completed my design
To keep the Menai bridge† from rust
    By boiling it in wine.
I thanked him much for telling me
    The way he got his wealth,
But chiefly for his wish that he
    Might drink my noble health.

And now, if e'er by chance I put
    My fingers into glue,
Or madly squeeze a right-hand foot
    Into a left-hand shoe,
Or if I drop upon my toe
    A very heavy weight,
I weep, for it reminds me so
Of that old man I used to know—
Whose look was mild, whose speech was slow,
Whose hair was whiter than the snow,
Whose face was very like a crow,
With eyes, like cinders, all aglow,
Who seemed distracted with his woe,
Who rocked his body to and fro,
And muttered mumblingly and low,
As if his mouth were full of dough,
Who snorted like a buffalo—

---

*Carriages with two wheels, common around the turn of century; frequently hired out.
†Located in Wales.

> *That summer evening, long ago,*
>   *A-sitting on a gate. "*

As the Knight sang the last words of the ballad, he gathered up the reins, and turned his horse's head along the road by which they had come. "You've only a few yards to go," he said, "down the hill and over that little brook, and then you'll be a Queen— But you'll stay and see me off first?" he added as Alice turned with an eager look in the direction to which he pointed. "I shan't be long. You'll wait and wave your handkerchief when I get to that turn in the road? I think it'll encourage me, you see."

"Of course I'll wait," said Alice: "and thank you very much for coming so far—and for the song—I liked it very much."

"I hope so," the Knight said doubtfully: "but you didn't cry so much as I thought you would."

So they shook hands, and then the Knight rode slowly away into the forest. "It won't take long to see him *off*, I expect," Alice said to herself, as she stood watching him. "There he goes! Right on his head as usual! However, he gets on again pretty easily— that comes of having so many things hung round the horse—" So she went on talking to herself, as she watched the horse walking leisurely along the road, and the Knight tumbling off, first on one side and then on the other. After the fourth or fifth tumble he reached the turn, and then she waved her handkerchief to him, and waited till he was out of sight.

"I hope it encouraged him," she said, as she turned to run down the hill: "and now for the last brook, and to be a Queen! How grand it sounds!" A very few steps brought her to the edge of the brook. "The Eighth Square at last!" she cried as she bounded across,

       *   *   *   *   *
          *   *   *   *
       *   *   *   *   *

and threw herself down to rest on a lawn as soft as moss, with little flower-beds, dotted about it here and there. "Oh, how glad I am to get here! And what *is* this on my head?" she exclaimed in a tone of dismay, as she put her hands up to something very heavy, that fitted tight all round her head.

"But how *can* it have got there without my knowing it?" she said to herself, as she lifted it off, and set it on her lap to make out what it could possibly be.

It was a golden crown.

CHAPTER IX.

QUEEN ALICE.

Well, this *is* grand!" said Alice. "I never expected I should be a Queen so soon—and I'll tell you what it is, your Majesty," she went on in a severe tone (she was always rather fond of scolding herself), "it'll never do for you to be lolling about on the grass like that! Queens have to be dignified, you know!"

So she got up and walked about—rather stiffly just at first, as she was afraid that the crown might come off: but she comforted herself with the thought that there was nobody to see her, "and if I really am a Queen," she said as she sat down again, "I shall be able to manage it quite well in time."

Everything was happening so oddly that she didn't feel a bit surprised at finding the Red Queen and the White Queen sitting close to her, one on each side: she would have liked very much to ask them how they came there, but she feared it would not be quite civil. However, there would be no harm, she thought, in asking if the game was over. "Please, would you tell me—" she began, looking timidly at the Red Queen.

"Speak when you're spoken to!" the Queen sharply interrupted her.

"But if everybody obeyed that rule," said Alice, who was always ready for a little argument, "and if you only spoke when you were spoken to, and the other person always waited for *you* to begin, you see nobody would ever say anything, so that—"

"Ridiculous!" cried the Queen. "Why, don't you see, child—" here she broke off with a frown, and, after thinking for a minute, suddenly changed the subject of the conversation. "What do you mean by 'If you really are a Queen'? What right have you to call yourself so? You can't be a Queen, you know, till you've passed the proper examination. And the sooner we begin it, the better."

"I only said 'if'!" poor Alice pleaded in a piteous tone.

The two Queens looked at each other, and the Red Queen remarked, with a little shudder, "She *says* she only said 'if'—"

"But she said a great deal more than that!" the White Queen moaned, wringing her hands. "Oh, ever so much more than that!"

"So you did, you know," the Red Queen said to Alice. "Always speak the truth—think before you speak—and write it down afterwards."

"I'm sure I didn't mean—" Alice was beginning, but the Red Queen interrupted her impatiently.

"That's just what I complain of! You *should* have meant! What do you suppose is the use of a child without any meaning? Even a joke should have some meaning—and a child's more important than a joke, I hope. You couldn't deny that, even if you tried with both hands."

"I don't deny things with my *hands*," Alice objected.

"Nobody said you did," said the Red Queen. "I said you couldn't if you tried."

"She's in that state of mind," said the White Queen, "that she wants to deny *something*—only she doesn't know what to deny!"

"A nasty, vicious temper," the Red Queen remarked; and then there was an uncomfortable silence for a minute or two.

The Red Queen broke the silence by saying to the White Queen, "I invite you to Alice's dinner-party this afternoon."

The White Queen smiled feebly, and said "And I invite *you*."

"I didn't know I was to have a party at all," said Alice; "but if there is to be one, I think *I* ought to invite the guests."

"We gave you the opportunity of doing it," the Red Queen remarked: "but I daresay you've not had many lessons in manners yet?"

"Manners are not taught in lessons," said Alice. "Lessons teach you to do sums, and things of that sort."

"Can you do Addition?" the White Queen asked. "What's one and one and one and one and one and one and one and one and one and one?"

"I don't know," said Alice. "I lost count."

"She can't do Addition," the Red Queen interrupted. "Can you do Subtraction? Take nine from eight."

"Nine from eight I can't, you know," Alice replied very readily: "but—"

"She can't do Subtraction," said the White Queen. "Can you do Division? Divide a loaf by a knife—what's the answer to that?"

"I suppose—" Alice was beginning, but the Red Queen answered for her. "Bread-and-butter, of course. Try another Subtraction sum. Take a bone from a dog: what remains?"

Alice considered. "The bone wouldn't remain, of course, if I took it—and the dog wouldn't remain; it would come to bite me—and I'm sure *I* shouldn't remain!"

"Then you think nothing would remain?" said the Red Queen.

"I think that's the answer."

"Wrong, as usual," said the Red Queen, "the dog's temper would remain."

"But I don't see how—"

"Why, look here!" the Red Queen cried. "The dog would lose its temper, wouldn't it?"

"Perhaps it would," Alice replied cautiously.

"Then if the dog went away, its temper would remain!" the Queen exclaimed triumphantly.

Alice said, as gravely as she could, "They might go different ways." But she couldn't help thinking to herself, "What dreadful nonsense we *are* talking!"

"She can't do sums a *bit!*" the Queens said together, with great emphasis.

"Can *you* do sums?" Alice said, turning suddenly on the White Queen, for she didn't like being found fault with so much.

The Queen gasped and shut her eyes. "I can do Addition," she said, "if you give me time—but I can't do Subtraction under *any* circumstances!"

"Of course you know your A B C?" said the Red Queen.

"To be sure I do," said Alice.

"So do I," the White Queen whispered: "we'll often say it

over together, dear. And I'll tell you a secret—I can read words of one letter! Isn't *that* grand? However, don't be discouraged. You'll come to it in time."

Here the Red Queen began again. "Can you answer useful questions?" she said. "How is bread made?"

"I know *that!*" Alice cried eagerly. "You take some flour—"

"Where do you pick the flower?" the White Queen asked. "In a garden, or in the hedges?"

"Well, it isn't *picked* at all," Alice explained: "it's *ground*—"

"How many acres of ground?" said the White Queen. "You mustn't leave out so many things."

"Fan her head!" the Red Queen anxiously interrupted. "She'll be feverish after so much thinking." So they set to work and fanned her with bunches of leaves, till she had to beg them to leave off, it blew her hair about so.

"She's all right again now," said the Red Queen. "Do you know languages? What's the French for fiddle-de-dee?"

"Fiddle-de-dee's not English," Alice replied gravely.

"Who ever said it was?" said the Red Queen.

Alice thought she saw a way out of the difficulty this time. "If you'll tell me what language 'fiddle-de-dee' is, I'll tell you the French for it!" she exclaimed triumphantly.

But the Red Queen drew herself up rather stiffly, and said "Queens never make bargains."

"I wish Queens never asked questions," Alice thought to herself.

"Don't let us quarrel," the White Queen said in an anxious tone. "What is the cause of lightning?"

"The cause of lightning," Alice said very decidedly, for she felt quite certain about this, "is the thunder—no, no!" she hastily corrected herself. "I meant the other way."

"It's too late to correct it," said the Red Queen: "when you've once said a thing, that fixes it, and you must take the consequences."

"Which reminds me—" the White Queen said, looking down and nervously clasping and unclasping her hands, "we had *such* a thunder-storm last Tuesday—I mean one of the last set of Tuesdays, you know."

Alice was puzzled. "In *our* country," she remarked, "there's only one day at a time."

The Red Queen said "That's a poor thin way of doing things. Now *here*, we mostly have days and nights two or three at a time, and sometimes in the winter we take as many as five nights together—for warmth, you know."

"Are five nights warmer than one night, then?" Alice ventured to ask.

"Five times as warm, of course."

"But they should be five times as *cold*, by the same rule—"

"Just so!" cried the Red Queen. "Five times as warm, *and* five times as cold—just as I'm five times as rich as you are, *and* five times as clever!"

Alice sighed and gave it up. "It's exactly like a riddle with no answer!" she thought.

"Humpty Dumpty saw it too," the White Queen went on in a low voice, more as if she were talking to herself. "He came to the door with a corkscrew in his hand—"

"What did he want?" said the Red Queen.

"He said he *would* come in," the White Queen went on, "because he was looking for a hippopotamus. Now, as it happened, there wasn't such a thing in the house, that morning."

"Is there generally?" Alice asked in an astonished tone.

"Well, only on Thursdays," said the Queen.

"I know what he came for," said Alice: "he wanted to punish the fish, because—"

Here the White Queen began again. "It was *such* a thunderstorm, you can't think!" ("She *never* could, you know," said the Red Queen.) "And part of the roof came off, and ever so much thunder got in—and it went rolling round the room in great lumps—and knocking over the tables and things—till I was so frightened, I couldn't remember my own name!"

Alice thought to herself, "I never should *try* to remember my name in the middle of an accident! Where would be the use of it?" but she did not say this aloud, for fear of hurting the poor Queen's feelings.

"Your Majesty must excuse her," the Red Queen said to

Alice, taking one of the White Queen's hands in her own, and gently stroking it: "she means well, but she can't help saying foolish things, as a general rule."

The White Queen looked timidly at Alice, who felt she *ought* to say something kind, but really couldn't think of anything at the moment.

"She never was really well brought up," the Red Queen went on: "but it's amazing how good tempered she is! Pat her on the head, and see how pleased she'll be!" But this was more than Alice had courage to do.

"A little kindness—and putting her hair in papers*—would do wonders with her—"

The White Queen gave a deep sigh, and laid her head on Alice's shoulder. "I *am* so sleepy!" she moaned.

"She's tired, poor thing!" said the Red Queen. "Smooth her hair—lend her your nightcap—and sing her a soothing lullaby."

"I haven't got a nightcap with me," said Alice, as she tried to obey the first direction: "and I don't know any soothing lullabies."

"I must do it myself, then," said the Red Queen, and she began:

> *"Hush-a-by lady, in Alice's lap!*
> *Till the feast's ready, we've time for a nap:*
> *When the feast's over, we'll go to the ball—*
> *Red Queen, and White Queen, and Alice, and all!"*

"And now you know the words," she added, as she put her head down on Alice's other shoulder, "just sing it through to *me*. I'm getting sleepy too." In another moment both Queens were fast asleep, and snoring loud.

"What *am* I to do?" exclaimed Alice, looking about in great perplexity, as first one round head, and then the other, rolled down from her shoulder, and lay like a heavy lump in her lap.

---

*Curlers.

"I don't think it *ever* happened before, that any one had to take care of two Queens asleep at once! No, not in all the History of England—it couldn't, you know, because there never was more than one Queen at a time. Do wake up, you heavy things!" she went on in an impatient tone; but there was no answer but a gentle snoring.

The snoring got more distinct every minute, and sounded more like a tune: at last she could even make out words, and she listened so eagerly that, when the two great heads suddenly vanished from her lap, she hardly missed them.

She was standing before an arched doorway over which were the words QUEEN ALICE in large letters, and on each side of the arch there was a bell-handle; one was marked "Visitors' Bell," and the other "Servants' Bell."

"I'll wait till the song's over," thought Alice, "and then I'll ring the—the—*which* bell must I ring?" she went on, very much puzzled by the names. "I'm not a visitor, and I'm not a servant. There *ought* to be one marked 'Queen,' you know—"

Just then the door opened a little way, and a creature with a long beak put its head out for a moment and said "No admittance till the week after next!" and shut the door again with a bang.

Alice knocked and rang in vain for a long time, but at last a

very old Frog, who was sitting under a tree, got up and hobbled slowly towards her: he was dressed in bright yellow, and
had enormous boots on.

"What is it, now?" the Frog said in a deep hoarse whisper.

Alice turned round, ready to find fault with anybody.
"Where's the servant whose business it is to answer the door?"
she began angrily.

"Which door?" said the Frog.

Alice almost stamped with irritation at the slow drawl in
which he spoke. "*This* door, of course!"

The Frog looked at the door with his large dull eyes for a
minute: then he went nearer and rubbed it with his thumb, as
if he were trying whether the paint would come off; then he
looked at Alice.

"To answer the door?" he said. "What's it been asking of?"
He was so hoarse that Alice could scarcely hear him.

"I don't know what you mean," she said.

"I speaks English, doesn't I?" the Frog went on. "Or are you deaf? What did it ask you?"

"Nothing!" Alice said impatiently. "I've been knocking at it!"

"Shouldn't do that—shouldn't do that—" the Frog muttered. "Wexes it, you know." Then he went up and gave the door a kick with one of his great feet. "You let *it* alone," he panted out, as he hobbled back to his tree, "and it'll let *you* alone, you know."

At this moment the door was flung open, and a shrill voice was heard singing:

"To the Looking-Glass world it was Alice that said,
'I've a sceptre in hand, I've a crown on my head;
Let the Looking-Glass creatures, whatever they be,
Come and dine with the Red Queen, the White Queen and me!'"

And hundreds of voices joined in the chorus:

"Then fill up the glasses as quick as you can,
And sprinkle the table with buttons and bran:
Put cats in the coffee, and mice in the tea—
And welcome Queen Alice with thirty-times-three!"

Then followed a confused noise of cheering, and Alice thought to herself, "Thirty times three makes ninety. I wonder if any one's counting?" In a minute there was silence again, and the same shrill voice sang another verse:

" 'O Looking-Glass creatures,' quoth Alice, 'draw near!
'Tis an honor to see me, a favor to hear:
'Tis a privilege high to have dinner and tea
Along with the Red Queen, the White Queen, and me!'"

Then came the chorus again:

"Then fill up the glasses with treacle and ink,
Or anything else that is pleasant to drink;
Mix sand with the cider, and wool with the wine—
And welcome Queen Alice with ninety-times-nine!"[8]

"Ninety times nine!" Alice repeated in despair. "Oh, that'll never be done! I'd better go in at once—" and in she went, and there was a dead silence the moment she appeared.

Alice glanced nervously along the table, as she walked up the large hall, and noticed that there were about fifty guests, of all kinds: some were animals, some birds, and there were even a few flowers among them. "I'm glad they've come without waiting to be asked," she thought: "I should never have known who were the right people to invite!"

There were three chairs at the head of the table; the Red and White Queens had already taken two of them, but the middle one was empty. Alice sat down in it, rather uncomfortable at the silence, and longing for some one to speak.

At last the Red Queen began. "You've missed the soup and fish," she said. "Put on the joint!" And the waiters set a leg of mutton before Alice, who looked at it rather anxiously, as she had never had to carve a joint before.

"You look a little shy; let me introduce you to that leg of mutton," said the Red Queen: "Alice—Mutton; Mutton—Alice." The leg of mutton got up in the dish and made a little bow to Alice; and Alice returned the bow, not knowing whether to be frightened or amused.

"May I give you a slice?" she said, taking up the knife and fork, and looking from one Queen to the other.

"Certainly not," the Red Queen said, very decidedly: "it isn't etiquette to cut* any one you've been introduced to. Remove the joint!" And the waiters carried it off, and brought a large plum-pudding in its place.

"I won't be introduced to the pudding, please," Alice said rather hastily, "or we shall get no dinner at all. May I give you some?"

But the Red Queen looked sulky, and growled "Pudding—Alice; Alice—Pudding. Remove the pudding!" and the waiters took it away so quickly that Alice couldn't return its bow.

However, she didn't see why the Red Queen should be

_____

*Fail to acknowledge someone's greeting.

the only one to give orders so, as an experiment, she called out "Waiter! Bring back the pudding!" and there it was again in a moment, like a conjuring-trick. It was so large that she couldn't help feeling *a little* shy with it, as she had been with the mutton; however, she conquered her shyness by a great effort, and cut a slice and handed it to the Red Queen.

"What impertinence!" said the Pudding. "I wonder how you'd like it, if I were to cut a slice out of *you*, you creature!"

It spoke in a thick, suety sort of voice, and Alice hadn't a word to say in reply: she could only sit and look at it and gasp.

"Make a remark," said the Red Queen: "It's ridiculous to leave all the conversation to the pudding!"

"Do you know, I've had such a quantity of poetry repeated to me to-day," Alice began, a little frightened at finding that, the moment she opened her lips, there was dead silence, and all eyes were fixed upon her; "and it's a very curious thing, I think—every poem was about fishes in some way. Do you know why they're so fond of fishes, all about here?"

She spoke to the Red Queen, whose answer was a little wide of the mark. "As to fishes," she said, very slowly and solemnly, putting her mouth close to Alice's ear, "her White Majesty knows a lovely riddle—all in poetry—all about fishes. Shall she repeat it?"

"Her Red Majesty's very kind to mention it," the White Queen murmured into Alice's other ear, in a voice like the cooing of a pigeon. "It would be *such* a treat! May I?"

"Please do," Alice said very politely.

The White Queen laughed with delight, and stroked Alice's cheek. Then she began:

> " *'First, the fish must be caught.'*
> *That is easy: a baby, I think, could have caught it.*
> *'Next, the fish must be bought.'*
> *That is easy: a penny, I think would have bought it.*
>
> *'Now cook me the fish!'*
> *That is easy, and will not take more than a minute.*
> *'Let it lie in a dish!'*
> *That is easy, because it already is in it.*
>
> *'Bring it here! Let me sup!'*
> *It is easy to set such a dish on the table.*
> *'Take the dish-cover up!'*
> *Ah, that is so hard that I fear I'm unable!*
>
> *For it holds it like glue—*
> *Holds the lid to the dish, while it lies in the middle:*
> *Which is easiest to do,*
> *Un-dish-cover the fish, or dishcover the riddle?"*

"Take a minute to think about it, and then guess," said the Red Queen. "Meanwhile we'll drink your health—Queen, Alice's health!" she screamed at the top of her voice, and all the guests began drinking it directly, and very queerly they managed it:

some of them put their glasses upon their heads like extinguishers, and drank all that trickled down their faces—others upset the decanters, and drank the wine as it ran off the edges of the table—and three of them (who looked like kangaroos) scrambled into the dish of roast mutton, and began eagerly lapping up the gravy, "just like pigs in a trough!" thought Alice.

"You ought to return thanks in a neat speech," the Red Queen said, frowning at Alice as she spoke.

"We must support you, you know," the White Queen whispered, as Alice got up to do it, very obediently, but a little frightened.

"Thank you very much," she whispered in reply, "but I can do quite well without."

"That wouldn't be at all the thing," the Red Queen said very decidedly: so Alice tried to submit to it with a good grace.

("And they *did* push so!" she said afterwards, when she was telling her sister the history of the feast. "You would have thought they wanted to squeeze me flat!")

In fact it was rather difficult for her to keep in her place while she made her speech: the two Queens pushed her so, one on each side, that they nearly lifted her up into the air: "I rise to return thanks—" Alice began: and she really *did* rise as she spoke, several inches; but she got hold of the edge of the table, and managed to pull herself down again.

"Take care of yourself!" screamed the White Queen, seizing Alice's hair with both her hands. "Something's going to happen!"

And then (as Alice afterwards described it) all sorts of things happened in a moment. The candles all grew up to the ceiling, looking something like a bed of rushes with fireworks at the top. As to the bottles, they each took a pair of plates, which they hastily fitted on as wings, and so, with forks for legs, went fluttering about in all directions: "and very like birds they look," Alice thought to herself, as well as she could in the dreadful confusion that was beginning.

At this moment she heard a hoarse laugh at her side, and turned to see what was the matter with the White Queen; but, instead of the Queen, there was the leg of mutton sitting in the chair. "Here I am!" cried a voice from the soup-tureen, and Alice turned again, just in time to see the Queen's broad good-natured face grinning at her for a moment over the edge of the tureen, before she disappeared into the soup.

There was not a moment to be lost. Already several of the guests were lying down in the dishes, and the soup-ladle was walking up the table towards Alice's chair, and beckoning to her impatiently to get out of its way.

"I can't stand this any longer!" she cried as she jumped up and seized the table-cloth with both hands: one good pull, and plates, dishes, guests, and candles came crashing down together in a heap on the floor.

"And as for *you*," she went on, turning fiercely upon the Red Queen, whom she considered as the cause of all the mischief— but the Queen was no longer at her side—she had suddenly dwindled down to the size of a little doll, and was now on the table, merrily running round and round after her own shawl, which was trailing behind her.

At any other time, Alice would have felt surprised at this, but she was far too much excited to be surprised at anything *now*. "As for *you*," she repeated, catching hold of the little creature in the very act of jumping over a bottle which had just lighted upon the table, "I'll shake you into a kitten, that I will!"

CHAPTER X.

SHAKING.

She took her off the table as she spoke, and shook her backwards and forwards with all her might.

The Red Queen made no resistance whatever; only her face grew very small, and her eyes got large and green: and still, as Alice went on shaking her, she kept on growing shorter—and fatter—and softer—and rounder—and—

268

CHAPTER XI.

WAKING.

—and it really *was* a kitten, after all.

CHAPTER XII.

WHICH DREAMED IT?

"Your Red Majesty shouldn't purr so loud," Alice said, rubbing her eyes, and addressing the kitten, respectfully, yet with some severity. "You woke me out of oh! such a nice dream! And you've been along with me, Kitty—all through the Looking-Glass world. Did you know it, dear?"

It is a very inconvenient habit of kittens (Alice had once made the remark) that, whatever you say to them, they *always* purr. "If they would only purr for 'yes,' and mew for 'no,' or any rule of that sort," she had said, "so that one could keep up a conservation! But how *can* you talk with a person if they always say the same thing?"

On this occasion the kitten only purred: and it was impossible to guess whether it meant 'yes' or 'no.'

So Alice hunted among the chessmen on the table till she had found the Red Queen's then she went down on her knees on the hearth-rug, and put the kitten and the Queen to look at each other. "Now, Kitty!" she cried, clapping her hands triumphantly. "Confess that was what you turned into!"

("But it wouldn't look at it," she said, when she was explaining the thing afterwards to her sister: "it turned away its head, and pretended not to see it: but it looked a *little* ashamed of itself, so I think it *must* have been the Red Queen.")

"Sit up a little more stiffly, dear!" Alice cried with a merry laugh. "And curtsey while you're thinking what to—what to purr. It saves time, remember!" And she caught it up and gave it one little kiss, "just in honor of its having been a Red Queen."

"Snowdrop, my pet!" she went on, looking over her shoulder at the White Kitten, which was still patiently undergoing its toilet, "when *will* Dinah have finished with your White Majesty,

I wonder? That must be the reason you were so untidy in my dream.—Dinah! Do you know that you're scrubbing a White Queen? Really, it's most disrespectful of you!

"And what did *Dinah* turn to, I wonder?" she prattled on, as she settled comfortably down, with one elbow on the rug, and her chin in her hand, to watch the kittens. "Tell me, Dinah, did you turn to Humpty Dumpty? I *think* you did—however, you'd better not mention it to your friends just yet, for I'm not sure.

"By the way, Kitty, if only you'd been really with me in my dream, there was one thing you *would* have enjoyed—I had such a quantity of poetry said to me, all about fishes! To-morrow morning you shall have a real treat. All the time you're eating your breakfast, I'll repeat 'The Walrus and the Carpenter' to you; and then you can make believe it's oysters, dear!

"Now, Kitty, let's consider who it was that dreamed it all. This is a serious question, my dear, and you should *not* go on licking your paw like that—as if Dinah hadn't washed you this morning! You see, Kitty, it *must* have been either me or the Red King. He was part of my dream, of course—but then I was part of his dream, too! *Was* it the Red King, Kitty? You were his wife, my dear, so you ought to know—Oh, Kitty, *do* help to settle it! I'm sure your paw can wait!" But the provoking kitten only began on the other paw, and pretended it hadn't heard the question.

Which do *you* think it was?

A BOAT, beneath a sunny sky,
Lingering onward dreamily
In an evening of July—

Children three that nestle near,
Eager eye and willing ear,
Pleased a simple tale to hear—

Long has paled that sunny sky:
Echos fade and memories die:
Autumn frosts have slain July.

Still she haunts me, phantomwise,
Alice moving under skies
Never seen by waking eyes.

Children yet, the tale to hear,
Eager eye and willing ear,
Lovingly shall nestle near.

In a Wonderland they lie,
Dreaming as the days go by,
Dreaming as the summers die.

Ever drifting down the stream—
Lingering in the golden gleam—
Life, what is it but a dream?[9]

Endnotes

ALICE'S ADVENTURES IN WONDERLAND

1. (p. 18) *she very soon finished it off:* Carroll placed asterisks after Alice takes a drink from the bottle and again in chapter 5 after she eats cake, to indicate those moments immediately before Alice's adventures become more unbelievable.
2. (p. 26) "How doth the little crocodile.... With gently smiling jaws!": This short ballad is a parody of British minister and hymnwriter Isaac Watts's song "Against Idleness and Mischief," from *Dream Songs for Children* (1715). The first two stanzas of Watts's song are: "How doth the Little busy Bee/Improve each shining Hour,/And gather Honey all the Day/From every opening Flower!//How skillfully she builds her Cell!/How neat she spreads the Wax;/And labours hard to store it well/With the sweet Food she makes."
3. (p. 57) *"Repeat* 'You are old, Father William' ": This poem is a parody of "The Old Man's Comforts, and How He Gained Them" (1799), by Robert Southey. The first two stanzas of Southey's poem are: "You are old, Father William, the young man cried,/The few locks which are left you are grey;/You are hale, Father William, a hearty old man,/Now tell me the reason, I pray.//In the days of my youth, Father William replied,/I remember'd that youth would fly fast,/And abused not my health and my vigour at first/That I never might need them at last."
4. (p. 79) *"Why is a raven like a writing-desk?":* Carroll provided an answer to this riddle: "Because it can produce a few notes, though they are *very* flat; and it is nevar [*sic*] put with the wrong end in front!" (see p. 3).

THROUGH THE LOOKING-GLASS

1. (p. 164) JABBERWOCKY: When Carroll first wrote "Jabberwocky," he titled it "A Stanza of Anglo-Saxon Poetry" and had it printed in what looked like Old English script. See the "Comments &

Questions" section in this edition for the author's annotations on the poem.

2. (pp. 167–168) *This time she came upon a large flowerbed:* The incident of the live flowers is taken from Alfred, Lord Tennyson's *Maud* (1855), in which a lover awaits his beloved in a garden filled with talking flowers.

3. (p. 169) *"It says 'Bough-wough!'":* Carroll here philosophizes upon the etymologies of words, questioning whether they have any intrinsic meaning or are merely arbitrary signs.

4. (p. 191) "The sun was shining on the sea . . .": This poem is composed in the same meter as "The Dream of Eugene Aram" (1829), by Thomas Hood, about a schoolteacher who is also a murderer.

5. (p. 215) *"Must a name mean something?" . . . "With a name like yours, you might be any shape almost":* Humpty Dumpty argues that words have an intrinsic relationship to the things they name. Elsewhere he will argue that names are entirely arbitrary.

6. (p. 237) *This time it was a White Knight:* Many commentators have speculated that the White Knight is in fact Carroll.

7. (p. 246) 'I give thee all, I can no more': Alice is referring to "My Heart and Lute," by Thomas Moore (1779–1852). The first line of Moore's poem is: "I give thee all,—I can no more,/Though poor the off'ring be;/My heart and lute are all the store/That I can bring to thee."

8. (p. 261) "To the Looking-Glass world. . . . ninety-times-nine!": This poem is a parody of "Bonny Dundee" (1830), by Sir Walter Scott. Following is Scott's first stanza: "To the Lords of Convention 'twas Claver'se who spoke./'Ere the King's crown shall fall there are crowns to be broke;/So let each Cavalier who loves honour and me,/Come follow the bonnet of Bonny Dundee./Come fill up my cup, come fill up my can,/Come saddle your horses, and call up your men;/Come open the West Port and let me gang free,/And it's room for the bonnets of Bonny Dundee!'"

9. (p. 272) *A boat, beneath a sunny sky. . . . Life, what is it but a dream?:* The first letters of each of the lines combine to spell "Alice Pleasance Liddell."

Inspired by Alice's Adventures in Wonderland *and* Through the Looking-Glass

FILM ADAPTATIONS

The wonderfully curious Alice has been appearing on the silver screen since 1903, the year she debuted in British director Cecil Hepworth's *Alice in Wonderland,* a silent, eight-minute movie that depicts the young girl's propensity to grow and shrink. Alice, played by May Clark, encounters the White Rabbit and the Queen (both played by Hepworth's wife), the Frog-Footman (Hepworth himself), and a slew of playing cards who walk upright in the Tenniel-drawn fashion. In 1910 Thomas Edison's film company produced the second *Alice* adaptation, also a silent film, this time ten minutes long. Shot in the Bronx, *Alice's Adventures in Wonderland (A Fairy Comedy),* features similar growing and shrinking effects on the part of Alice, played by Gladys Hulette. The first full-length *Alice in Wonderland* (running time: fifty-two minutes) premiered in 1915 under the stewardship of director W. W. Young. Starring Viola Savoy as Alice and shot on Long Island, this film's imagery derives, as faithfully as the technology of the time would allow, from Tenniel's illustrations.

The first "talkie" of *Alice* was released in 1931, a film with Ruth Gilbert as Alice that was eclipsed in popularity by Paramount's all-star production of 1933, directed by Norman McLeod. The Paramount *Alice in Wonderland* features Charlotte Henry as Alice, Gary Cooper as the White Knight, W.C. Fields as Humpty Dumpty, and Cary Grant as the Mock Turtle. In the first film to blend elements of *Alice* with *Through the Looking-Glass,* director McLeod remained consistently loyal to Tenniel's visual style. Walt Disney's well-known animated feature *Alice in Wonderland* was released in 1951, with Kathryn

Beaumont as the voice of Alice. Disney used seven songwriters to score this musical adaptation of the Alice books. William Sterling's musical *Alice's Adventures in Wonderland* (1972) took the story back to live action. Featuring music by John Barry and lyrics by Don Black, this stunningly colorful production stars such British notables as Dudley Moore and Peter Sellers.

Alice's adventures have also been the subject of numerous films made for television, most notably the BBC's 1966 production directed by Jonathan Miller and, in 1999, a three-hour epic, directed by Nick Willing, with an all-star cast: Robbie Coltrane, Whoopi Goldberg, Ben Kingsley, Miranda Richardson, Martin Short, and Gene Wilder, among others. In 1977 Monty Python's Terry Gilliam made his directorial debut with *Jabberwocky*, a loose interpretation of Carroll's nonsense poem that showcases an amazingly nasty monster. *Dreamchild* (1985) details the real-life events of Alice Liddell's trip to America in 1932, the centennial of Lewis Carroll's birth. The film intercuts scenes from the journey with fantastical flashbacks of Alice's childhood spent with Carroll, who is played by Ian Holm.

"WHAT THE TORTOISE SAID TO ACHILLES"

Lewis Carroll published the following short piece, with the title given above, in the April 1895 issue of the journal Mind.

Achilles had overtaken the Tortoise, and had seated himself comfortably on its back.

"So you've got to the end of our race-course?" said the Tortoise. "Even though it does consist of an infinite series of distances? I thought some wiseacre or other had proved that the thing couldn't be done?"

"It *can* be done," said Achilles. "It *has* been done! *Solvitur ambulando.* You see the distances were constantly *diminishing*; and so—"

"But if they had been constantly *increasing*?" the Tortoise interrupted. "How then?"

"Then I shouldn't be *here*," Achilles modestly replied; "and you would have got several times round the world, by this time!"

"You flatter me—*flatten*, I *mean*," said the Tortoise; "for you are a heavy weight, and *no* mistake! Well now, would you like to hear of a race-course, that most people fancy they can get to the end of in two or three steps, while it *really* consists of an infinite number of distances, each one longer than the previous one?"

"Very much indeed!" said the Grecian warrior, as he drew from his helmet (few Grecian warriors possessed *pockets* in those days) an enormous note-book and a pencil. "Proceed! And speak *slowly*, please! *Shorthand* isn't invented yet!"

"That beautiful First Proposition of Euclid!" the Tortoise murmured dreamily.

"You admire Euclid?"

"Passionately! So far, at least, as one *can* admire a treatise that won't be published for some centuries to come!"

"Well, now, let's take a little bit of the argument in that First Proposition—just *two* steps, and the conclusion drawn from them. Kindly enter them in your note-book. And in order to refer to them conveniently, let's call them *A, B,* and *Z:*—

(*A*) Things that are equal to the same are equal to each other.

(*B*) The two sides of this Triangle are things that are equal to the same.

(*Z*) The two sides of this Triangle are equal to each other.

Readers of Euclid will grant, I suppose, that *Z* follows logically from *A* and *B,* so that any one who accepts *A* and *B* as true, *must* accept *Z* as true?"

"Undoubtedly! The youngest child in a High School—as soon as High Schools are invented, which will not be till some two thousand years later—will grant *that.*"

"And if some reader had *not* yet accepted *A* and *B* as true, he might still accept the *sequence* as a *valid* one, I suppose?"

"No doubt such a reader might exist. He might say 'I accept as true the Hypothetical Proposition that, *if A* and *B* be true, *Z* must be true; but, I *don't* accept *A* and *B* as true.' Such a reader would do wisely in abandoning Euclid, and taking to football."

"And might there not *also* be some reader who would say 'I accept *A* and *B* as true, but I *don't* accept the Hypothetical'?"

"Certainly there might. *He*, also, had better take to football."

"And *neither* of these readers," the Tortoise continued, "is *as yet* under any logical necessity to accept *Z* as true?"

"Quite so," Achilles assented.

"Well, now, I want you to consider *me* as a reader of the *second* kind, and to force me, logically, to accept *Z* as true."

"A tortoise playing football would be—" Achilles was beginning.

"—an anomaly, of course," the Tortoise hastily interrupted. "Don't wander from the point. Let's have *Z* first, and football afterwards!"

"I'm to force you to accept *Z*, am I?" Achilles said musingly. "And your present position is that you accept *A* and *B*, but you don't accept the Hypothetical—"

"Let's call it *C*," said the Tortoise.

"—but you *don't* accept

(*C*) If *A* and *B* are true, *Z* must be true."

"That is my present position," said the Tortoise.

"Then I must ask you to accept *C*."

"I'll do so," said the Tortoise, "as soon as you've entered it in that note-book of yours. What else have you got in it?"

"Only a few memoranda," said Achilles, nervously fluttering the leaves: "a few memoranda of—of the battles in which I have distinguished myself!"

"Plenty of blank leaves, I see!" the Tortoise cheerily remarked. "We shall need them *all*!" (Achilles shuddered.) "Now write as I dictate:—

(*A*) Things that are equal to the same are equal to each other.
(*B*) The two sides of this Triangle are things that are equal to the same.
(*C*) If *A* and *B* are true, *Z* must be true.
(*Z*) The two sides of this Triangle are equal to each other."

"You should call it *D*, not *Z*," said Achilles. "It comes *next* to the other three. If you accept *A* and *B* and *C*, you *must* accept *Z*."

"And why *must* I?"

"Because it follows *logically* from them. If *A* and *B* and *C* are true, *Z must* be true. You don't dispute *that*, I imagine?"

"If *A* and *B* and *C* are true, *Z must* be true," the Tortoise thoughtfully repeated. "That's *another* Hypothetical, isn't it? And, if I failed to see its truth, I might accept *A* and *B* and *C*, and *still* not accept *Z*, mightn't I?"

"You might," the candid hero admitted; "though such obtuseness would certainly be phenomenal. Still, the event is *possible*. So I must ask you to grant *one* more Hypothetical."

"Very good. I'm quite willing to grant it, as soon as you've written it down. We will call it

(*D*) If *A* and *B* and *C* are true, *Z* must be true.

"Have you entered that in your note-book?"

"I *have*!" Achilles joyfully exclaimed, as he ran the pencil into its sheath. "And at last we've got to the end of this ideal race-course! Now that you accept *A* and *B* and *C* and *D*, *of course* you accept *Z*."

"Do I?" said the Tortoise innocently. "Let's make that quite clear. I accept *A* and *B* and *C* and *D*. Suppose I *still* refused to accept *Z*?"

"Then Logic would *force* you to do it!" Achilles triumphantly replied. "Logic would tell you, 'You can't help yourself. Now that you've accepted *A* and *B* and *C* and *D*, you *must* accept *Z*!' So you've no choice, you see."

"Whatever Logic is good enough to tell me is worth *writing down*," said the Tortoise. "So enter it in your book, please. We will call it

(*E*) If *A* and *B* and *C* and *D* are true, *Z* must be true.

Until I've granted *that*, of course I needn't grant *Z*. So it's quite a *necessary* step, you see?"

"I see," said Achilles; and there was a touch of sadness in his tone.

Here the narrator, having pressing business at the Bank, was obliged to leave the happy pair, and did not again pass the spot until some months afterwards. When he did so, Achilles was still seated on the back of the much-enduring Tortoise, and was writing in his note-book, which appeared to be nearly full. The Tortoise was saying, "Have you got that last step written down? Unless I've lost count, that makes a thousand and one. There are several millions more to come. And *would* you mind, as a personal favour, considering what a lot of instruction this colloquy of ours will provide for the Logicians of the Nineteenth Century—*would* you mind adopting a pun that my cousin the Mock-Turtle will then make, and allowing yourself to be re-named *Taught-Us*?"

"As you please!" replied the weary warrior, in the hollow tones of despair, as he buried his face in his hands. "Provided that *you*, for *your* part, will adopt a pun the Mock Turtle never made, and allow yourself to be re-named *A Kill-Ease!*"

This dialogue, restoring the beloved Tortoise and the Mock Turtle, has inspired mathematicians for generations, among them Douglas R. Hofstadter. In his book *Gödel, Escher, Bach: An Eternal Golden Braid* (1979), he intersperses among his chapters further colloquies between the Tortoise and Achilles. In this way, Hofstadter introduces complex geometrical puzzles through the allegorical Carrollian heroes. *Gödel, Escher, Bach* received a Pulitzer Prize in 1980.

Comments & Questions

In this section, we aim to provide the reader with an array of perspectives on the text, as well as questions that challenge those perspectives. The commentary has been culled from sources as diverse as reviews contemporaneous with the works, letters written by the author, literary criticism of later generations, and appreciations written throughout the works' history. Following the commentary, a series of questions seeks to filter Lewis Carroll's Alice's Adventures in Wonderland *and* Through the Looking-Glass *through a variety of points of view and bring about a richer understanding of these enduring works.*

LEWIS CARROLL

A Stanza of Anglo-Saxon Poetry

> *'Twas bryllyg, and ye slythy toves*
> *Did gyre and gymble in ye wabe:*
> *All mimsy were ye borogoves;*
> *And ye mome raths outgrabe.*

The meanings of the words are as follows:

Bryllyg   (derived from the verb to *bryl* or *broil*). "The time of broiling dinner, i.e. the close of the afternoon."

Slythy   (compounded of *slimy* and *lithe*). "Smooth and active."

Tove   A species of Badger. They had smooth white hair, long hind legs, and short horns like a stag. Lived chiefly on cheese.

Gyre   Verb (derived from *gyaour* or *giaour*, "a dog"). "To scratch like a dog."

Gymble   (whence *gimblet*). "To screw out holes in anything."

Wabe   (derived from the verb to *swab* or *soak*). "The side of
               hill" (from its being soaked by the rain).
Mimsy   (whence *mimserable* and *miserable*). "Unhappy."
Borogove   An extinct kind of Parrot. They had no wings, beaks
               turned up, and made their nests under sun-dials;
               lived on veal.
Mome   (hence *solemome*, *solemone*, and *solemn*). "Grave."
Rath   A species of land turtle. Head erect: mouth like a
               shark: the front forelegs curved out so that the ani-
               mal walked on its knees: smooth green body: lived
               on swallows and oysters.
Outgrabe   Past tense of the verb to *outgribe* (it is connected
               with the old verb to *grike* or *shrike*, from which are
               derived "shriek" and "creak"). "Squeaked."

Hence the literal English of the passage is:

> "It was evening, and the smooth active badgers were scratching
> and boring holes in the hill-side; all unhappy were the parrots,
> and the grave turtles squeaked out."

There were probably sun-dials on the top of the hill, and the
"borogoves" were afraid that their nests would be undermined.
The hill was probably full of the nests of "raths," which ran out,
squeaking with fear, on hearing the "toves" scratching outside.
This is an obscure, but yet deeply affecting, relic of ancient
Poetry.

—from *Mischmasch*, one of Carroll's
private periodicals (1855)

THE NEW YORK TIMES
The time may come when Lewis Carroll's name will be forgotten, but the tale of "Alice in Wonderland" is immortal. Few persons have ever heard of Perrault, and yet everybody knows "Little
Red Riding Hood." The qualities which were necessary to write
the adventures of these little heroines are, in a measure, analogous
to those which the composition of an epic poem exacts. The
authors had to be artists, and their minds were complex, but

they reinstated themselves into the naïveté, the charming simplicity of childhood. Perrault had a foundation in folk lore, but
Carroll had to add a new fable to those that nations have told for
ages. He was a man of genius when he created Alice.

—October 9, 1893

ISA BOWMAN

To have even known such a man as he was is an inestimable
boon. To have been with him for so long as a child, to have
known so intimately the man who above all others has understood childhood, is indeed a memory on which to look back
with thanksgiving and with tears.

Now that I am no longer "his little girl," now that he is
dead and my life is so different from the quiet life he led, I
can yet feel the old charm, I can still be glad that he has kissed
me and that we were friends. Little girl and grave professor!
it is a strange combination. Grave professor and little girl!
how curious it sounds! yet strange and curious as it may seem,
it was so.

—from *The Story of Lewis Carroll* (1899)

THE NEW YORK TIMES

It is not to speak hyperbolically, in the circumstances, to say
that "Through the Looking-Glass" is a book of all time. It is as
fresh and charming to-day as it was thirty odd years ago.

—November 8, 1902

ALICE LIDDELL HARGREAVES

Nearly all of *Alice's Adventures Underground* was told on that
blazing summer afternoon with the heat haze shimmering
over the meadows where the party landed to shelter for awhile
in the shadow cast by the haycocks near Godstow. I think the
stories [Carroll] told us that afternoon must have been better
than usual, because I have such a distinct recollection of the
expedition, and also, on the next day I started to pester him
to write down the story for me, which I had never done
before.

—*Cornhill Magazine* (July 1932)

W. H. AUDEN
I have always thought one might learn much about the cultural history of a country by going through the speeches made by its public men over a certain period, in legislatures, in law courts, and at official banquets, and making a list of the books quoted from without attribution. So far as Great Britain is concerned, I strongly suspect that, for the past fifty years, the two *Alice* books and *The Hunting of the Snark* have headed it.
                    —*The New York Times Magazine* (July 1, 1962)

QUESTIONS

1. What do the denizens of Wonderland have in common?

2. Is Wonderland a place of adventure, romance, or escapism? A daydream? Or an oblique collision with reality?

3. Is there satire in the Alice books? If so, what is its target?

4. In the Alice books there is no direct treatment of such serious matters as how to make a living, the vicissitudes of love, marriage, raising children, and the like. Instead there are impossible situations, absurd characters, animals who talk. But is there, amid the fun, some comment on a serious aspect of human life? If so, what is it?

5. Does Alice herself have any character, any signs of an inner life, or is she just a device to stand in contrast to the others, to be a foil for them?

For Further Reading

BOOKS BY LEWIS CARROLL

Carroll, Lewis. *Alice in Wonderland.* Edited by Donald J. Gray. Second edition. New York: W. W. Norton, 1992. Includes *Through the Looking-Glass* and *The Hunting of the Snark,* as well as critical essays.

Carroll, Lewis. *Diversions and Digressions of Lewis Carroll.* Edited by Stuart Dodgson Collingwood. New York: Dover, 1961. A selection from Lewis Carroll's unpublished writings and drawings.

Carroll, Lewis. *Symbolic Logic and the Game of Logic.* New York: Dover, 1958.

BIOGRAPHICAL

Gordon, Colin. *Beyond the Looking-Glass: Reflections of Alice and her Family.* San Diego: Harcourt Brace Jovanovich, 1982.

Cohen, Morton N. *Lewis Carroll: A Biography.* New York: Alfred A. Knopf, 1995.

———. *Reflections in a Looking-Glass: A Centennial Celebration of Lewis Carroll, Photographer.* New York: Aperture, 1998.

Hudson, Derek. *Lewis Carroll: An Illustrated Biography.* London: Constable, 1976.

Wood, James Playsted. *The Snark Was a Boojum: A Life of Lewis Carroll.* New York: Pantheon Books, 1966.

CRITICISM

Bloom, Harold, ed. *Lewis Carroll.* Modern Critical Views series. New York: Chelsea House, 1987.

Gardner, Martin. *The Annotated Alice.* New York: Clarkson N. Potter, 1960.

Gardner, Martin. *More Annotated Alice.* New York: Random House, 1990.

Phillips, Robert. *Aspects of Alice.* New York: Vanguard Press, 1971.

OTHER WORKS OF INTEREST

Deleuze, Gilles. *The Logic of Sense.* New York: Columbia University Press, 1990.

Sewell, Elizabeth. *The Field of Nonsense.* London: Chatto and Windus, 1952.